FIRE AWAY

THE BUNKHOUSE SERIES

LAINEY LAWSON

ISBN: 9798329839371

Cover illustration and design by Sonia GX

Editing by Dani Galliaro

This book is for you if you read to escape your pain.
Take a deep breath, be kind to yourself, and here's another cowboy
romance to help keep you sane.

DISCLAIMER

To avoid spoilers, the full list of trigger and content warnings have been included at the end of this book. If you prefer to vet them before starting the story, please skip to that section first. Happy and safe reading!

1

SAVANNAH

Spending the day in jail isn't so bad. In a small town like Westridge, they bring you coffee with extra sugar and turn the TV toward your cell. Not having paperwork in front of me or a million emails to answer is a welcome bonus too. The only downsides so far have been the smelly drunk in the corner and not having anyone to call who is willing to come bail me out.

I've been here before. Not on the wrong side of the bars, exactly, but in the misery of another all-time low. Each time I find myself in the throes of it, I ask myself the same question. *Is this it? Is this the time that I finally push the limits of my self-destruction so far that there's no coming back?* I always beg and plead with the universe to get me out and give me another chance.

I won't put myself in this situation again, I swear. I've learned my lesson this time, I promise. But the outcome never changes, and I know even without a crystal ball that this will not be the last time I land on the jagged sharp surface of rock bottom.

I wasn't dumb enough to expect my dad to come to my rescue today. Bad news travels fast, so I'm sure without even speaking to me to get my side of the story, he's created his own narrative that what happened was completely my fault.

Maybe it was. Maybe I'm the problem.

I'm not sure it matters at this point, though. He hasn't gone out of his way to help any other time that I've gotten myself into some form of trouble regardless of whether or not I was to blame.

Even though he considers me a disappointment, you'd think he'd at least still answer my call. A clear vision of him huffing out a breath and rolling his eyes as the collect call flashes across the screen of his phone plays in my mind. The mental image is enough for shame to heat my cheeks.

Feeling like I'm not worth his time or effort is an inevitable sentiment for me. But even as familiar as it is, it's still hard to stomach.

According to the black framed digital clock above the door on the other side of the room, I've been stuck in here going on seven hours. My feet are beginning to throb in my heels because I'm too scared to take them off and let my bare feet touch the cold concrete floor. It doesn't *look* too dirty, but I can't even begin to imagine the amount of invisible germs swimming around on it. Shifting my full weight from one foot to the other every so often will have to do for now.

I could sit, but that would mean cozying up with the unfortunately smelly drunk sharing the cell with me.

I set my coffee down on the scratch-covered bench along the wall inside the holding cell and then turn to lean my back against the bars keeping me from the outside world. What's next? Is the ceiling going to cave in on me? With my string of luck lately, adding in a broken leg from falling debris would fail to surprise me.

Tilting my head back, I stare up at the textured brown edges of the water-stained ceiling tiles. I squint, pretending they're clouds instead. The urge to surrender to my impending breakdown is creeping in. Since the prospect of someone coming to get me out of here tonight is looking bleak, my adrenaline from the day will crash soon and the tears will start. It happens every time I have a major screw-up, and no one is there to keep me from spiraling.

"I'm sorry your dad didn't answer," Justin, the officer on duty, says from the other side of the room. "But I'll let you make another call if you need to, Savannah."

I look over my shoulder to see him sitting at his desk in a flimsy office chair. He's leaning back and pulling his eyebrows together, deep in thought. Justin and I met when I first moved here not long ago. I became quickly acquainted with most of the local law enforcement due to the nature of my job, and he's been kind and generous toward me from the start. Unlike most of the others. I'm not so defeated that I can't appreciate his empathy toward my current situation.

"Thank you," I reply, puffing out a sigh. "I just don't have anyone else to call."

Pathetic, I know. But it's the truth.

My co-workers and I have had a rocky start. I don't bond quickly or easily with others, and my experience so far with the other people in my office has been no exception. I'm not sure they'd jump at the chance to help the newcomer who's making them all look bad at the moment.

Then there's my mom and my brother, both of whom always take my father's side. They're too scared of him not to. I don't see either of them burning a bridge with him just to lend me a hand. God forbid.

No one else comes to mind either, not even an acquaintance that I've made in town. My difficulty warming up to new people extends to making new friendships, and being in a new town hasn't helped that.

I've lived in Westridge all of one month and already I've managed to throw fuel on the fire that is my bad reputation.

When it comes to strangers, I have a thicker skin. It's easier to care less how people feel about you when you hardly know them. To date, their opinions haven't been an issue. But attitude doesn't do me any favors when I need someone to get me the hell out of this jail cell.

Justin flattens his lips and his eyes soften, so I blow out a breath and look away. I may be embarrassed by my lack of options, but I don't want him to feel sorry for me.

The television mounted on the wall adjacent to my holding cell plays a 2000s era game show rerun on mute, and I turn to stare at it, resting my chin on my folded arms against the bars.

When minutes go by and I don't have any names to give Justin to call, I assume he'll drop it and leave me to rot in here for the time being.

"Want me to get a bail bondsman on the phone then?" he asks. "You don't want to spend the night here, I'm sure."

I most definitely do not. No heating pad for my tight lower back, no sound machine, and having to sleep with my clothes on? I shudder at the thought. No, thank you.

"I guess that's my only choice," I mumble and shrug. I hate how discouraged I feel right now and the fact that I don't have the energy to hide it. "The sooner I get out of here, the sooner I can try to fix the mess I've gotten myself into."

I switch my weight to my left foot and wiggle my right ankle above the floor to lessen the soreness. Justin nods and goes silent again.

I wish the inside of my head was as quiet as the space around me. My fists clench as I work to dampen my discouraging thoughts and focus on what few positive ones I have left.

No matter how low I get, I need to remember that I'm still an expert at picking up the pieces. If self-sabotage was an Olympic sport, I'd have a case of gold medals and my picture on a special edition Wheaties box for crying out loud. I can get through this. I've done it a hundred times before, and I can do it again.

"Hey," Justin abruptly sits up tall in his chair with his eyebrows raised, "I have an idea! You might not like it though."

It's nice that he's still trying to help but I can't imagine what he's come up with. I cock an eyebrow and shift my gaze to him without fully turning my head. I don't like the sound of it, but given my lack of options, I'm all ears.

"How about calling Warren?" he suggests. He delivers the sentence slowly, like he's walking on eggshells. As he should, because over my dead body will I be phoning in a favor from that douchebag and he knows it.

"On second thought, I think this rock-hard bench looks just fine for a night's stay," I quip back with no hesitation.

"Oh, he's not as bad as you think. He's bailed his buddy Tripp out of here at least twice before, so he knows how it works. He'd get you out and I bet he'd even give you a ride home too."

There's not a chance in hell I'm calling Warren Farrow. He can gag on a Pogo stick for all I care.

"I don't even have his number anymore," I lie while tipping up my chin. It's still very much in my contacts.

Three weeks ago, I attended a small fundraiser in town with the rest of the attorneys at my firm. I didn't want to go, but in an attempt to integrate myself into the community, I tagged along. In hindsight, a terrible decision.

When I first saw Warren standing near the stage with a

crowd of people around him, I might have ogled a little bit. Okay, a lot. I could blame it on the two drinks I'd already had, but the truth is that somehow his smile sparkled when his lips spread wide in an easy laugh. I couldn't look away. He was charisma personified.

I can't put a finger on how I was able to stifle my anxiety that night. But there was a certain type of magic between us that put me at ease.

By the time the evening was over, he'd introduced himself to me, talked with me for at least an hour, and asked me on a date. He was so friendly, and I was helplessly pulled into his glow. To say I was thrilled about the idea of going out with someone so stupidly handsome is an understatement. I'm not used to other people going out of their way to ask me to spend more time with them, and his attention toward me felt like snuggling up with a clean hot blanket fresh out of the dryer.

I thought at that moment that with a new job and meeting Warren, things were really starting to look up for me.

But it was all a game to him.

What I'd give to go back and turn him down.

"Warren is a good guy," Justin continues to gently disagree with me. Here we go again with the endless praise for this man from every person I've ever spoken to in this town.

With Warren and Justin being friends, I'm sure he heard about our first date disaster. Surely, he didn't get the other side of the story if he still thinks so highly of him.

"Are we talking about the same person?" I ask, rolling my eyes. "Because the one I'm thinking of is a selfish prick."

That makes Justin chuckle while shaking his head. "I know you two got started on the wrong foot, but he'd show up and get you out. I know he would."

No. Part of the reason I left the city and moved to Westridge was to distance myself from people who treated me poorly, not the least of which being my own flesh and blood. I'll be damned if I let a boy with nothing better to do than string me along and play games with me take their place.

Behind me, a rustling of movement echoes in the small space.

"So make him post the bail," my cellmate who's been silent up until now suggests. "Never pay him back. Stiff him, you know?" His words are slurred, but his expression is straight and serious, like it's an obvious idea.

Wouldn't that be something? For the first time in days, the corners of my mouth turn up in a sly smile.

"He's still drunk," Justin laughs. "Maybe not the best advice."

"Revenge is *always* good advice," the still slightly drunk man defends himself. "Got anything stronger than this here coffee by the way?" He lifts his cup and twists his face hoping to gain the same sympathy from Justin that I've received.

"You know I don't, Mr. Wright. And if I did, I wouldn't give it to you," Justin lectures as he crosses his arms.

Before Mr. Wright has a chance to further plead his case, the office phone on Justin's desk rings and he snaps it up.

"Yeah," he says into the receiver. A few moments pass as he listens to the person on the other end of the call, and I take the opportunity to mull over the idea of calling Warren.

How funny would it be if I stiffed him after he shelled out a few thousand bucks to bail me out? The idea of pissing him off sounds better than a cool evening rain in the middle of this miserably hot Texas summer.

Justin covers the receiver with his free hand and holds it in the air to get my attention.

"They're asking if someone's coming to get you or not," he says.

I stand up straight, smooth my hands over the front of my pencil skirt, and pull down the hem of my blazer that's buttoned up all the way to hide my torn-open blouse.

This day can't get much worse, so I might as well have a little fun with it. I nod sharply.

"Fine. I'll call him."

2

WARREN

Nights like this don't happen as often as they used to. Not too long ago, they were a common occurrence at the ranch. We had a routine and it suited us all just fine. It did me, at least.

We grilled food and hung out at the bunkhouse after a long day's work nearly every night. The times that we weren't hosting a party or out at the bar, that is.

Lately, though, I've had to split my time between here and my new business. It opens in a few months and I'm up to my eyeballs in preparations. Bills and to-do lists demand my attention from my already-cluttered desk, but I haven't had the heart or the cash flow to leave my job here at the ranch just yet.

Gage was the first to shake things up around here by getting engaged to my sister, Blythe, and moving out to the big house across the property with her. He's still on the ranch every day, seeing as how he owns the place, but it's just Tripp, Heston, and myself living in the bunkhouse now.

Tripp has taken on most of my responsibilities while I'm

not able to be here. And he's more preoccupied with adding notches to his bedpost than he's ever been.

Heston seems more distant lately, too. Taking off to who knows where at any given time. We know better than to ask him questions or dig into that.

It used to be the four of us guys, living on the edge like a rowdy bunch of young bachelors.

Things have changed so quickly. It's not all for the worse, but it's out of the norm just the same. Change has never been comfortable for me and I'm still getting used to it.

The fact that we're all here together on the same night means I should be enjoying myself and spending time with my sister and friends inside right now. Instead, I'm in the mood for some silent brooding on the patio out back.

Above the summer breeze and a few cicadas, laughter and music can easily be heard from the house behind me. It's a comforting background noise until the guilt sets in that I'm not up for a night of drinking and conversing like I don't have a care in the world. I've never been good at faking emotions, I guess.

My thumb runs along the side of the water bottle resting on my knee. There's condensation pooling in the ridges of the plastic and for a short minute, I fixate on the pad of my finger in contact with the cool drops of liquid.

I've been doing that a lot recently. Zoning out. Trying not to think about all the risks and different ways my lofty business venture could go wrong. Or about the girl who's taken up permanent residence in my brain since the moment I met her.

Savannah Chase. Her name drifts through my thoughts on a regular basis. That and the look on her face when I asked her if she'd go out with me when we met that night three weeks ago. I couldn't think of anything more beautiful if I tried.

The one that got away isn't a fair way to describe her. I never had her to begin with. Somehow, I managed to accidentally fuck things up with her a week later before our first date had even ended.

And my brain keeps warning me that I could do the same with my business before it has a chance to get off the ground too.

Interrupting my failed attempt at pushing away all the overwhelming thoughts swirling around in my head, the back door to the bunkhouse creaks open. Without turning, I know that it's Heston.

If the lack of greeting wasn't a dead giveaway, the stealthy footsteps were.

I lean my head against the back of the chair while he takes the seat next to mine. I'm not surprised that he's joined me. It's not uncommon to find him out here alone at night. He prefers the quiet. What shocks me is that he strikes up a conversation.

"Private pity party?" he asks in his typical low-pitched voice.

I tear a piece of the label away from the plastic bottle in my hand and nod. In my peripheral vision, he brings a can of beer to his lips for a drink and then spreads his legs to get more comfortable. He isn't one for small talk, so I wait for him to reveal what's on his mind. Long beats of silence are expected with him.

"Emma stopped me in town today," he finally says.

I wince but eventually right my expression. Emma is my ex-girlfriend. We dated for a short period of time during which she became a little overly obsessed. Not only that, but she had a very unattractive infatuation with nose candy. I broke things off knowing I didn't feel the same about her as she did about me.

"Oh yeah? She doing good?"

I don't think there's any bad blood between Emma and me. At least not on my end, there isn't. But my friends, including Heston, couldn't stand her when we dated. So it's weird that he brings her up.

"Fine, I guess," he shrugs. "It was awkward as hell, though. She's still dating Spencer. And she demanded I tell you that I saw her with him."

Ah, so she's showboating him around town now. Spencer Chase is a little bitch. Not to mention he's also Savannah's brother. We do not get along in the slightest.

When Emma liked me, he liked Emma. I had the girl that he wanted, and he hated me for that, which he made abundantly clear whenever I was with her. It was annoying as hell.

In the time that Emma and I were together, Spencer did nothing but sit in his posh air-conditioned office in the city just thinking of all the ways he could piss me off. Well that, and making more money than he knows what to do with. We couldn't be any more different.

Now I'm hard up for his sister who hates me, and I've become the shining star of my own little backwoods soap opera. Yee-fucking-haw.

I raised my white flag in his little pissing match pretty quickly, though. Breaking things off with Emma got him off my back until recently, when I asked Savannah on a date having no idea they were siblings.

"Is it bad that I'm kind of hoping for them to work out so that Emma moves to the city with him and they both stay the hell out of Westridge?" I chuckle.

It sounds bad, wishing someone would leave town. I get the feeling that she's using Spencer to try and make me jealous. If she's going out of her way to show him off to Heston, who she knows would rather dig a well by hand than participate in small-town drama, then it confirms that she's willing to try anything to get my attention.

Heston just shakes his head with the tiniest of smirks.

"Nah," he says under his breath before another drink of his beer. "She's certifiable. Wouldn't want her around either if I was you."

"Did you say anything to her?"

"Nope. Walked away."

I laugh as I picture Emma trying to show off her rich boyfriend only to be met with Heston's unimpressed glare. Against my better judgment, I ask the question on the tip of my tongue.

"Was Savannah there with them?"

With a knowing quirk of his eyebrow, he shakes his head.

My phone vibrates on the arm of the chair as the screen lights up with an incoming call. Heston takes that as his cue to leave. What Heston doesn't make clear with words, he does with his actions. He knows Spencer and I have been at each other's throats in the past—and that Emma can get a little over the top. His bringing them up was a heads-up that Spencer is in town and Emma is clearly trying to use him to stir up some envy on my end.

Once Heston is back inside, I lift the phone and read the unfamiliar caller ID number. It's local, but not in my contacts. Not wanting to miss a call that could pertain to my business, I slide my thumb across the bottom of the screen and answer in my most professional voice.

"This is Warren."

My brows instantly pull together when an automated robot speaks back to me.

"This is a collect call from an inmate," there's a short pause while it switches to a recorded voice, "Savannah Chase."

I jump up from my seat.

Inmate? Savannah? I twist my face and fight the urge to laugh at first. She's got to be pulling some kind of prank on me.

I wouldn't be surprised, considering we just had the world's worst first date. One that I never even got to explain myself for.

If she's really in jail I highly doubt she'd call me, anyway.

The look of disgust on her face flashes through my mind, and for the millionth time, I mull over the disastrous dinner we had. Trying to bring back my focus, I rub the pinch in my forehead away.

"Do you accept the charges?" the automated voice chimes in again.

I hesitate for a moment until the same message plays a second time and warns me that if there is no response, the call will be terminated.

"Yes," I answer while scratching my head and trying to predict what sort of trouble Savannah might have gotten herself into if this call is legit. There's a short pause followed by a click on the line.

"Warren?"

Her voice is only slightly less irritated than the last time it graced my ears. I swallow hard and close my eyes long enough to fight off the urge to pace around the patio like a nervous madman.

"Are you in jail right now?" I ask in the most even voice that I can manage.

The tension in my shoulders eases slightly when she clears her throat and softly laughs. I hide my small smirk with the back of my hand even though she can't see me right now.

"I—yes. I am."

My eyes widen. The sudden practiced confidence in her voice is obvious. If we were standing face to face right now, I bet I'd see her whipping her hair off her shoulder and forcing herself to stand taller and appear unfazed.

I have no idea why she'd be calling me of all people at a

time like this. She hates my guts. This was evidenced by the fact that our last encounter involved an entirely full glass of water being splashed in my face. Plus, she's been dodging my calls and texts as I've been trying to get a hold of her for the better part of the last ten days.

It hits me that something terrible could have happened and that she clearly needs my help. My tone lowers as I fail to conceal the concern in my voice.

"Are you hurt?"

"I'm fine. Just a little misunderstanding is all. Are you busy right now?"

I look behind me to the bunkhouse where a warm glow of light spills out of the windows.

"Kinda, yeah," I admit. It's not that I'm not willing to offer her the help that she's inconspicuously asking for right now, but if I had to choose between a night with my family and friends and coming to the rescue of a girl who hates me and has refused to hear me out until she needed something from me? I might choose the former.

"Right. Of course, silly me!" she quips back in a tone too sweet to be genuine. "Enjoy your evening then!"

"Wait—"

"Yes?" I swear I can hear her smile through the phone. It's probably a satisfied one, thinking she's got me right where she wants me after a subtle guilt trip.

I huff out a heavy breath and tilt my head to the sky. This woman is fucking complicated. Sure, she's brilliant. Smarter than most people could ever hope to be. I knew that within minutes of meeting her. And yeah, she's a brunette bombshell with the kind of body I could waste years of my life just daydreaming about.

But she's still . . . *complicated*. And stubborn as hell.

So why is my brow starting to sweat at the thought of her

being locked up? Why do I care? And why am I walking back inside right now to grab my keys?

Maybe so I can try to explain myself again. Or maybe so I can figure out why I haven't been able to get her out of my head since the night I first met her. I wish she didn't have a hold on me, and that I could cross her off the list of things that have been giving me hell lately.

"Hang tight," I tell her with a sigh.

"Okay. Thanks, Warren."

She hangs up and the line goes silent as I shove the soles of my boots back and forth against the welcome mat before opening the door and stepping inside. The back patio is just off the kitchen, and the first thing I see when I walk in is Gage kissing my sister, Blythe. It's not a rare sight to see around here these days. The two don't even *try* to keep their hands off each other. He lifts her into his arms and spins her around while she laughs.

"Look," Blythe says as she points to the large TV screen in the living room. I don't bother looking at first, preoccupied with scowling at the crack on my phone screen that I just discovered, but then Savannah's name comes through the speakers.

I was expecting to see a commercial or something for the law firm where she works, but when I snap my head toward the screen, it's much worse than that. It's the nightly prime-time news, and a reporter is talking about the arrest of a local attorney earlier today.

The headshot in the corner of the screen is of a smiling Savannah, perfectly polished and put together as usual. That only lasts about three seconds before they've replaced her picture on the screen with video footage of her being escorted out of the courthouse. She's cooperating but clearly displeased. In less than ten seconds, she shouted a few curse words and threw her hair aggressively out of her face before stepping into the cop car.

I'm so shocked and distracted by the video, even as the car is driving away with her in it, that I barely catch the next few words out of the reporter's mouth. He said physical altercation and alleged indecent exposure? What the hell happened in there today? I look down to check the time, seeing that it's just now a little bit past eight.

Blythe gasps and snaps her fingers as the breaking news story segment ends.

"Hey, am I crazy, or is that the girl you went on a date with a few weeks ago, Warren?" she asks.

I purse my lips, set my phone down on the table, and shove both of my hands in the pockets of my jeans. I don't exactly have the time or energy to chat and explain it, but I look up to the ceiling and reply to my sister with a resounding sigh anyway.

"That's her."

"No shit," Tripp laughs and plasters an amused grin on his face. He's leaning his hip against the back of the couch with one boot crossed over the other. After looking down at his phone for a moment, he lifts it and points the screen toward me. "Damn, this story is going viral."

I hate social media, so I don't even attempt to lean forward and read what's on the screen. He flips the screen back toward him and reads it out loud anyway.

"Breaking News: New-in-town Westridge attorney arrested after courthouse altercation. It's got a shit ton of comments," Tripp laughs. "Damn, what the hell happened?"

"I don't know," I sigh. "I'm sure they're blowing it out of proportion for clicks."

"Well, I can't say this is what I had in mind when I said you needed to get out there and start dating again," Blythe points out. "But good grief, she is *pretty*."

It's obvious when the wheels start spinning in my sister's mind. If I don't get out of here quickly, she's going to have a thousand more questions that I don't have the answers to.

Heston shakes his head and rubs at his temple in his spot on the recliner. I pin him with a stare before he has a chance to give me any shit. He wouldn't normally have a comment in a conversation like this. But something tells me he wouldn't miss an opportunity to make fun of my less-than-impressive dating track record.

"A rancher and a jailbird. Classic," Gage says while leaning down and resting his chin on Blythe's shoulder to hide a smile.

"Save it," I roll my eyes and swipe my keys from the bowl on the island.

"Wait," Tripp smirks and folds his arms, still leaning against the couch. "Are you ditching us to go bail out your girlfriend?"

"She's not my girlfriend," I mumble.

Grabbing my phone from the table and swinging my keys around my index finger, I trudge toward the front door.

"Bring her back here so we can get the full story!" Blythe yells when I'm halfway out the door.

"Ask them if you can keep the handcuffs—" I slam the door shut behind me, cutting Tripp off before he gets a chance to finish his sentence. I may be outside now, but I can still hear him and Gage howling with laughter.

Even with the sun down, it's still hot in West Texas. The air hangs heavy and humid, making my shirt stick to the skin on my back and my breaths feel deeper than they should.

My truck's driver's side window slides down as I hold the button before firing up the engine. I need to feel the air as I make my way into town. It's about a fifteen-minute drive from the ranch. Plenty of time to figure out how to wipe the nervous sweat off my palms while talking to Savannah Chase without her noticing.

3

SAVANNAH

"You're free to go, Ms. Chase," the clerk says in an uninterested monotone.

She looks to be about my age, late twenties, and not too thrilled about working the night shift. She smacks her gum and doesn't make eye contact with me from behind the thick glass barrier as she pushes my bag of belongings across the counter. Just as I pick it up and open the flap, my movement stills, and my knees lock at the deep sound of the unmistakable voice behind me.

"Guess you can't get out of letting me take you home this time."

My face fixes in a scowl and I turn around slowly on my heel. There's no point in pretending to be pleasant with him now, he's clearly already signed the papers and paid my bail. It was probably a poor decision to turn and look at him. God, he's distracting. I wish he wasn't so tall and his jeans didn't fit like they do. It'd make hating him a whole lot easier. I take a breath and avert my gaze to clear my thoughts.

This is the guy who pretended to like you just to make his ex jealous, Savannah.

The urge to make a scene and cuss him out is strong now that I've reminded myself of that little fact, but I'm not sure it's worth the risk of making even more of a fool of myself in public than I already have in the last twenty-four hours. Lifting my chin, I tuck the bag of belongings under my arm and walk straight toward the door.

"Oh, Warren! So nice to see you! Careful on the ride home, it's supposed to storm tonight," the clerk calls out. It's clear how much more excitement and warmth she has in addressing him compared to how she spoke to me.

"Will do," he answers her and tips the brim of his hat. "See you at the ranch next weekend?"

She beams and nods enthusiastically like she's just won the lottery. Give me a fucking break. And why would she be seeing him at the ranch next weekend?

"Awesome. Have a great night." Warren flashes her a charming smile over his shoulder and waves.

At first, I found it fascinating how much the people in this community obviously adored him. The night we first met, our conversation was constantly interrupted by different people fawning over him, going in for an earnest handshake or hug, and gushing over him and his family. Now, I just find it irritating.

My hand doesn't make it to the door handle fast enough before he pushes it open for me and waits for me to walk through. With pursed lips and an eye roll, I step outside. As I pass by him, my traitorous senses inhale his unavoidable scent. The same intoxicating cloud of leather and musk that I remember.

Attempting to put some distance between us, my determined steps make my heels click-clack against the sidewalk. Even when the door to the police station slams behind us, I don't slow down, in hopes of finally leaving this dreadful day behind.

"Hey," Warren calls out. I can hear him jogging to catch up with me, and it doesn't take him long with legs nearly twice the length of mine. "I'm actually parked that way," he says, pointing over his shoulder.

Looking straight ahead, I keep up my pace and ignore him. That is until he takes three more long strides and turns around, stopping right in front of me. He's blocking the narrow sidewalk, so I practically skid to a halt so as not to crash right into his chest.

Face to face with him and no escape in sight, my chest rises and falls. For the briefest second, I indulge in the sight of him. All tan skin, broad shoulders, and barely there scruff. My eyes narrow to a slit, trying to blur away the outline of him in front of me.

"The office where I parked my car this morning is just down a few streets. I'll be just fine to walk there," I say and add a hand to my hip to prove how casual this is for me. Truthfully, it's a little bit farther than just a few streets down. And my feet are killing me. But nothing good has ever come out of spending time with this guy. I'd rather just be on my way.

"It's dark out. Just let me take you home."

"Why? Are you hoping Emma hears about you giving me a ride and turns green with envy? Or maybe you're hoping it will piss off my brother?" I point my finger in the air like it's a novel idea, but then roll my eyes. "I'm not falling for your tricks again. And anyway, my brother cares a lot less about who I happen to be with than you think. Trust me, acting like you want to drive me home is not worth your time."

He lets out a long, exhausted breath and flexes his jaw. If my stubbornness annoys him, then so be it. He won't be the first to be annoyed by me, nor will he be the last. I take a step to the right in an attempt to get around him, but he mirrors my movement to stay in front of me. I shift to the left, hoping he doesn't block me again, but he does.

Our eyes meet once again and my eyes search for something to focus on other than the striking blue of his irises.

"Come on, Savvy. It's not like that," he says.

"I'm not stupid. It most definitely *is* like that," I argue. "Now if you could kindly step aside, I would *really* like to go home now."

"I can't do that," he says with a shake of his head and a firmer tone than before like his patience is wearing thin.

I open my mouth to give him one last protest before I end up taking a shoe off and throwing it at his head, but he takes the bag from under my arm before I get the chance to do either of those things.

"Hey! I need that, my phone is in there!" I jump up to try and snatch it back from him, but he holds it high in the air where I can't possibly reach it. Stepping closer, he looks down and waits until I reluctantly meet his gaze.

"If you want to go to the office to get your car, I'll drive you there," he states. "But I'm not about to let you walk a mile there by yourself at night and that's final."

Slowly, he lowers the bag and places it back in my hands. His brow quirks up as he waits for me to give in to him. I crumple the clear plastic bag in my fists, damn near ripping it open with my grip. I don't want him to be a reasonable gentleman right now. I need him to be the slime bag that I know he is.

I'm tired. So fucking tired. From this day, the last few months, hell the last five years.

I see in his determined expression that I won't be able to change his mind about letting me walk to the office right now.

I also won't be able to go back in time and undo everything else that took place today.

And I certainly can't erase what happened between Warren and me either.

Everything feels so out of my control and it's paralyzing.

With that realization, the fight that I've been holding on to for dear life in me dims and my shoulders fall in a slump. I sniff back the threat of tears and spin on my heel to head for his truck so he doesn't detect the emotions on my face.

If he wants to take me to my car so I'm not walking alone in the dark, *fine*. Apparently, I don't have a choice in the matter, let alone the strength to argue with him or anyone else any further tonight.

On my trek along the sidewalk, I pass the police department building and scan the side parking lot for his truck. After a minute, I finally spot it parked under a single streetlight, looking even more black and shiny than I remember. The last time I was walking toward this vehicle, I was actually excited. I shake my head at the memory. So naive.

Warren somehow passes me again, making it to the passenger door first and opening it for me.

"Oh, cut the crap, cowboy." I scoff and slide into the seat.

He closes the door and I sink into the luxurious leather. As soon as he climbs into the driver's side and roars the engine to life, I push the seat heater button and kick the heels off my now-swollen feet. God, that's comfortable. He may be a pain in the ass, but at least he has a nice truck. The worst ones always do.

4

WARREN

W hen we pull out of the parking lot and onto Main Street, rolling clouds blacken the already dark night sky and tiny drops of rain sprinkle the windshield. That brings a smile to my face. I get why some people might not be a huge fan of rainstorms. They leave behind a bit of a mess. But I love the fresh earthy smell of them. And I know the farmers and ranchers in the area need the moisture as bad as ever.

I take my eye off the road for a split second to roll down the window and then chance a peek at Savannah. We're creeping along at the speed limit so I can drag out this short drive as much as possible.

The expression on her face is a mix of exhaustion and irritation. She makes no secret of how unhappy she is to see me again. I don't fucking like it one bit.

As much as I'd like to take this opportunity to talk to her, I don't want to make her night even worse. Though, there's no telling when I'll get this chance again seeing as how she's been ignoring me for weeks. I glance her way again and decide to rip off the band-aid.

"I know you're mad at me, but—"

"Of course, I'm mad at you," she cuts me off. "As a matter of fact, I dislike you very much, Warren." My face falls as she enunciates each word, but I can't ignore the slight hesitation in her voice. After a moment of contemplation, she continues to rake me over the coals.

"You embarrassed me for your own personal gain. But you picked the wrong girl to use." Her pointer finger aims straight for my face and I see it waving out of my peripheral while I drive. "I'm not going to give you a pass just because you bailed me out tonight. I don't have time for your shit, and if you're half as smart as the rest of this town thinks you are, you'll just drop me off and leave well enough alone."

By the time she's done with her little speech, she's sitting straight up in her seat and cutting me in half with a heated stare. I'd like to correct her with the fact that I most definitely did not embarrass her on purpose, but I hate fighting and she argues for a living. Going back and forth with her would be pointless. And I'd have to be an idiot not to realize that now is not the time to push her.

"Yes ma'am," I sigh. It's a little sarcastic, I admit. But what am I supposed to do? Cover her mouth with my hand and force her to listen to me? I'd rather not get kicked in the balls, so no.

"Thank you." She nods once, turns in her seat until she's facing forward again, and looks straight out the front windshield with her arms crossed.

I bet she thinks her demands were bold enough to wear me down for good. But in reality, I'm just picking my battles and biding my time. Something about this girl has me determined to win her over. Someone as strong-willed as she is would never give in unless she truly wanted to.

The walls she's put up around herself are twenty feet

high, but I want to know what it's like for Savvy to want me. I'm going to find out if it's the last thing I do.

Outside, lightning flashes and raindrops fall faster, so I close the window. The fresh air isn't worth a soaked shirt. I flip up the lever to turn on the windshield wipers and take a turn down her office's street.

"It's coming down pretty good out there. Want me to just drop you at your house so that you don't have to drive in this?"

"No," she sulks.

I shake my head, but smirk at the same time. She's not giving me a single inch here.

As soon as the office comes into view, Savannah unbuckles her seat belt and pulls her bag close to her chest, ready to jump out the second I pull to a stop and put the truck in park.

"I'm the black SUV," she says, pointing to one of only a few cars parked on the street in front of the dark red brick building. The hanging business sign sways back and forth from gusts of wind, and if I didn't already know that it said Law Offices of Powell and Grant, I wouldn't be able to read it from the sheets of rain blurring the letters.

Without even saying goodbye, the little firecracker next to me swings open the passenger door and jumps right out. It takes her a few tries to slam it back shut due to the blustery wind. Then she puts her head down and trudges toward her car. I was taught to stay put until the person you're dropping off starts their car and pulls away before leaving, so I wait. While she fumbles through her bag for her keys, my phone buzzes in the cupholder with a group text notification.

TRIPP

Rain, baby!!

GAGE

Sitting on the porch right now listening to it. I almost forgot what rain even looked like.

TRIPP

Isn't it an hour past your bedtime old man?

GAGE

yes.

TRIPP

Go to sleep then cause we're muddin tomorrow boys

GAGE

Last time we did that Heston high centered your Bronco and Warren fucked up the light bar on the side by side.

lol worth it

GAGE

How's the Savannah situation going?

I look up from my phone at the reminder of her. She's sopping wet, still not in her car, and her shoulders are shaking. *Shit.* Without thinking, I place my hat on the center console and step out into the relentless downpour.

"Hey, what's—"

I stop in my tracks and cut off my sentence when I notice that her bag is on the ground beneath her and she's covering her face with both hands. If she looked up at me right now, there's a good chance I'd see her tears mixed with the rainfall streaming down her face.

As I walk closer and step in front of her, I wrap my hands around her wrists. Not wanting to uncover her face, she shakes her head and tries to back up. But I don't let her. My first instinct should be to give her space. Let her sob for another minute before I try and figure out how to make her feel better.

But we're standing on the side of the dark street, drenched. Not the most ideal place to cry it out. Plus, another second of seeing her so upset might split me in two.

Feisty Savannah, I fully expected. This version? Not so much.

My grip on her wrists tightens and I pull her closer. Slowly, because I anticipate her jerking away again.

If you've ever tried to help a hurt animal, you know the helpless feeling. There's nothing you can do but be patient and hope they trust that you're just concerned about them. You can sense the hesitation in their body language, the fight with their common sense, and their curiosity as they question whether or not you're trying to attack them. Savannah heaves another sob and it's clear whatever battle she's been fighting has finally broken the surface.

Even over the deafening rain and whistling wind, I can feel the moment that a massive breath finally leaves her body. The stiffness in her limbs fades, and when her forehead hits my chest, she melts completely.

"It's stupid," she sniffs into my shirt. "All I've been through lately, and it's the lost keys that do me in."

Tentatively, I release my grip on her wrists, and she finally drops her arms from her face to wrap them around my waist. Resting my chin on the top of her head, I smooth one hand over the back of her head and the other across her shoulder blades. Back and forth.

I look down at her, a mess from the rain and the storm inside. When her guard is down, we move so naturally together like this. There's no stopping the flood of memories from when we first met.

Her curious smile, the way my body unconsciously leaned toward hers . . .

She was relaxed, and we talked for hours. I know it's borderline diabolical to feel so strongly about someone so soon after meeting them, but I didn't give a shit. I was helpless to fight against the thought that we were perfect together.

An unsettling ache builds beneath my rib cage, and I work to ignore it and focus on the version of her that's currently in my arms instead.

I know she hates me. Or at least she *thinks* she does. Hugging is the last fucking thing I thought I'd be doing with her right now. I'm not complaining, but still.

No matter how she feels about me, I can't help but comfort her when she's so obviously upset like this. It seems like she needed it too. Because with every second, she leans more into my embrace, to which my body automatically responds with a tighter hold.

Maybe I can't fix whatever problems she has right this second, but for now, I want her to feel a little less alone. Lightning cracks through the clouds in a flash, and a few seconds later thunder echoes around us.

"You don't have your keys?" I say, nearly shouting so that she can hear me despite being buried in my chest and the downpour that surrounds us.

If she says anything, I don't hear it, but she's nodding. God, I shouldn't be thinking about how cute it is when she nuzzles her nose into my chest like that. Or how much I don't want to lead her back to my truck, effectively putting an end to our spontaneous embrace. But she's starting to feel cold, and there's no hope of getting into her car right now, so I back away to take her hand.

Or at least, I try to. It takes less than a second for realization to cross her face and she takes two large steps away from me.

After another loud crack of lightning, she squeals and jumps, running away from me and getting into my truck. I jog to the driver's side and hop in too, all the while thinking once again how complicated and confusing this woman is.

She could have slapped me when I hugged her, but she didn't. She could have ended the hug herself, but she didn't. And I'm starting to get whiplash from her hot and cold reactions to every little thing I do.

When I slide into my seat and shut the door behind me, I look over and see Savannah holding her face in her hands again.

"Hey," I say just above a whisper. "It's gonna be alright. I'll take you home and you can track your keys down tomorrow."

"My brother is going to give me so much shit for this. Even more than he already does."

"*Fuck* your brother," I blurt before I find the decency to not say it out loud.

Her head whips in my direction and she glares at me like I put a bag of burning dog shit on her doorstep. The way her nose crinkles up and her eyes narrow is adorable though and I don't think she looks half as scary as she thinks she does.

"Sorry," I mumble. "Not trying to be a dick, but he's a grade-A asshole and you know it."

"Okay he's an ass, I know that. But—" She stops herself and turns away. "I don't know why I'm talking to you about this. I just need to go home."

"You can talk to me about it, Savvy." I leave out the part where I *want* her to talk to me about it. I'm unbelievably drawn to anything that she has to say. It's the reason I asked her out a few weeks ago in the first place. I hung on her every

31

word and when the night was over, I knew I wanted to hear more. Now, trying to get her to talk to me again feels like blowing out a trick birthday candle that just keeps lighting.

"I don't want you to be upset. I'm a good listener. Just ask my sister. I know it sucks how things ended with our date and—"

The hand in front of my face shuts me up real quick.

"I'm going to stop you right there. Thank you for the hug and for calming me down," she says quietly. "But I'm certainly not going to trauma dump on you. I'm cold, wet, and *tired*."

Sucking in a long, exaggerated breath, I fire up the truck and put it in drive to take her home.

The way she's avoiding a conversation with me right now is maddening, not just because pining after a woman who wants nothing to do with me is different from what I'm used to, but more because we have unfinished business.

We had something real; I could feel it. I want to get back to that, but I'm going to have to earn her trust again in order for that to happen.

If the ignored calls and texts, angry looks, and refusals to talk it out weren't enough to deter me, I'm not sure anything will.

If she ever slips and lets me get a word in edgewise, I'll find a way to convince her to give me another chance.

5

SAVANNAH

My eyes are as puffy and red as they've ever been. My head throbs like I just got home from an all-night rager. And I may very well get fired today.

"Damn thing," I curse as I throw the beauty sponge across the bathroom and it bounces off the vintage coral tile, landing somewhere behind the woven basket in the corner.

It doesn't matter how expensive my concealer is or how much blending I attempt. I place my hands on either side of the sink, leaning toward the vanity mirror. This mug is going to look as rough as I feel and there's not much I can do about it at this point. Little to no sleep and hours of crying will do that to a girl.

I spent half the night wide awake and trying to figure out a world-class speech that might help save my career. The other half, warding off the guilt from how hard I was on Warren after he saved my ass when no one else would.

In truth, I appreciated that he was willing to come pick me up and take me home even when I acted like an absolute ice queen toward him. I don't think anyone has ever helped me calm down so fast, but he did somehow. His body was irresistibly warm in the middle of the nearly frigid rain. His voice was sure and soothing.

For a moment, with the way he touched me and his reaction to my mental breakdown, it was almost as if he cared.

I'd love nothing more than to believe that to be true, but I can't trust my feelings around him. I can't trust him in general. No matter how charming or handsome he is, he's not cunning enough to fool me twice.

The long hours of overthinking last night did nothing to erase the familiar rush of disappointment about my job either. Knowing I have to walk into that office today and face the consequences of the stunt I pulled yesterday brings a whole new meaning to the word failure.

Now would be a great time for me to call a friend. Isn't that what most girls do on a morning like this when one of them feels like booking a one-way ticket to Antarctica? FaceTime while they do their hair and get dressed. Vent about the latest drama, hype each other up, or maybe tell each other how good they look in their outfits.

I wouldn't know, I'm just assuming. The closest I've ever come to having that is propping up my phone to watch a complete stranger's "get ready with me" videos or makeup tutorials online while I get ready.

But I could use a real friend right now. I sure as hell am not going to get a nurturing pep-talk from my aloof parents, pretentious brother, or nonexistent gal pals. The only thing I can do is down the rest of this berry smoothie, slap on a little extra lip gloss, and hope for the best.

With one last glance in the mirror and a quick smoothing of my curls, I finish putting on my gold jewelry and camel blazer on top of my signature crisp white blouse. I almost went with a more plain sensible black that I laid out yesterday, but I'll be damned if I'm going to get canned looking like I showed up for my own funeral.

Looking down, I slip my feet into a pair of my favorite sling-back heels. Fake it 'till you make it, but *never* in ugly shoes.

Hooking my bag in the crook of my elbow, I walk out of the bathroom and across the hardwood floor to the kitchen. It's only a few feet away, nestled in the corner of the studio layout cottage by the sliding barn door that leads to the backyard.

This rental fell into my lap when I posted my apartment in the city as a sublet after I was hired at the firm in Westridge. I commuted for a while since it was about an hour away. On a good day. That got old after a few weeks, and I realized that I needed to move.

Luckily, a girl about my age who only lives a few minutes from Westridge emailed me and offered me a trade situation. She needed a place to live in the city while she taught a class at the university for the summer and fall semesters, and I needed to live closer to work until I found something more permanent. There aren't a lot of options for renting around here, so I was elated when she emailed me.

After a few conversations on FaceTime to make sure she wasn't scamming me, I agreed to take care of her little cottage and the "exorbitant amount of plants," her words, while she took over my lease until the end of the year.

My eyes about bugged out of my head when I arrived with my things to move in. When she said that she had a lot of plants for me to take care of, I wasn't expecting to find a damn botanical garden for a home.

She has a greenhouse off the side of the modest property, a yard overflowing with colorful blooms, vines framing the gates and front door, and more green succulents and other various plants inside than there is space to sit down.

She patiently walked me through the maintenance and care of them, and I could tell right away that they meant a lot to her. I was happy to find out that almost everything outside was hooked up to an automatic water system, so it hasn't actually been as much work as I feared it would be.

Still, I've spent a decent amount of time picking the occasional weed, monitoring soil, deadheading, and sending her pictures and videos. But I don't mind. It's a perfect arrangement for us to trade places. Her dreamy mix of vintage and zen sense of style is growing on me too.

I know it's probably because we haven't spent much time together, and neither of us has spare time for small talk or casual conversation, but she's been incredibly kind to me and I'm grateful that I can stay at her house while I'm here.

She seems like the type of girl I'd like to have as a friend. Under different circumstances, maybe we could be.

That may not be for much longer unless I can save my job today. I'll miss this place if I have to leave soon. With a sigh, I rinse out my smoothie glass and load it in the dishwasher.

A horn honks from the front yard and I put my sunglasses on, masking my eye-roll even though no one is inside with me to see it.

Plastering on a look of confidence, I walk out the door, locking it behind me and doing a quick scan of the yard to make sure everything is in order before I get into my brother's ridiculous vehicle of choice. It's a stupidly expensive white sports car with a full custom borderline neon red interior. Bright enough to give you a headache just from sitting in it. It fits his outlandish personality, I guess.

Immediately, I cringe when I spot the tiny white bag of white powder sticking out from under a piece of paper in the center console. And as I expected, he didn't waste a second before making me feel like the size of an ant. I can take his terrible attitude, but he better not be high.

"You could have told me it was this far out of town and off dirt roads. You owe me a fucking detail."

36

More worried about getting the dust off his precious car than helping me. He sounds like my father when he says things like that and it makes me cringe once again.

I place my bag on my lap and gently close the passenger door, although I'd like to slam it. Maybe even run a key along the pristine paint on the outside once he drops me off for good measure.

Spencer and I have always had a rocky relationship. He's competitive, outgoing, and has been successful in pretty much everything he's ever set out to do. My parents dote on him with his fancy Ivy League degree and going into the family business with my dad. Unfortunately, they don't find his conceited comments and finance bro attitude as annoying as I do.

I still texted him once I got home last night begging for a ride to the office since my keys were nowhere to be found. I did not want to call and beg him for a ride to work. I didn't even want to call him when I needed help getting out of a damn holding cell either.

But this morning I didn't have much choice. A recurring theme for me, it seems. I needed someone to take me into town. And at least with Spencer, I know what I'm getting. Calling Warren was out of the question, of course. I've come to terms with letting him help me get home. I wasn't about to tack on getting me to work too.

"You're lucky I was still in town," Spencer says through a mouthful of what looks like a breakfast sandwich. "Next time you mess shit up and need a ride to work, just call Emma. I should already be back in the city. I don't have time for this."

It's been awkward working with my brother's girlfriend, Emma. For some reason, she feels the need to fill me in on all the dirty details of their fling and I have to stop myself from saying something rude every time she brings him up in the office. And anyway, she's probably been at work for hours already and wouldn't have come to get me this morning anyway.

"She was asked to come in early and help with pro bono day. I knew she wouldn't be able to pick me up, so I called you," I explain in a flat voice while staring out the window at the passing fields of green.

"Whatever," he mumbles as he swallows his food. "The hell is pro bono day?"

"People from all over the county come into the firm for a free consultation. They're either taken on as clients free of charge or referred to someone else who can help them."

"Sounds dumb."

I shake my head and cross my ankles. If he didn't have such a complete lack of empathy, he'd bother to educate himself on giving back to the community.

Mariana Powell and Henry Grant, partners at the firm, host the pro bono day once per quarter. There are no appointments, first come first serve. Despite what some may assume, It's more than just a tax write-off in the form of literal charity cases. I haven't experienced it before today, but from what I've heard, they've helped a multitude of families, single parents, and struggling businesses get the representation they need but can't afford.

Spencer looks down at his phone to answer a text and I grab the handle of the passenger side door, hoping we make it to town in one piece before we either crash or I kick him out with the spike of my heel, leaving him on the dirt road to drive there myself.

I know deep down that he's a good guy. Or that he could be. But he's followed in our dad's footsteps and unfortunately, that means that image reigns supreme in his mind. Nothing I ever do measures up to their expectations and it's exhausting.

By the time he drops me off and I walk into the law firm

office, it's already buzzing with the sound of the copy machine, clients in the waiting area, and classic country music streaming softly through the speakers. I'm not late, for once, but I expected that with pro bono day happening.

"Psst!" A voice hisses from behind the freakishly tall fiddle leaf fig tree next to the front desk. I step toward it curiously and crane my neck, finding Emma hiding and trying to get my attention.

When I started working here, I thought Emma hated my guts. But after about a week or so, she started dating my brother and conveniently warmed up to me. I'll admit, she's given me countless helpful tips on how to deal with our coworkers and firm partners in an attempt to settle in here and plant the seed of a hopefully successful career. But despite her help, things haven't been going as well for me as I'd hoped.

"There are policemen in the conference room," she whispers. "Come on."

6

SAVANNAH

I peer around as Emma grabs my hand and tows me down the hallway toward the supply closet. When we're safe inside and she shuts and locks the door behind us, I tuck a strand of hair behind my ear and give her a baffled look.

"What in the world are we doing?" I ask.

"I've been waiting for you to get here! You *cannot* go to your desk."

"It doesn't matter, Emma. I'm going to get fired. I literally got arrested yesterday."

"Well, I think you might be in more trouble than you thought. I'm sure they heard you made it home last night and would be showing up here today so they called the cops for security. Do you want to be escorted out of a building like that again?"

I twist my face and pull one brow down. That doesn't make any sense. Other than what happened at the court-house, which I was already reprimanded for, I haven't done anything that would elicit them having the police here waiting for me. Nothing that I can think of anyway.

"Give me your keys. I'll pull your car around, you can slip out the back door, and be gone before they see you!"

"I don't have my keys," I sigh.

I contemplate an escape plan I'm not entirely sure I even need when feet shuffle accompanied by muffled voices down the hallway. As they get closer to the storage closet, their conversation becomes more clear and we press our ears to the door to try and catch what they're saying.

"That's great news. Thanks for stopping by."

That sounded like Mrs. Powell's voice. I press the shell of my ear closer to the wooden door until the side of my face is squished up against the flat surface.

"Sure thing. I'm headed out. Holler if you need anything," another voice says, this one deeper, more gruff, and a lot like the Chief of Police who I've had a few professional conversations with in the past.

My eyes widen and lock with Emma's.

"Don't chance it," she whispers. "You should go home."

This is silly. I'm not a coward and I'm no stranger to getting my ass chewed. I'll be damned if I'm going to tuck my tail between my legs and leave without showing my face. In one swift motion, I open the door and step out into the hall.

"You need to chill out. I'm dreading this, but I'm not going to leave and it sounds like the police you saw earlier are gone now. It'll be fine," I say.

Emma scrunches her nose and shrugs, taking off in the direction of her office near the staff lounge. I hate when this happens. I'm face to face with a potential relationship whether it be a friend or coworker or otherwise, and then proceed to say the wrong thing or act a certain way that makes them walk away.

I don't know why I'm so hell-bent on marching to the beat of my own drum. But those traits have done a number on my job experiences, friendships, and other relationships.

I've learned that most people prefer someone who goes along with whatever they have to say. Someone agreeable and bendable.

That fact is part of why I was so shocked that Warren not only agreed to come help me last night, but he hugged me too. Actually hugged me when I was crying and in the middle of a breakdown. I don't know why he didn't leave me alone after the second time I bit his head off, and I didn't know how to react to that either.

Maybe he's the type of person to show his disgust behind a person's back instead of to their face. He probably laughed at me on his way home and made fun of me to his friends for being a walking catastrophe.

A small twinge of anxiety floods my insides, making me grab the sleeve of my blazer and tug it down over my wrist. It helps to keep myself busy and occupied when feelings like this arise, so I lift my gaze and walk to my desk.

I don't have my own private office yet, being at the bottom of the food chain here so to speak. But my side of the cubicle is right next to the window so I still call that a win. It looks like they weren't angry enough to throw my things out the door yet. My mini fridge still sits under the left side of the desk. My millions of sticky notes are still scattered along the edges of the computer monitor. And even my stacks of case files remain next to the keyboard.

My desk phone rings, and I lean over to see that the caller ID is coming from the main conference room. I clear my throat and scramble to pick it up.

"Hello?"

"Answer the phone by stating your name so that the person calling knows they've reached the correct line of communication, dear."

Mariana. She owns half of this law firm technically but runs the whole damn thing literally. I've never met anyone as sharp as she is. It's part of the reason I all but begged for this job. I was desperate to work with her and soak up every bit of knowledge she was willing to give.

Lucky for me, not a lot of big-shot lawyers are jumping at the chance to move out of the city and to the town of Westridge. After researching Mariana's stellar track record of mentoring young attorneys, I went for the opportunity.

"Right. Yes ma'am," I say back to her.

"Meet us in the conference room, please."

The dial tone blares through the receiver after she hangs up, and my hand immediately massages the tension on the back of my neck. Her voice was not unpleasant, but I know she's displeased with me. I can *feel* it, and it doesn't feel good. I'm really beginning to hate this recurring feeling of letting people down.

"Have a seat," Mr. Grant says as I enter the conference room. He's seated to the right of Mrs. Powell, who is at the head of the table. Steam rises from his coffee and he blows on the surface before taking a sip.

"Is there a reason you were late this morning Ms. Chase?" he says as the bottom of his mug clinks against the glass-top table. "We tried to reach you at your desk a few times before you finally answered. There are several prospective clients waiting on meetings and we need to get this over with beforehand."

My forehead wrinkles, knowing I definitely wasn't late. In fact, I was a few minutes early. Then I remember Emma's little freakout that had me inconveniently detained and I take a deep breath. Instead of trying to explain that whole situation, I try for once to keep things simple.

"Sorry about that," I say. The brown office chair squeaks as I lower myself into it and adjust the height for my short legs. Instead of giving into the urge to use the lever as a fidget to calm my nerves, I fold my hands on the table and wait for the inevitable lecture to proceed with a stack of termination papers being smacked down in front of me.

"I was happy to see that when I stopped by the police station last night, you had already been released. I attempted to call, but I imagine your phone must have died," Mariana chimes in. Normally I can appreciate her typical power move of standing behind her chair like that, but right now it's intimidating as hell. "You'll be happy to know that I've been working with law enforcement for the charges against you to be dropped immediately."

My eyes widen and dart between them. It hasn't even been twenty-four hours. Oh, she's good.

"But . . . how?" I'm sure they sense the relief in my voice. It's not a completely out-of-the-woods feeling, but it's damn close. I have a much better chance of keeping my job if there are no criminal charges.

"Henry gathered video surveillance evidence from the courthouse while I contacted witnesses. It was only a matter of hours before the chief viewed the footage and agreed that you were not only provoked but acting in self-defense," she explains. "As for the indecent exposure, well, that was clearly an accident. The complainant had no choice but to drop the charges when I emailed him all that information."

"You mean after you threatened him with a countersuit for mental anguish," Mr. Grant scoffs.

"Semantics. The point is, it's all been taken care of. And I need you in the archives so we can prepare for new cases coming up while the pro bono meetings take up the rest of the workload today. It's a big slate. All hands on deck," she says while tapping on the screen of a tablet at the same time. There's a pen tucked behind her ear and she's biting the corner of her lip, already on to the next thing in her mind. I'm convinced that even during a serious conversation, this woman never stops working.

"I don't know what to say. Thank you," I breathe out, relief flooding my body.

I should have known the guy at the courthouse yesterday didn't have much of a leg to stand on. One minute I was looking for Emma and the next, the grumpy asshole who we just beat in a civil case bumped straight into me.

It wouldn't have bothered me if he would've settled for an angry glare and moved on. But he couldn't help himself. *"Maybe I wouldn't have lost if I had tits like yours,"* he'd said as he shouldered past me with an eye roll. Loud enough for an entire group of people to hear as we were walking out of the room.

I'd turned to face him, already on edge from a circus of a morning that included a flat tire and a broken button on my blouse. When he widened his stance and got in my face, I whipped my purse up from my side as if I was going to put it over my shoulder, knowing it would smack him in the process. Two men had to hold him back when he flopped back dramatically like I'd struck him with a damn baseball bat. It wasn't the Oscar-worthy performance that he was hoping for, but it was enough to get a few gasps from the crowd and attention from security.

The cherry on top was when I tripped over his leg as he flopped around on the floor. It caused my blouse to pop open, thanks to the missing button on top, and exposed my entire torso. He whined and cried to the security guards about my indecent exposure and assault on him and I left the place in fucking handcuffs.

Just once, I wish I could have kept my composure. I'm not naturally hot-headed, but I let my emotions get the better of me before I even arrived for the hearing. You'd think I'd be able to handle distress more eloquently, being so used to it. But that certainly wasn't the case yesterday. His behavior toward me was like a loud clap at the bottom of a mountain of snow just waiting to bring down an avalanche.

I roll my shoulders back, attempting to shake off the urge to cry. If I were back in the city a few hours from here where I grew up right now, I'd be cowering in front of my parents, enduring a painfully long lecture about how reckless I am. Most of the trouble that I got into as a child and a young adult was to get their attention. It worked, but they grew to resent me for not being able to match their perfectly polished and posh demeanor.

Stop embarrassing us, they'd say. *Be quiet and fall in line.*

I never did either of those things and on top of refusing to play their puppet in the family business, they've all but given up on any sort of relationship with me.

Now, my desperate attempts to make them see me have morphed into a deep-rooted habit of self-destruction and I *hate* it.

"No need to thank me. That man was in the wrong and it was all a misunderstanding," Mariana assures me.

Mr. Grant huffs as he stands from his chair and gathers his things. "I'll be in my office," he grunts. He and Mrs. Powell exchange a look.

When the door closes behind him, I stand up to leave, but sit again when Mariana sits down next to me.

"Savannah, I'd like to have a conversation just between us now if that's alright with you."

I nod but my chest tightens and I swallow hard.

"This law firm prides itself on professionalism and esteem garnered from our clients. Now, I have empathy and understanding for the unfortunate situation that happened yesterday. I think you have great potential and I'd like to keep you around. Mr. Grant, on the other hand, is more skeptical and has suggested that you remain employed here under probationary terms." Her voice is soft as she speaks to me. It's a soothing contradiction compared to the tidal wave of meaning behind her words.

"I—" My head shakes and I fail as usual to come up with the right thing to say. How did I get here *again*? It's uncomfortable and suddenly the weight of another crisis has me nauseous. "I'm going to do better. I promise."

Mariana places a hand on my shoulder and nods. "Can I offer you a piece of advice?"

"Of course," I choke out on the verge of tears.

"At the end of the year, performance reviews will take place," she says. "You're going to have to work to repair your reputation a little bit and it won't be easy. But I think if you focus on staying out of trouble, sharpening your skills, and showing us a new dedication toward conducting yourself in a way that aligns with our firm's standards, then everything will turn out just fine."

7

SAVANNAH

The smells of clean laundry and all-purpose cleaners float around the small space of the cottage. Right on cue, I began my rage cleaning the second I got home for the weekend after another week at work. I sincerely enjoy my job but it's significantly less enjoyable knowing I'm on probation.

There's no getting out of the mundane tasks thrown my way in place of real casework, and walking around the office on eggshells was unavoidable all week. I don't feel like I have control over any part of my life except for this one right now.

When things get dicey, as they often do, I drown my thoughts in scrubbing floors and dishes. I don't ever ask anyone to come visit whatever home I'm living in. But if they did, they wouldn't find a single speck of dust or item out of place. Which is honestly hilarious considering the mess that is my life outside these walls.

As I'm folding a navy-blue bath towel, my phone pings with a text notification from across the room. I place the towel on top of the neat pile of already folded ones and walk over to pick up the phone to see who texted me. My eyes bug out of their sockets when I see Warren's name. After pausing my music and ripping out my headphones, I slump onto the cream-colored loveseat to open the message.

WARREN

Hey Savvy

I know it's a text, but I swear I can almost hear him saying those words in his deep voice. We haven't spoken since he picked me up from jail. I thought he'd given up, and that should have made me feel satisfied. The reckless side of me perks up at the possibility that maybe he wasn't ready to quit after all.

That realization sends a shiver up my arms and I cross my legs tight to try and shake off the swoon. God, I'm pathetic. I know the bar for men must be in motherfucking hell right now because why am I still crushing over a guy I swore I'd stop thinking about just because he was nice to me a week ago?

WARREN

I was hoping you might want to come hang out this weekend. Are you busy?

The text bubbles continue to pop up underneath his last message, disappearing several times and it makes me laugh. I picture him typing up something to convince me to come and then erasing it seconds later. After watching this happen for another minute, I decide to put him out of his misery and text him back.

I have plans sorry.

Between the wine, way-too-long baths, and staring at the ceiling, my schedule is jam-packed for the weekend. Definitely no time to squeeze in hanging out with the confusingly sometimes awful, sometimes sweet man that I'm trying desperately to stop fantasizing about.

> **WARREN**
>
> Come on, I could come pick you up. The food's always good and the beer's cold. And I really want to see you.

What kind of food

> **WARREN**
>
> I've got a brisket on the smoker as we speak but I could go grab some other stuff whatever you want

We're not friends.

> **WARREN**
>
> A damn shame.

eye roll emoji

INCOMING CALL WARREN

Oh shit. Before I can think about it, I hit the decline button. It feels like there's a tennis match going on in my head with him. The yellow ball bounces back and forth between two sides: wanting to forget about what happened and give in to the urge to spend time with him and then back to the side of common sense where I remember that I don't know if I can trust this man.

INCOMING CALL WARREN

With a sigh, I stand up and stab the green button to accept his second call. Before saying anything, I put it on speaker so that I can set the phone on the counter and resume cleaning to distract myself at the same time.

"Savvy…" his voice rings through the small space around

me. My movement only falters for a split second when hearing it.

"Yes?" I answer back in a slightly shaky voice.

"Don't make me beg."

Now *that* I could potentially get on board with. I scrub the already gleaming sink even harder than before with the image in my head of Warren on his knees.

"I have more important things to worry about right now than messing around with fuckboys," I quip back. And it's the truth. The last thing I need right now is to let Warren toss me around for fun. My job is on the line and I need to come up with a plan to save it.

I've messed up too many times in the past. If I got fired from the law firm, not only would my brother and parents blow a gasket and ridicule me more than they already do, but I also have no other job prospects lined up and nowhere else to go. I *have* to make this work.

His huff comes through the phone and I smirk, hoping he took offense to me calling him out.

"I know you want to believe that I am, but I'm not a fuckboy. I just want to get to know you better, Savvy. Hang out with me."

He *sounds* sincere. But the most well-crafted acts are always convincing. I bet he's said this a million times before to a million other girls. He's got it down to an art.

"What's the point?" I ask. Because really, what's his angle here? It was obvious on our date that he never truly liked me in the first place. It was all a game to him. My face turns red just thinking about it. I'm not sure if it's anger or embarrassment or both, but either way, I'm not putting myself in that position again.

"The point is I want to talk to you. Just give me a chance."

I let out a sigh and stop what I'm doing for a moment to stare at the phone. During our meeting last week, Mariana gave me another chance. And as many times as I've screwed up in life, I've always had the opportunity to try again. Maybe it's unreasonable for me not to hear him out. Since I'm trying to turn over a new leaf with my job, I could take a stab at lowering my skepticism when it comes to friendships and relationships too.

Historically, those things have always been represented by a dark cloud of sadness for me. I could be setting myself up for more disappointment, but it might turn out differently this time.

"Alright, fine. I'll hang out with you, you stubborn mule."

It's silent for a second and even though I can't see him, I think he might be doing a quick happy dance because there's a smile in his voice when he finally replies.

"Hell yeah. It'll be fun, I promise."

"I got my keys from my purse that was left at the courthouse, so you don't need to pick me up. Just send me a pin. What are we going to be doing?" I try not to sound too eager, but his excitement is unavoidably contagious.

"Party at the bunkhouse."

B y the fourth turn on a dirt road, I'm starting to regret agreeing to come to *the bunkhouse*, whatever the hell that is. If this is some sort of creepy underground sex club in a big room full of crusty old bunk beds I swear I will punch Warren square in the face.

I'm trying to pay attention to the road so I don't crash, but my attention is split between straight ahead and the maps app on my phone that keeps glitching because I lose more service the farther I get from town. It'd be just my luck to get lost in the country with no bars.

Thankfully, the voice from the phone finally tells me that my destination is on the left. I drive through open iron gates sitting underneath a massive sign that reads "Prairie Rose Ranch." The fences on either side of the long driveway aren't painted, having a more natural and rustic look to them. I pass several groups of cows grazing on grass. The subtle rolling hills and wide open spaces are stunning in a way that I never thought I'd appreciate, growing up in a concrete jungle like I did.

Since it's a nice evening, I roll my window down and let the night air blow in around me as I drive slowly toward the ranch up ahead. The closer I get, the more I wonder where the hell I'm going to park. There are lines of trucks and cars just outside of a large pole barn style building that I'm guessing is where the party's at.

Luckily a lifted red Jeep pulls out of a spot near the front and passes me down the drive, so I swoop in. Now time to sit in the car and decide whether or not I'm even going to go in. It sucks feeling anxious. I never thought there would be this many people here and I wish I could have prepared myself a little better. What really causes me to flake on stuff like this is the thought of people talking to me and not liking what they hear.

I already know my reputation in this town is tarnished with the local news segment about my arrest. It wouldn't surprise me if everyone I met here turned their nose up and wasn't a fan of anything I had to say. It's so much easier to stay home and avoid that possibility, and the possibility of everyone not being my fan once they get to know me.

I think back to the courage it took for me to agree to dinner with Warren when we met at the fundraiser in town. The fact that I agreed to go on a date with him at all when he asked was incredibly rare for me.

Now, here I am stepping out of my comfort zone again just to hang out with him. I blame it on the thick wavy hair curling around the nape of his neck and that damn dimple in his cheek.

Tap Tap

A hand flies to my chest and I whip my head toward the driver's side window where someone just knocked. My mouth drops open when I see her, decked out in cut-off shorts and a faded black crop top with a rooster on it that says "Turnpike Troubadours." Her long dark blonde hair falls in soft waves almost to her waist and she pushes it over one shoulder while smiling at me. I can't stop staring at her perfect teeth and she looks like she belongs on the cover of a magazine rather than in the middle of a red dirt parking lot.

While the window rolls down, she quickly pulls out her phone and types on it, then looks back at me.

"Hi! Savannah?"

I nod nervously.

"I thought I recognized you. Come on, girl! I need a partner!" She opens my door and takes my hand without hesitation. I stumble out, barely grabbing my phone from the dash as I go.

"Wait, I need to take my keys out and lock my car."

She rolls her eyes playfully and waves her free hand as she leads me away from the vehicle.

"Two things about parking your car on this ranch. Always leave the keys in it in case you're in the way and one of the guys needs to move it. And never worry about someone stealing it or something. My fiancé has a thousand security cameras and the people around here are as good as gold anyway." the warmth in her voice makes me believe every word she says, and in a trance, I follow her into the building.

I drop my hand from hers as soon as I come face to face with the sea of happy people drinking and talking inside.

Music fills the large space, sounding vintage and slightly scratchy like it's coming from an old jukebox.

In the circle I grew up in, being invited to a "party" meant dressing up. But everyone here has casual jeans or shorts on, nothing fancy. They look comfortable and I feel like an idiot in my strappy heeled sandals and coral summer dress with puffy sleeves. It's cute. But it's not right.

The blonde girl that brought me inside skips toward the back of the room and I spin on my heel to turn around and walk out. I don't belong here. This was a mistake. Instead of making my way to the door as I turn though, I slam into a wall of muscle with an "oof."

Two large hands come up to wrap around my forearms to keep me from stumbling back. They're large and strong and . . . familiar. These hands have been around my wrists before.

"And just where do you think you're going?" he asks.

"Something came up and I need to leave," I blurt out trying not to be distracted by his hands on me and his sexy low voice.

"Bullshit. You just got here, you can't dip out already. B!" He shouts above the noise across the room.

I look to see whose attention he's trying to get and the girl who brought me in waves us over.

"That's my sister, Blythe. Let's get a drink." Placing his hands on my shoulders, he spins me around and gently pushes me toward the kitchen.

When he reaches the fridge that looks as old as my grandpa and holds up a can of beer, I nod. He pops the top and hands it over to me. The first sip is bitter, but it helps with the nerves, so I take another drink and a deep breath.

"Is this where you live?" I ask, trying to channel the type of easy conversation that most people might start in a situation like this.

"Mmhm," he nods while swallowing a drink of his beer.

"Me, Tripp, and Heston. You'll meet them too, they're around here somewhere. Gage runs the place, but he and Blythe live at the big house past the creek. Come on, I'll show you around."

Tripp. Heston. Gage. Blythe.

I repeat the slew of new names in my head to memorize them. The more I fight social situations, the more I tend to disassociate and forget everything that was said to me. I can't do that right now. I don't want to seem rude and I don't want to come off uninterested so I continue to roll the names around in my mind until they plant roots there. They're not going to like me anyway, but it's worth the effort to avoid complete disgust from them.

"Who are all these other people?" I ask. Who has this many friends?

"Some guys work here part-time. Others are just buddies from around town."

Apparently, he and his sister have a thing for handholding because he wraps his fingers around mine. His palm is rough in a delicious way and his hold is so firm as we weave our way through groups of people. I haven't held hands with many guys before, but the ones I did always had soft skin and a delicate touch. This feels different and I don't hate it at all.

"Up these stairs," he points to a steep black iron staircase just off the kitchen, "is the loft. And down this hall is the bathroom if you need it. Past that are the bedrooms."

The walls are a simple stained pine, reaching all the way up to a high ceiling lined with matching exposed beams. It's not lavish or gaudy, but the sheer scale of the building has me looking up in awe.

Echoes of conversation and music continue to fill the area as he pulls me along, not stopping when he speaks. It's a whirlwind of information and I quickly study the space around us and what he's saying.

I don't miss the way a few people do a double-take as we walk by them. It doesn't feel scrutinizing, but most definitely curious. Instinctively, I shuffle closer to Warren hoping his large frame can hide me.

We come up to a long rectangular table covered in red plastic cups. It looks a little sticky and I have to blink away to stop thinking about how much I'd like to wipe it off.

"Sav, you're with me!" Blythe beams. She holds her hand out toward me with a face-breaking grin. She's standing at one head of the table with a bottle of beer and a ping pong ball in her hand that isn't outstretched.

The wall of security that was Warren's body moves toward the end of the table opposite his sister where he starts arranging the cups in a triangular shape and splashing a little bit of water from a pitcher in all of them.

Tentatively, I step toward Blythe and let her pull me in next to her. While she racks up our cups, I look around for something to fixate on so that I don't think about what a terrible shot I am and how disappointed she'll be when she finds that out. My gaze lands on a group sitting on a huge sectional in front of a stone fireplace that isn't lit. They all erupt in laughter as a guy with a full sleeve of tattoos tells a story.

"That's Tripp," Blythe says with a laugh. "He's a little insane but lovable. Great guy."

Again, something in her voice makes me believe her. The task of repairing my reputation pops back into my head and I make a mental note to maybe keep my distance from this Tripp guy tonight if I can. If he's so well loved, they'll be sure to listen to him if he has anything negative to say about me.

"Okay here's the deal. No one *ever* beats these guys," she says as she glares across the table where Warren and another man are standing. I snicker seeing them so concentrated. They obviously take this seriously. "Warren likes to bounce it

57

in, so watch for that. And Heston is a swatter. Don't let his silence fool you, he's quick. And—"

She's cut off by a whoosh and splash as a ping pong ball lands right in the front and center cup on our side. Her mouth drops open and a hand goes to her hip.

"You little *shit*," she seethes.

Warren claps his hands once and leans back laughing. I can't help but stare. His shirt sleeves are tight around his biceps, but not so much that he looks like he's trying to show off. His thighs fill out his jeans in a way that makes my hands sweat. And somehow the light around him is brighter than anywhere else in the room.

It's almost mesmerizing enough to make me forget about what he did.

Almost.

The guy standing next to him, who I think is Heston, casually tosses his ball and it bounces off the rim of one cup and into another. His body barely moved, and it only took one simple flick of his wrist to make the perfect shot. I find his presence a bit frightening if I'm being honest. There's something in his cold stare that makes me think he could easily break this table in half at any moment if it wasn't a waste of his time and a bitch to clean up.

Blythe stomps her foot and groans with frustration.

"That's three, ladies. Bottom's up.," Warren croons. He's got both hands on the table and he's leaning toward us with a mischievous look on his face.

Blythe and I remove the cups that had balls land in them, putting them to the side. Then she raises her beer in front of me. She's obviously annoyed by being three cups down on the very first round already, but there's still a glimmer of joy in her eye.

"Cheers!" she says with a smile as she taps her drink against mine and then tips hers back for a gulp.

I don't know if she took one drink or two, but I take two of mine just in case to cover the amount we're supposed to drink. Wiping my mouth with the back of my hand, I pick up the ball on my side and get ready to miss. Just as I'm about to toss it over to the other side, Blythe leans in and whispers in my ear.

"Get ready. As soon as I bounce mine over, bounce yours right behind mine right away, don't wait."

I squeeze the little orange ball in my hand and nod, determined to follow her plan of action. Warren is staring me down with his eyes narrowed like he knows Blythe is up to something. She puts her hands at her side like she's not ready to shoot yet and I mirror her casual posture.

"Oh, *god,*" Blythe gasps. "What is Hattie doing here?"

Heston's face goes white as a sheet of paper and he about falls over his own boots spinning to look toward the door. At the same time, Blythe leans far forward with her bottom lip between her teeth. Her arm stretches out and in a flash, her ball bounces across the center line. Before it lands in a cup, I close one eye and throw mine with as much sharp precision as I can. With two almost-simultaneous plops, our shots land in two cups in the front. My eyes widen.

"GOTCHA!" Blythe squeals, jumping up and down several times. The room blurs and I realize that she's taken my hands and I'm jumping with her. The laugh that escapes me is accidental, but I can't stop from joining in on her infectious celebration.

I don't know who Hattie is, but she must be someone to Heston. Blythe's little plan worked like a charm. We're out of breath by the time we stop jumping and I place a hand on my cheek to feel the warmth there.

It's strange, having a girl who's so vibrant and fun celebrate with me like we're old friends. Something in my chest aches and I tug at a strand of my hair to bring myself out of this weird feeling that I don't know how to handle.

Heston's shaking his head knowing he just got bamboozled. And Warren has both hands on his hips, lips in a firm line. After shooting us a frustrated look, he turns and whacks Heston on the arm.

"Balls back," Blythe shouts and holds her hand out above the cups.

"That's just embarrassing," a freakishly tall man with a dark and short trimmed beard strolls by the table. In a few long strides, he's invaded our space and picked Blythe up off her feet so she's at eye level with him.

"You smell like smoke," Blythe says as she kisses a trail up the side of his neck. This must be Gage.

I feel awkward now and should probably look away, but I just can't. The way he's holding her looks like nothing short of a death grip and her legs are wrapped around him in such a way that even if he let go, she'd still be attached. I lean on the edge of the table with one arm, mesmerized by them and listening in on their conversation.

"I've been grilling." As he says those words into the shell of her ear he squeezes under her thighs. His voice lowers and he whispers in her ear now, but it's loud enough for me to hear. "Are you done here, or do I have to wait to eat you for dessert?"

As soon as those words come out of his mouth, my body weight collapses onto my hand and it juts off the slippery table. My elbow crashes into the remaining cups, and each and every one of them topples over like dominoes, spilling across the table and onto the floor.

"*Shit*," I mumble as I right myself and try to regain my balance.

"Undefeated," Heston says as he fist-bumps Warren and walks off, satisfied.

"Damn!" Blythe says as she wiggles out of Gage's grasp and picks up the cups.

I bend to help clean up the mess, drooping my shoulders and muttering incessant apologies all the while.

"Did you hurt your arm? Let me look," she says as we finally stand. There's a small red mark on the heel of my hand that scraped down the edge of the table, but it doesn't hurt too bad.

"Oh, I'm fine," I reassure her and pull my hand back to my midsection. "I'm so sorry. I lost us the game."

"It's okay! Don't be sorry, we can just put the cups back up and keep going. I think we can beat them," she says and winks at me.

I half expected her to be angry that I ruined everything. It's what usually happens when I do that.

"Nah. You lose," Warren's voice sounds from behind me as he rounds the table to our side. If I could stop either getting embarrassed or making a fool of myself in front of this man that'd be great.

Blythe whips around and looks at Gage, no doubt looking for someone else to jump to our defense so that Warren and Heston don't get to extend their notorious winning streak by default.

Gage just shrugs and bends to kiss Blythe on the cheek. "Sorry, baby. That's a party foul. Game over, house rules."

I feel so bad and I start to spit out more apologies when I hear Warren's name being yelled above the crowd at a high-volume shriek.

"Warren! Over here!"

A frantic hand waves above the heads of people surrounding her, but I can't see her face. But whoever she is, she's headed right for us and neither Warren nor his friends seem the least bit excited about that fact.

"You're *kidding* me. She's here again?" Blythe groans.

Gage turns and mumbles a drawn-out "Yikes."

"Warren!" the shrill voice calls out again.

Without a warning and before I can get a good look at her, a hand wraps around the side of my neck, turning me completely around. I'm stunned as Warren's face is coming right for me.

When we're inches apart, he stops his advance and I suck in a sharp breath. Without thinking, I grab each of his arms to regain the balance that I never seem to have around him.

"Sorry," he whispers, helping to steady me with a tighter grip around my neck.

"What are you doing?" I say back under my breath, mimicking his suddenly hushed voice.

I focus on his blue eyes while he bites his lower lip with a mix of anticipation and urgent desperation.

"My ex," he looks away toward the crowd and then quickly shifts his gaze back to mine. "Shit. I don't have time to explain."

My face turns for just a moment, looking for an explanation. It's an involuntary response given the confusing current situation.

"Savvy," he says with a thumb hooked under my chin to bring my focus back to him. "Can I kiss you?"

Miraculously, I swallow the lump in my throat and manage not to make a scene after hearing his wild and spontaneous suggestion.

"Heads up, man," Gage says from behind us.

Copying his previous motion, Warren looks to the crowd and back to me again, but quicker this time. The inner corners of his eyebrows tip up, waiting for me to either punch him in the gut or agree and close the distance between our lips.

Absolutely not, the angel on my shoulder screams.

Just a little taste, the devil on the other shoulder cackles.

He shifts on his feet, and I realize he's running out of time to enact this stupid idea. This stupid, stupid, tempting idea.

Then just like the night I met him, I fold. I'm so weak when it comes to him, that it isn't just my lips that meet his. My entire body leans in to get its fair share of attention too.

8

WARREN

For ten whole seconds, I'm powerless.

A peck from her would have sufficed, and that's what I'd anticipated. But Savvy has something else in mind and even though this is all for show, I know this girl doesn't half-ass anything.

Like an idiot, my eyes remain wide open at first, studying the girl currently attached to not only my lips, but my torso and hips as well.

My eyebrows shoot up to the top of my forehead when she smashes her mouth against mine with more pressure as each second passes.

I inhale, realizing I haven't breathed in yet, and the perfectly light aroma of her fresh citrus perfume invades my senses.

It's a tug of war to anchor my focus. Her soft lips, her scent, and her hands on my arms all demand my attention. It's overwhelming and exhilarating all at once. Before I can process how perfect it is, it ends too soon with Emma's grating voice in the background as she refuses to let us go on another moment without making sure we know that she's now standing right next to us.

"Excuuuse me? Hello?"

The moment Savannah steps away and puts a few feet of distance between us, her hand flies up to her mouth. Her cheeks are fully flushed—whether it's from arousal or embarrassment, I'm not sure.

Immediately, I regret how flustered I was, stunned and frozen in place during that kiss. It was supposed to be performative, but it didn't feel that way and I wasn't ready. I want to try again. Fast. Ideas of where I'd touch her to coax more sounds or reactions out of her flood my mind and I rub the side of my jaw in frustration.

"Were y'all playing spin the bottle or something? That's so cute," Emma scoffs.

Unfortunately, she's not walking away, so my plan to get rid of her by kissing someone else was an epic failure in that sense. But the kiss itself? It had my heart racing. It was meant as a distraction, but it was sweet like nothing I've ever tasted. I look down to my boots, expecting to see them hovering above the ground but they're not. Strange, because the rest of me feels like it's floating.

I turn my gaze to see Savannah's mouth open in shock as she stares at Emma. With the crowd that gathered around us and the jealous glare on Emma's face that she's doing a terrible job of hiding, she glances around frantically.

I've seen that look on her face before. She's scouting a fast way out.

"I missed you—" Emma says as she turns in my direction, but I cut her off when Savannah spins and darts down the hallway.

"I don't have time right now, Emma." I'm not trying to be mean to her, but I've never wanted her to shut up and leave me alone as much as I do right now. In the split second that I made eye contact with her, I could tell she was a little bit high too.

I push through a group of people who are all giving me confused looks. It doesn't take long to catch up to Savannah, but I'm not fast enough to keep her from pushing through the nearest door she could find. Which just so happens to be Tripp's room. She's not even halfway through the doorway when she squeals and slaps a hand over her eyes.

Over her head, I can see Tripp making out with a shirtless girl on the edge of his bed. His head pops up and he smirks over her shoulder while the girl straddling his lap latches onto his neck. Blowing out a heavy breath and shaking my head, I reach around Savannah to grab the knob and pull the door back closed.

"Ugh," Savannah groans.

"In here," I say as I usher her to my room a little further down the hall.

She hesitates, no doubt hating the fact that I followed her when she was clearly looking to escape alone. I couldn't help but follow her though. Partly because I could see the wheels spinning in her head and partly because I wanted to ask her when we could kiss again. With a glare, she follows me into the room and I close the door.

"Is there a back door I can use?" She crosses her arms over her middle, holding her elbows in each hand.

"There's a mudroom at the end of the hallway with a door that leads to the back, yeah." I scratch a nonexistent itch at the nape of my neck, deep in thought. "You want to leave?"

"I don't know," she sighs and then starts walking across the room, pacing as if the movement might help her put together pieces of a complicated puzzle in her mind.

My lips roll inward as I watch her. Her delicate heels tap against the wooden floorboards that have seen better days, her feminine dress a stark contrast to my slightly messy and simple room. She's beautiful, elegant even, as she glides back and forth to gather her thoughts.

"You know," she says when she stops pacing and spins to face me, "when I decided to go along with your kiss to get your ex to go away out there, I didn't realize it was Emma. *Again*. I feel like a pawn in some sort of scheme at this point, and this is the *second* time you've used me to make her jealous."

She holds two fingers in the air and emphasizes the word *second* to drive home her point. My chest expands with a deep breath and in my head, I start trying to come up with an honest explanation that doesn't sound like a measly excuse.

The first time she's referring to is when we went out on our first date. I took her out to the only decently nice restaurant in town three weeks ago, and things went great at first. We clinked our glasses, ordered food, and smiled stupidly at each other the way you can't help but do when you're as happy as you are excited about who you're with.

I don't know exactly how Savannah was feeling, but I was into her more than anyone else that I had ever been on a first date with. I'm not saying I knew for sure that we were endgame yet, but I knew that I'd been waiting for that butterflies-in-your-chest feeling that she was giving me for a long time.

In true Emma fashion, it only took a few minutes for her to show up and ruin things. Shit hit the fan after she stomped over to our table. She got right in my face and started berating me with questions like *how could you do this to me?* and then spitting out allegations like *you knew I'd be here tonight and you brought a new shiny toy just to make me jealous.*

Fucking ridiculous, honestly. I'd be willing to put money on her having followed us. But I understand how it made me look from Savannah's point of view.

"Okay, this needs to be cleared up right now," I say with a

newfound demanding tone. I'll be damned if I let this miscommunication make Savannah think I'm some manipulative asshole who's hung up on his ex any longer.

"The way I see it, Emma is the one with the agenda here, not me. I know she showed up during our date, but I had no idea she'd be there, trust me," I put a hand on my chest and take a few steps toward her. "If I'd have known she was there, I wouldn't have been caught dead in that restaurant. I wasn't trying to make her jealous, or even see her. I just wanted to go on a date with you. That's all, I promise."

It takes a minute, but the shields of defense and skepticism in her expression fade enough for me to drop my shoulders a notch. She's still looking away from me and biting the corner of her lip, though. I don't think I'm totally in the clear yet.

"Explain what just happened then," her hand juts out toward the party, referring to the kiss. "Is *that* why you invited me here?"

"What?" I shake my head and furrow my brow. "No. That didn't even cross my mind until I heard her yelling my name and coming toward us."

Yes, I wanted Emma to see me with someone else, hoping it'd finally send the message that I was not interested in getting back with her and that her efforts to keep squirming her way into my proximity were pointless. But it wasn't a preconceived plan.

And admittedly, it wasn't just about scaring off Emma. I couldn't stop staring at Savvy across the table during that game of beer pong. I *wanted* to kiss her.

But I leave out that part of the reasoning and stick to the main point.

"I've been letting her down easy for too long. Trying to be nice and let her figure out for herself that there was no way I was getting back with her. But she keeps trying, and you were there, and I thought—" my right boot shuffles across the hardwood floor and I struggle to keep the nerves at bay as I try to make her understand. "I thought if she saw me kiss you, she'd finally drop it and move on."

"That doesn't make sense, though. She's with my brother. Why would she still be coming after you if she has a boyfriend?"

"She doesn't even like your brother," I scoff. "She runs around town with him on her arm hoping it'll stir me up. I know it sounds complicated. It *is* complicated, but believe me, I wouldn't orchestrate all of this. I wouldn't do that to you."

"Sounds like something an envious ex-boyfriend would say," she argues. Her eyes narrow and she begins pacing again, this time walking toward the window and looking out across the open field filled with one too many tumbleweeds.

I run my palm over my face, but then my hands find their way to my pockets, the only other option that doesn't involve me touching her right now. I'm trying to resist the instinct to take her hand or hug her, resolving to wait patiently for her to respond.

When she walks over to the far side of my bed, using it as a barrier between us, she finally turns back to face me.

"That's not the case, Savvy. I don't want her. I want her to leave me alone. Plain and simple," I state.

"Why does shit like this always happen to me," she whispers, closing her eyes. Her head is pointed toward the ceiling now and she looks almost as defeated as the last time we had a one-on-one conversation like this. I've never made such a fool of myself so many times in front of a girl that I'm into like I have with the one standing in front of me.

"So . . . you're not using me for your own personal gain, and you're not in love with your ex who happened to crash our date as well as this party."

I smirk at the way she thinks out loud, running over every detail. It makes me think that she's probably a kick-ass lawyer and I admire that about her. Even if our conversations sometimes make me feel like I'm on the stand about to plead my case.

The fact that she states it more like a realization than a question gives me hope that she might be beginning to believe me, though. I stand across from her on the opposite side of the bed and shake my head.

"No."

She nods and looks down, still contemplating.

"Why is your bed so huge?" She's wrinkling her brows together now, both hands on her hips, looking at the bed from the foot all the way to the headboard. Her eyes land on the pair of briefs I left lying on top of the comforter earlier this morning and I catch her rolling her lips into her mouth and subtly running her tongue over them.

I hate having to stand up so far to get out of bed in the morning, so I got a pretty tall bed frame not long ago. The kind that dogs need stairs for instead of being able to jump onto. Between that and the four-inch mattress pad, it nearly covers her entire body, and I can only see her from her rib cage up when I face her from the opposite side.

She closes her eyes and shakes her head suddenly. "Never mind. Back to the kiss. I can't imagine what was going through your head thinking that being seen with me like that would even be believable. There's no way Emma, let alone anyone else in that room, thought it was anything other than a joke."

My head pulls back, and I twist my face trying to figure out what she means. Why would it not be believable?

"Obviously one person believed it. You kissed me like you meant it."

Instantly, her face turns from its natural color to a shade

of bright pink I've only ever seen on the late spring peonies in my mama's front yard. One corner of my mouth lifts ever so slightly as I remember the way she fisted the sleeve of my shirt and pulled me toward her.

"I didn't want to kiss you for the first time in front of a bunch of people like that, but I'm not sorry it happened. Next time there won't be anyone else around," I say in a low voice, trying not to fantasize about all the ways it could end differently if we were alone.

I nearly miss it, but the edges of her mouth tip up in an almost smile and the corners of her eyes wrinkle just enough to notice. Just as quickly, she changes her expression to one of indifference.

"Okay," she whispers, nodding. She tries to walk past the bed and toward the door, but I move in front of her and gently hold her forearm.

"Do you believe me?" I ask.

Her eyes lock with mine and she lets out a sigh.

"Yes. I think so," she answers. "But this has turned into more drama than I can handle right now. Not with everything happening at my job. A job where your crazy ex-girlfriend is my coworker, nonetheless. And . . ." the soft and loose brown curls on either side of her heart-shaped face bounce back and forth while she shakes her head, "I'm barely staying afloat as it is. This is just too much. I'm not sure there'll be a next time, Warren."

9

SAVANNAH

Glaring at the computer monitor in front of me, I toss a handful of dried cranberries that I wish were french fries in my mouth. You'd think my email would be pretty empty on a Friday, but in this line of work, the weekend is fair game for billable hours and the flood of tasks and requests never seem to stop landing in my inbox.

Still being on probation, it's the same drudgery they've had me doing since the jail incident. It's frustrating. How can I prove myself as a capable attorney when everything they're giving me could very well go to a paralegal? But for the last two weeks, this is how it's been.

"Hey, girl!" A chipper voice sounds over the top of the cubicle wall to my left. I turn to see that it's Emma and I inwardly cringe, but force a smile. I've successfully avoided her all week since the bunkhouse debacle thanks to the big case she's been working on with the senior partners. I want to be the one on cases with the senior partners, jealousy gnawing at my gut. I suck in a deep breath to push it away, realizing that my luck in staying away from her has finally run out.

"Hi, Emma."

"A peace offering," she smiles brightly as she lifts an iced coffee over the top of the wall and extends it toward me.

"Oh, thank you. That's not necess—"

"I know most of the time, new girlfriends don't get along with the ex, but since we work together, I thought maybe we could be friends instead." Aside from the minuscule twitch in her right eye, her face is the picture of sweet enthusiasm, so I take the drink from her.

Wait . . . girlfriend? Does she think Warren and I are dating?

"Let's double date soon! I know *all* the places Warren loves, so it'd be super easy and fun, right?" Her ponytail swings from side to side with her overly animated way of talking. I instinctively squirm away from her, scooting back in my chair. This woman is *a lot.*

I guess I can give her credit for being pleasant with me at the office despite seeing me kiss Warren. I had fully prepared myself for her to be a total bitch to me after hearing how obsessive she's been over him.

"I think you have the wrong idea. Warren and I aren't—"

"You don't want to be friends with me?" Her question comes out like a devastated and child-like whine while the size of her eyes grows and she pouts out her bottom lip.

It's not that I don't want to be friends with her. It's that she mistakenly believes that Warren and I are together, which couldn't be further from the truth. God, that'd be awkward if that were true considering she still has pent-up feelings for him. And she's been stringing along my brother at the same time. The more I run the ridiculous scenario over in my head, the less I feel like I'm at work right now, instead on an episode of *The Jerry Springer Show.*

"No, that's not it at all." I take a quick sip of the iced coffee and offer a soft smile. Just as I'm about to correct her on the misunderstanding, my desk phone rings.

"One second," I say to Emma and then pick up the receiver. "Hel—I mean, this is Savannah."

"This is Henry. Can you come to my office for a quick meeting, please?"

"Sure thing, see you in a minute." I hang up the phone and quickly stand, gathering a pen and my padfolio. "I'll be right back."

Emma nods and I turn to head toward Mr. Grant's office.

"Don't forget your drink, you don't want it to get all watery just sitting there!"

"Right," I lightly laugh and go back to grab the drink, lifting to her in cheers, a wordless way of me saying that all is good between us, and I want no part in her little circle of drama.

The inside of Henry Grant's office isn't lavish or gigantic like most managing partners' offices are. It's not on the corner of a city skyscraper with a view or furnished with fancy bookshelves and golden-hued lamps. It's humble and welcoming with warm tones and pictures of his family decorating the walls. I take a seat in one of the soft taupe chairs across from him at his desk and put on my most attentive face.

"What can I do for you, Mr. Grant?"

"First off, call me Henry, please." He lifts a glass of murky-looking water to his lips, takes a big gulp, and winces. "My wife's pulling out all the stops after our doctor hounded me for my cholesterol. She's got me drinking this crap." He adds a good-natured laugh.

I smile at him, thinking how cute it is that he's downing a foul-looking drink per his wife's wishes.

"She cares about you," I point out, which I realize a

second later was a redundant thing to say. *Obviously she cares about him, you idiot.*

Henry slowly nods with a content grin taking over his face. "That she does. Now," his tone turns more business-like, "we've got a lot to discuss."

I pray he doesn't notice how hard I swallow. In my experience, no good news ever follows words like those.

"The first of which being I had no idea that you were in a relationship with Warren Farrow."

What? For the second time in less than ten minutes, someone I work with is under the impression that Warren is my boyfriend. I thought the impromptu kiss at the bunkhouse party was behind us, but now I feel more like killing him for it. Never underestimate small-town gossip in situations like this. It's fast and potent. And in my case, will fuck with your job that's already hanging by a thread.

My mouth opens halfway, but then I wonder why in the world my boss would care who my "boyfriend" is, or whether I had a boyfriend at all.

"Sensational," he claps his hands once and leans back a bit in his office chair. "They don't make them any better than the Farrow family. He's a catch, you did well."

In my six weeks of working here, Henry has never spoken to me this way. I thought maybe he'd be angry for some reason. But he's reacting to his own assumption with such . . . joy? Comradery?

He seems genuinely pleased with me like I made some sort of incredible decision by dating Warren Farrow. For a second, I bask in the unexpected approval. It's a hit of serotonin that I haven't felt in a very, *very* long time.

"It's wonderful what he's done, getting his business ready to open in such a short time. I'm great friends with his dad, you know. We should all have a get-together soon," he says, still wearing that smile.

God, I wish I could roll my eyes right now. What is it with the people in this town being so obsessed with Warren? I get that he's charming and good-looking and . . . well, that's beside the point.

This is such a stark contrast to my last conversation with Henry, which reeked of disappointment. That must be why I don't have the heart to correct him on the gossip about my romantic life. It's ridiculous. I know. Honesty is always the best policy, but if there's one thing I know about myself, it's that I'm an expert at doing stupid shit. This is no exception.

"Of course. That'd be great," I reply with a shaky voice.

What are you doing?!

I internally smack myself upside the head, but continue to go along with it anyway.

"Fantastic. Oh, and I've seen the extra work you've put in lately. You are doing well, Savannah. I have room at the table for an associate next Monday for the Sweeney hearing. Plan on being there." He lifts a stack of papers and straightens their edges on the surface of the hardwood desk.

Hiding the blinding smile threatening to take over my entire face, I nod several times. "Thank you. Thank you so much. I'll be ready."

I'm nervous about going to the hearing knowing it'll be a multi-hour trial of my ability to prove myself. I'm going to have a daunting amount of reading to do this weekend to prepare. But I don't think those hours of struggle will hold a candle to trying to figure out how to tell my boss that I'm not actually dating the town golden boy that he loves so much.

Either that or convince Warren to go along with it.

10

WARREN

"What if, and hear me out, you just went and cried in the shower by yourself like every other self-respecting man instead of whining to me about it?" Tripp suggests. He's leaning back with his face toward the sun, one hand casually holding the reins and one hand on the back of the saddle.

"You're a dick," I huff and shake my head.

"No, I just thought it was more interesting the first hundred times you brought her up. Now it's just pathetic, dude. She's got you all kinds of fucked up."

I squint toward the sky and run a hand through my hair, trying to find the part of his sentence that's a lie. For the hundredth time today, I wish a spontaneous cluster of clouds would roll in and give us a break from the scorching summer heat.

"She doesn't want anything to do with me," I sigh.

"And?" Gage butts into the conversation and I turn to glare at him. "You're awfully touchy about it for someone who has his pick of women in this town."

"Oh, *that's* why you're hung up on her," Tripp teases.

"Because she's the only one that won't give you the time of day. It all makes sense now."

"No that's not it. She's . . . I don't know."

"Not like other girls," Tripp says in a fake and impressively high-pitched girly voice, flipping his nonexistent long hair over his shoulder.

I take the opportunity to throw the last bit of my sandwich, and it hits him right on the cheek.

"Really," he deadpans, wiping the side of his face. "You know I hate mustard."

"It's more than that," I explain.

"You should have tried taking her on an actual date again instead of inviting her to a party last weekend," Gage suggests. "She looked uncomfortable as hell at times, not gonna lie."

I groan and squeeze my eyes shut. "I know. I'm surprised she showed up at all, to be honest."

"Mauling her with your mouth in front of Emma's ass and everyone else didn't help," Tripp says.

That earns a chuckle from Heston who's running the blade of his pocket knife over the end of a stick. While the rest of us are in the saddle, he's sitting on the ground, back against a big tree and hat pulled down low. We had to bring out some t-posts and a post driver to fix fence today, so he drove the side-by-side instead of riding his horse.

"Give her another call," Gage continues, trying to help my pitiful situation.

I didn't get hung up on a girl that kind of hates me on purpose. It just happened, like I couldn't control it. I miss her and we're not even *friends*. Her words.

"You don't think I've tried that? She's gun shy and won't even talk to me," I say.

"Give me your phone," Tripp demands.

"Yeah right. I'm not—"

He snatches it out of my hand before I finish my sentence and immediately starts typing away on it. My heart sinks because I know it was already unlocked and he's probably about to make a bad situation even worse. When I move my horse closer to his to try and take it back, he signals to his horse to move back without even touching the reins.

Most people wouldn't expect Tripp to be such a skilled rider. Of all of us, he spends the most time in the saddle. He barely has to move his feet and legs, and his horse knows exactly what to do. I sigh and drop my shoulders knowing there's no stopping whatever he's about to do without literally jumping on him.

He brings the phone up to his ear and holds one finger up like he's waiting for someone to answer. I almost throw up when his eyebrows shoot up and he starts talking.

"Hi, is this Savannah?" he asks. I swat my arm out again and then even throw my hat. All failed attempts to stop him. Gage is laughing his ass off behind me and Heston is leaning back and looking up at us, scowling at Tripp's antics, but still interested in how they're going to play out.

"My friend Warren here is down bad for you, and I was wondering if maybe you could come over and put him out of his misery. He said he'll rub your back and kiss your feet every day for a year if you'll be his girlfriend," Tripp says.

"You're fucking kidding me right now," I seethe as I finally get close enough to him to grab his arm. With a huge shit-eating grin, he turns the phone toward me, showing the home screen and no phone call.

"Psych," Tripp laughs. Between coughs and gulps of breath from cackling so hard, he hands the phone back over.

Ding

He's lucky a text chime comes through because I was about to chuck the phone right at his nose. With one last glare at him, I turn my gaze to the phone screen. The smile

79

that curves onto my face is impossible to hide when I see who it's from.

"She texted me," I say, shocked.

"Never underestimate manifestation," Tripp grins. "You're welcome."

SAVANNAH

Can we talk?

Before I get the chance to text back, a call from my dad comes in. I answer it right away like I always do when it's someone from my family.

"What's up, Dad?"

He grunts like he's standing from a sitting position. "Just had some lunch at the house. You still out in the pasture?"

"Yeah, we're finishing up. Should be done before the heat gets too bad this afternoon."

"Good deal," he says. "Anything else been going on lately?"

"Not really, just splitting my time between here and the business still until it's up and running," I answer. One of my brows quirks up while I turn my horse to follow the rest of the guys who are heading back to the ranch. He's using the curious tone reserved for when Mom puts him up to fishing for information. He's not very good at making it seem nonchalant. "Why?"

"No reason."

I realize it sounds like he's on speaker and my suspicions are pretty much confirmed. "Hi, Mama," I say and roll my eyes.

"Oh hi, sweetie!" she answers too quickly. There's no chance she wasn't standing right next to him listening the entire time.

"What's going on?" I laugh.

"Nothing," she says. "We were just wondering when we were going to get to meet your girlfriend. Savannah, is it? We didn't even know you were dating someone! This is so exciting!"

"Huh? Mama, Savannah and I aren't dating."

"Warren, you know better than to lie to your mother like that," she says. "Now, we're having a little dinner at the Grants' on Sunday night. Do you think you might want to bring her?"

"I'm confused. I don't have a—" Another text comes through from Savannah and I'm starting to wonder if whatever it is that she needs to talk to me about has anything to do with the fact that my parents think we are in a relationship.

Obviously, I don't hate the idea at all. But I have a hard time believing that she suddenly changed her mind and then told the town we were together. Something else is definitely going on here.

SAVANNAH

Preferably soon?

"Can I give you a call back?" I say to Mom and Dad.

"Of course! Make sure to text me if she has any allergies soon though so I can plan what to bring to the Grants'."

"I'll get right on that, Mama. Love you."

"Love you!" they say in unison as I hang up and text Savannah back.

Where are you?

11

SAVANNAH

W arm blazes of red and orange bleed into the sky while the sun sets and I'm starting to get impatient waiting on Warren. I'm hoping to get ahead of this and talk to him about the fact that the whole town thinks we're dating before anyone else does.

I turn away from the window where I've been staring down the empty gravel driveway for half an hour to pick up my spray bottle. If I'm going to sit here and look through it, I might as well clean it. I push the gauzy linen curtains to the side, soak the entire window in cleaner, and then grab a microfiber towel to wipe it down.

"Finally," I sigh as Warren's black truck pulls into the drive. I rush to toss the microfiber towel into the laundry basket and tuck away the cleaning spray, scanning the rest of the space for anything out of place before he parks and inevitably comes inside. There's nothing that needs sprucing up, of course, but it never hurts to triple-check.

The front of the cottage consists of two large bay windows on either side of the front door, so I have a perfect view of Warren stepping out of his truck and walking this way. I'm frozen in place next to the couch and trying not to sweat.

It's never comfortable for me to have someone in my safe space, no matter who it is. But I don't have much of a choice. This has to be a private conversation with no chance of anyone overhearing.

God, I *hate* how he's wearing that soft cotton T-shirt and those damn jeans with the crease down the center. Is it necessary to have them so deliciously tight around his thighs? Couldn't he just wear something baggy or unflattering?

Knock knock.

I shake out of my daze to harness my focus and walk toward the door to open it. As the handle clicks and the door swings inward, he looks at me straight on, wearing the same stupidly charming smirk I've seen on him so many times before, dimple and all.

"Savvy."

"Warren." I flatten my lips and keep my face as serious as I can, knowing what I'm about to explain to him.

Stepping aside, I open the door wider allowing him to stride in. The cottage is already a relatively small studio design and is filled to the brim with various plants and other bohemian-style decor. With the space he takes up now though, it feels even more cramped than usual.

Aside from his tall frame, his energy fills any room and I'm reminded of the familiar nervous feeling that takes over any time I'm near him. For now, I shove those emotions to the side and remember why I had to invite him here.

"Can I get you something to drink or would you like to take a seat?" I ask.

He smirks and chuckles softly. "You don't have to be so formal with me."

He doesn't have to tell me that, I already know. But I'm

terrible at talking to people if it's not in a professional setting. It's usually best if I treat situations like this more like a meeting rather than a social conversation.

I hate how strongly I sense his effortless confidence right now. How he always seems so comfortable is beyond me. I wish I could feel that way, but I don't, and the best thing to do right now is cut right to the chase.

"My boss, Henry Grant, is under the impression that you and I are in a romantic relationship. Along with the rest of the office and most likely the entire town by now, I'm sure. I just wanted you to be aware of that," I say in a monotone and matter-of-fact voice as if it's not the most ridiculous thing that's ever come out of my mouth.

Warren's face isn't giving anything away. But he crosses his arms and leans a hip against the kitchen island.

"You tell 'em I was your boyfriend?"

My knees lock up and my mouth drops open. Surely, he doesn't actually think I would lie about that to the person that I work for. Or anyone for that matter. I didn't deny it like I should have, sure, but that's different.

"No!" I defend myself.

"Well, this makes sense," he says and nods, running his tongue along his upper teeth. Is he mad? Upset? I half expected him to storm out of here.

"What do you mean?" I ask.

"I mean my parents already called me to invite you to dinner," he laughs.

"Oh, for fuck's sake! I was hoping to get ahead of this." I spin around so I'm not facing him anymore and start pacing the room, my usual tendency when I need to think. His parents are going to hate me. I was hoping maybe we could keep them out of this.

"This is my fault," his voice suddenly turns more apologetic. "I brought up the idea of kissing you in front of a shit ton of people at the party and I'm guessing if it wasn't you that told anyone we were together, they put two and two together on their own."

"You're damn right it's your fault," I shoot back at him while coming to a stop in front of the window, nibbling my thumbnail. "But I went along with it I guess."

Contrary to popular belief, staring out of a window in despair does not bring on brilliant revelations. I'm still stuck on my original idea which was to get him on board with embracing the town gossip instead of correcting it.

When I peer over my shoulder at him, he looks to be hiding a grin.

"Okay, here's the plan. I cannot afford to lose my job and start over again, but it's not looking good at the moment. Mr. Grant was over the moon about this whole thing and after putting me on probationary terms, it was the first time I've seen him approve of me. I think we should keep up the ruse for a while until I'm in a better place with my career."

"Is that right?" he asks, and I can hear the satisfaction in his voice. He thinks I *want* this. "It'd be a lot easier if you just admitted you liked me."

I stalk toward him, stopping when I'm close enough to see the faint dusting of freckles over the bridge of his nose and under his eyes.

Warren is infuriatingly handsome, effortlessly smooth, and charming. He's friendly and beloved–everything I'm not but need to be if I want to avoid getting canned.

But I don't want to like him. Liking complicates things. If I let this be anything other than fake, he'd have power over me. I already feel like my control is slipping in every other aspect of my life. Feeling devastated when the jig between us is up is not something I can add to the mix and still survive.

He could crush me.

Plus, if Emma found out I liked him, but our relationship was a trick of sorts, the humiliation would be unbearable. I'd have to leave town. To wither away in this studio cottage. To have Mesa discover me months from now and say what a shame it was that Savannah Chase died not of a broken heart, but a completely mortified one.

I *cannot* like Warren Farrow and this entire idea might be my worst yet. But I'm not above unearthing some vulnerability and begging him for help anyway.

"I cannot afford to lose my job," I say while looking up at him with a fixed expression. "My feelings or lack thereof for . . . *you* have nothing to do with it. I don't want to get fired and if my boss thinks you see something in me, then it'll put me in his good graces while I try to prove myself at the firm. If you'll play along, that's all the information you need to remember to help you pull it off."

"Pull it off?" he laughs. The rich sound vibrates around me, and I realize now how close we're standing. "I don't need any tips on how to make people think that I want you."

"Right," I say, trying not to read too far into what he just said.

His chest rises and falls, and I don't back away. If I took even one tiny step forward, I'd trip right over his boot. His hands move upward and at first, I think he's going to touch me for some reason, but he pauses and his hands land on his hips.

"You sure about this?" he asks low and slow. "You'd have to talk to me. Maybe even touch me. And we both know how hard that'd be for you. Right?" The deep gruff to his voice sends a chill up my arms, making the hair stand up.

He looks down at me, waiting for me to answer. It's a good reminder of why I can't give in to him. That voice. That face. He's used to getting what he wants, and I don't have time to be a puddle on the floor at his feet. I am a successful and driven independent woman who hasn't ruined her career. At least, that's who I want to be.

"I think I'll manage," I say with narrowed eyes, over-enunciating each word.

"I feel bad about some of the wild shit that's happened every time we've hung out, and maybe I owe you one," he acknowledges. "I'll be your fake boyfriend."

Okay, then. We're doing this.

I give a closed-mouth smile and back away from him, headed to the door to send him on his way now that this is settled.

"Right after you admit that you need me," Warren's voice echoes behind me, stopping me in my tracks.

I scowl and ignore the tingle between my legs hearing his cocky request and I slowly turn back around to face him. I should have known it wouldn't be easy.

"I don't need you," I stand my ground. "If you don't want to help me, I'll figure something out."

He cocks one eyebrow. It nearly brushes against the thick lock of dirty blonde hair falling down the side of his forehead.

"You need me."

I take a sharp breath in and out of my nose, tilting my head and rolling my eyes at the same time. Hopefully, the slight shrug of my shoulders is enough to appease him. He knows the truth. I *do* need him.

"Say it," he demands.

I hate this. My teeth clamp together so hard my jaw cramps.

"I need you," I whisper without making eye contact with him.

He leaves the spot he was standing in and approaches me with a few even and steady strides. I swear my internal body temperature rises to a dangerous level when his lips meet my temple in a quick kiss.

"See you this weekend, then. *Sweetheart.*"

1 2

WARREN

It's the Sunday of the barbecue at the Grants' and I have a few hours before I go pick up Savannah. The only thing I could think to make the time go faster was to stop by my sister's house on the other end of the ranch. As happy as I am that she decided to move back here and take a residency within driving distance of Westridge, her busy schedule still keeps her in the city most of the time. If I know she's around for the weekend, I always make time and stop in.

I don't even make it up the first step of their porch before the door swings open and she's waving me inside. Good thing she hates surprises, because I'd never be able to sneak up on her around this place. Gage has it like Fort Knox nowadays. She's holding a plate of cookies and I snag one as I walk through the doorway and into the house.

"Damn, these are good. Did you make them?" I ask.

She snort-laughs and follows me into the kitchen. "Hell no. It's cute that you think I have time to cook."

"Right," I chuckle. "How's the job going by the way?"

"It's pretty great," she sighs as she sinks into one of the tall bar chairs. "It's more studying for boards and scut work than ideal, but I expected that. What are you all dressed up for?"

"I'm not dressed up," I scoff. Okay, maybe I wore jeans without holes or stains in them. And a button-up shirt. But it's short-sleeved, so I don't think it counts as dressing up but what do I know about clothes? Judging by my normal attire of old work pants and a threadbare T-shirt, I'd say not a whole lot.

"Yes you are, and I hope it's for Savannah." She claps her hands and smiles bigger than I thought was even humanly possible. "Mama told me about y'all and that she was coming over to the Grants' for Sunday lunch with you today." Her eyebrows wiggle and she shimmies her shoulders.

"Of course she did," I say with a straight face fighting off an eye roll.

"You're great and all but I've always dreamed of having a sister. I knew I had a good feeling about her." Her eyes close and she covers her hand over her chest. "I wish we didn't already have plans today so that I can get to know her better at the barbecue."

"Don't get your hopes up."

"About what?" Gage says as he rounds the corner. He has a bottle of wine in one hand and a book in the other. He places both of them in front of B and leans in to hug her from behind. "Picked this up on my way home from town and you left your book in my truck," he says to her.

She practically melts as his arms cage her in, and something foreign hits me. I don't like it one bit.

I've never been a lonely person. At least I never felt like I was. My family and I are extremely close, I see my friends every day, and it's rare for me to ever be isolated in the literal sense of the word. So it's weird that the feeling of loneliness slams to the bottom of my chest.

Realizing that I'm watching Gage with the love of his life

while I sit here by myself feels like hearing a record scratch. I want what they have. That's not something I'd like to dwell on at the moment, so I fill Gage in on the part of the conversation that he missed.

"About me and Savannah," I say. "It's not what you think."

Gage and Blythe stare at me, silent. Figures they wouldn't just change the subject after hearing that. I shift in my seat and take another bite of my cookie before explaining further.

I've lectured Gage about keeping things from his friends before, and Blythe is the one person in the entire world who can read me like the Sunday paper. Lying to them about it doesn't make sense and I don't think it would work anyway, so I blurt out the truth.

"It's not exactly *real*," I admit. "It's more of an arrangement."

Gage whistles and Blythe's jaw about hits the floor. She gathers her composure and sits back.

"That's . . . interesting," Blythe says as she studies my expression with narrowed eyes. "I don't get it. Why don't you just date for real?"

"I tried that," I mumble.

"Is this about the whole getting arrested thing?" Gage asks.

"Pretty much, yeah," I say. "Henry is her boss and he put her on probation or something like that. She's worried about losing her job and how people feel about her around here. I kind of owed it to her to help."

"Why do you owe her?" Blythe asks, confused.

"She thought I planned it when Emma showed up on our date at the restaurant. I think it embarrassed her and I looked like an ass who was just using her, I guess. And the random kiss last weekend. I don't know, it's a mess honestly. I've been fucking up every step of the way with her."

"That tracks," Gage says, and I clench my jaw and glare at him.

"Did you explain yourself?" Blythe asks.

"Yeah. I think we cleared things up, but she's still hung up on the drama of it all and I feel bad about it."

"Not to sound like a downer, but what's in it for you?" Gage contemplates.

That makes me stop and think. At first, it was just to help her. Her boss is basically a second father to me in a way, so I have a lot of swing there. She's been down on her luck with one thing after another lately and I honestly just felt bad for her and couldn't help but agree to the fake dating idea.

But truthfully, I know there's more to it. Something about Savannah Chase pulls me in like a fucking magnet. This is more than just helping her. It's selfish on my part, too.

I haven't stopped thinking about her. I can't stop picturing her lips on mine. It's been nearly impossible to drop my attempts at breaking through her stubborn exterior. There's more to her underneath it all and I want to dig it out.

"It's my chance to win her over," I admit. "If it helped get Emma off my back for good, that wouldn't hurt either."

"Jesus, you're whipped already," Gage teases. "You and your sister don't know how to rein it in when you have a crush on someone."

Blythe scoffs and rolls her eyes. "You have *no* room to talk."

"Yeah," I mumble, scratching the side of my head under my hat and then pulling it back down. "I have zero control over it. I can't stop thinking about her and after everything that's happened, all she wants to do is chew me up and spit me out."

"And you'd let her," Gage laughs. He strolls around the kitchen island and stops next to me, slapping his hand twice on my shoulder before walking away. "Good luck with that."

S avannah flips the visor down in the passenger seat, oversized sunglasses pushed to the top of her head and a tube of some sort of lipstick in her hand. The full-blast air conditioner blows her long curls back while she leans toward the mirror, applying a layer of soft glossy pink to her lips.

We're at a stop sign on our way into town, and there's no one behind us, so I keep the truck at a standstill while she finishes.

After rubbing her lips together in a way that makes my jeans a little tight in the crotch, she sits back in her seat and looks around in confusion.

"Why aren't we moving?"

I lift my foot off the brake and get us driving back down the road again with a smirk.

"Would you rather put makeup on in a moving vehicle on a bumpy dirt road?" I ask.

"No," she replies with narrowed eyes. I can feel her gaze on me, even as I look ahead through the windshield.

"Did you buy that house you're living in?" I ask as Westridge finally comes into view up ahead. I know pretty much everyone that lives in this town, having grown up here. But the place where Savannah lives was abandoned for as long as I can remember until recently. I never met who moved in before her, and it has me curious.

"No. The girl who owns it has been living in my apartment in the city for a while. We traded. Do you know her?"

I shake my head, flipping up the blinker and turning down the street that the Grants live on. Never heard of a trade living situation, but by the tone of her voice, it seems like it's working out well for her, so I don't question it. It makes sense to me that it's not actually Savannah's place. It's pretty, especially the landscaping. But it shocked me when I went inside. It didn't exactly fit her personality in the way I would have pictured her house to be.

She shrugs and stuffs her makeup back into her bag.

"Her name is Mesa. She's sweet," she explains while adjusting the chain of her gold necklace. "Pretty, too. With my string of luck, I thought she was another one of your exes or something."

The truck slows as I pull it into an open parking spot, and I slowly turn my head with a fake look of shock.

"Oh, now I remember. Yeah, we've dated. Bad breakup." I add in a dramatic cringe and a hand over my heart.

"Oh," Savvy says under her breath.

"I'm kidding," I chuckle. "Never heard of her."

She tries to swat me on the arm, but I've already started to get out. I hear a slew of curse words just as my boots hit the ground and I close the door, smiling to myself.

I parked behind my dad's old red and black blazer. The day Henry sold it to him was one of the best days of his life, and he's driven it every day since. The amount of times we've worked on it in the little shop behind our trailer keeps me smiling.

The same little dent I put in it in high school is still on the corner of the bumper. I'd like to think he didn't fix that on purpose. Gives it character.

I give it a good once over as I retuck the back of my shirt and walk around to the other side where Savannah is now standing.

But she's looking around like someone already has eyes on her every move and she bites down on her already worn-down thumbnail. A far cry from how she was when we were still in the truck.

"I don't know if I can do this. I shouldn't be here," she says in a panic. We're standing on the sidewalk next to a big tree in their front yard. I look over to the house, in its seemingly quiet state. I know good and well there is a bustle of people out back, though. The Grants are famous for their get-togethers.

"Don't be nervous, it'll be fun," I try to reassure her. But it didn't help much because she still looks like she's second-guessing coming here with me. "Talk to me."

"No. Let's leave."

She turns to walk back to the passenger door, but I grab her hand instead. She huffs as I pull her toward the back of the truck, hidden from the house by the tree.

With one hand, I keep her from running away, and with the other, I pull the latch on the tailgate and drop it down.

"We're going in there, and before we do, you're gonna sit here and tell me what's bothering you so much that your shoulders are almost as high as your ears and your hands are red from wringing them together," I say as I point to the bed of the truck.

"I'll do no such—"

I thought she might say that. In a flash, I cut off her protest by placing both of my hands on her hips and picking her up, then setting her ass down on the edge of the tailgate. I try to be gentle with her, but she still lands with a huff.

I fold my arms and stand in front of her, waiting until she makes eye contact with me. Which takes all of three minutes, but I'm in no hurry.

When her gaze finally meets mine, there's very little warmth to it. Her scowl is somehow angry and scared at the same time. The more I'm around her, the more I learn. It's hard to read her but I'm getting better at it.

"You're pushy," she says.

"And you're stubborn. But why are you so uptight?"

She looks around, deep in thought. Her bottom lip is

trapped between her teeth and she's swinging her legs back and forth as they hover above the ground.

"A lot is riding on this for me."

"I already know that. I'd rather hear the part you're not telling me."

She sniffs and pretends she has nothing else to say but I know better.

"I'm on your side here. Just talk to me," I say.

"Fine," she crosses her arms and finally locks eyes with me. "I don't like social situations because I'm self-conscious about what I say and how people perceive me. It never goes well," she blurts out in one quick breath. "Things are bad enough for me at work. Now I have to go in there and—" she waves her hand toward the house, "get them to like me outside of the office. And I'm not likable, Warren. I know I'm not."

She's speaking fast but I get the message. I don't know who fed her that bullshit or why she believes it. But I'm scratching my head trying to figure out where in the world this is coming from because I don't see her that way at all.

I pinch the bridge of my nose and take a breath so that I don't sound angry when I tell her that she's full of shit.

"That's not true," I don't know how to explain this to her so that she believes me, so I keep it simple. "You're in your head about it. Did someone tell you that you're unlikable? Because if they did, they're a dumbass."

"You're just saying that."

"I don't *just say* anything. I like you. Doesn't that count for something?"

Her legs still and her hands gripping the edge of the tailgate tighten, turning her knuckles white. She narrows her eyes in a skeptical glare. "Why?"

"Why what?"

"Why do you like me?"

Fair question. One that puts me on the spot, but I don't have a problem answering because I know that this is something that she needs to hear out loud to believe.

With one stride, I invade her space and place my hands on either side of her. The truck is hot from the summer sun underneath my skin, but I get a good grip and lean toward her.

Rambling on about how pretty or intelligent she is doesn't seem like the right way to go, even if there's truth to it. Instead, I say the first thing that comes to my mind when I think of Savannah.

"You're tenacious."

She purses her lips and tilts her head. Before I even had a chance to get the sentence out completely, the predetermined dissatisfied reaction was all over her face.

I arch a brow and lower my chin, hell-bent on convincing her that what I'm saying is true. "None of the shit that you've had to put up with lately has knocked you down so hard that you've given up. And hell, you never let me get away with a damn thing either. You're a force. Even when you don't feel like you are, I see it."

I *feel* it.

There are already enough people in my life who never question or deride me. But Savannah and I are different together. When I push her patience, she shoves right back. I don't just *like* that about her, I'm entranced by it.

"Oh, please. That's just a nice way of saying that I'm stubborn."

Case in point.

I shake my head and smirk. "No, that's different. But I like that about you too."

By her look of surprise, I'm guessing she expected me to argue with her.

I want her to believe me when I tell her things like this

97

but there's a disconnect. She can't fathom that I'm being honest with her. It kills me and makes me wonder what might have happened to make her so reluctant to accept compliments.

Aside from practically begging her to see herself the way I see her, I don't know what to do. With a deep sigh, she hops off the tailgate and I back up a few steps.

The look on her face is a war of contradicting emotions. Per usual, I can't pin down exactly what she's thinking, but I get the idea that she's uncomfortable after hearing all that from me. Good. Because her comfort zone is shutting me out, and I want her to step out of it.

Now that I'm not leaning over her and caging her in, she seems to have gathered her thoughts. "Thank you. For saying those things and for being here so that I can patch things up with my boss."

I nod and open my mouth to respond while lifting the tailgate back into place, but Savannah has already turned away to walk across the front lawn. Her dress blows to the side from the light breeze. She holds one side of it with one of her hands and smooths over her curls with the other.

Her favorite habit is walking away from me, but we actually got pretty far into that conversation before she bailed. Progress.

13

SAVANNAH

"Good, right? She makes it from scratch every summer," a warm voice says behind me.

I freeze with the glass to my lips and a mouth full of the ice-cold drink. I was trying to be sneaky and hide the fact that I was on my fourth glass of strawberry lemonade, but I guess someone noticed.

Swallowing the lemonade, I turn on my right foot and come face to face with a woman whose salt and pepper hair is pulled back into a sleek low bun. She plays with one of her dangling earrings and shoots me a friendly grin.

"It's delicious. Not too sweet," I say as I hold my glass up. "I hate it when lemonade is too sweet."

The woman's smile widens and she nods. "Her best lemonade is the blackberry one, but apparently those weren't ready to pick quite yet." Her face lights up as she animatedly explains about the world's finest lemonade.

We're standing under the minimal shade of a pergola just off the house in the Grant's backyard. It's a pretty addition but does little to fight off the summer heat so I dab my forehead with the back of my hand and take another sip of my drink.

"Who?" I ask. "I mean, who is *she* that you're talking about? That makes the lemonade?"

"Oh, that'd be Gayle!" She answers my question with a broad grin.

"Yes?" another lady pokes her head out in the doorway behind us after hearing her name. We turn to face her, and she smiles at us from around the corner of the sliding glass door that leads inside the house. She's wearing an apron with ruffles around the edges and holding a pair of tongs in her hand.

I'm not sure that I've ever seen someone with kinder eyes. Her light sandy hair and golden complexion send alarm bells off in my head warning me that this might be Warren's mom.

"Oh, we were just talking about your fabulous lemonade," she says to the lady in the doorway and then turns back to me. "And my name is LouAnn, by the way. LouAnn Grant," she says as she holds her hand outstretched toward me. I stare down at her delicate wrist iced with colorful bracelets that make a musical sound when they bump against one another.

"Savannah Chase. Nice to meet you." My palm meets hers in a gentle handshake.

I start to think of how to make the best first impression with her when out of nowhere, the other woman who was peering out at us from the doorway comes straight for me, her two arms wrapping around my shoulders and sweeping me into a hug.

My eyes shoot open, but out of instinct, I reciprocate the embrace. After a few squeezes and rocking back and forth, she finally pulls away and holds me at arm's length.

"That's my lemonade she's bragging on about," she beams.

"I'm Gayle Farrow, and you're my son's girlfriend, is that right?"

Last night while staring at the ceiling, I came up with as many believable responses as I could. What I didn't do was practice my facial expressions, because she looks confused when I accidentally wince at the suggestion that I'm dating Warren. It hasn't even been ten minutes at the cookout, and I'm already slipping up. I manage to replace my accidental reaction with a forced smile and nod in response.

"How long have you known each other?" Gayle asks.

"We met not long after I moved here," I say. "Not quite two months ago."

"That's a long time in Farrow years," she laughs loudly. "If he's anything like his sister, I'd bet y'all are already living together."

"God, no." I slap my hand over my mouth. Shit.

Your job is to convince them, I remind myself.

"I mean . . . yes. *Yes*, we're—*definitely* living together. At the same place. Living. One roof—" In a frazzle, I ramble out the most false and idiotic confession. My hand waves around above my head as I explain, and I can't stop the stupid words from spilling out of my mouth.

If she's surprised, she doesn't look it. In fact, a sheen of liquid covers her eyes and she tilts her head. I look over Mrs. Farrow's shoulder to see Mrs. Grant casually popping a cucumber slice into her mouth as she watches.

I start looking around, frantically this time, for a save from Warren. Where the hell did he disappear to?

I should take back everything that I just said immediately before word spreads that we're officially shacking up now. And in this town? That piece of gossip would spread like wildfire. But then I'd look like more of a nutcase than I already do.

"Mama."

I jump at the sound of his voice. Without turning around to look at him, a steady hand smooths its way over the middle of my back just in time before I dig myself a bigger hole with my mouth.

"Don't scare her off," he says. His fingers dance across the side of my rib cage and I'm pulled toward him, suddenly fitting tight under the crook of his arm.

Gayle shoos her hand toward her son. "Oh, please. If she agreed to live with you and your snoring and messy room didn't terrify her enough to leave, then she never will."

She winks and I slowly turn my head to look at Warren. His eyes narrow ever so slightly and his jaw flexes. It's the look you'd expect from someone who just found out they have a new and unwanted roommate.

He should be so lucky. I'm an excellent roommate. If you enjoy not talking and a spotless house, that is.

"Right . . ." he drawls and then side-eyes me. His grip around my middle tightens and I swallow hard enough for the group of people across the lawn to hear. Yet another part of the equation I couldn't have prepared for. Touching.

To get his gaze off me, I subtly shrug and snap my attention back to his mom. Before I get a chance to say anything though, a voice that I recognize as my boss calls from the grill by the pool.

"Steaks are done!"

"You kids hungry?" Gayle says over her shoulder as she turns away from us to walk back inside. I take the opportunity to step out of Warren's hold. The hand that was just on me is stuffed into his front pocket and his other hand runs over the facial hair above his top lip. Finally, he strides over to the screen door and holds it open. Keeping my eyes on the ground, I step inside the house.

I grew up in the city in a downtown high-rise. My parents owned the building we lived in and where they ran their investment firm. They spent most of their time at the office and were hardly ever in the penthouse a few floors up where our home was.

I, on the other hand, was stuck there most of the time before I was sent to boarding school. I hated the cold and monotone decor even though my mother described it as modern and sophisticated.

This home is the polar opposite of that.

There is sunshine everywhere. Not just in the natural light through the windows, but in the warm colors and soft furnishings that tell me people enjoy this space as more than just an aesthetic. It's not for show, it's for family. Friendship. Comfort.

Gayle places a bowl of fresh fruit in the center of the long table. It's not a formal dining room, but it fits nicely in the open space just off the kitchen.

"Warren, have a seat here. We have a lot to talk about," Mr. Grant says from his spot at the head of the table.

Warren walks toward the seat closest to Henry, but not before grabbing my hand and towing me along with him. He pulls the chair out for me, and I sweep the skirt of my sundress under my thighs to sit down. You'd think he'd sit down and leave it at that, but he cups the nape of my neck instead.

It's a firm grip and my spine instantly stiffens. There's nothing I can do to stop him from leaning down and pressing his lips against the wavy brown hair hanging over my ear.

"Relax," he whispers.

I fold my hands in front of me on the table while he takes his seat. It doesn't feel quite right, so I move them back to my lap. Then down at my sides and up to the table again.

To distract myself, I grab a nearby roll and put it on my

plate along with an assortment of other fresh and delicious-looking food.

"I need an update on how the business is going," Mr. Grant says through a mouthful of steak.

Warren nods a few times. He pushes the food around on his plate with his fork and presses his lips together tightly.

"Still on track to open in August," he finally answers. It's impossible to miss the discouraged undertone. "Hoping I didn't make a mistake sinking so much into it."

I don't look his way, but my ears perk up. We spoke about this briefly when we first met. I push a mandarin orange section around on my plate and smile softly remembering how obvious it was that he was extremely excited about his dealership and service center. His smile was radiant when talking about it at the time, but today he seems more hesitant.

"Cold feet?" A man who's sitting right across from us says. His face is weathered in a way that makes me think he works outside a lot. I recognize the familiar shape of his jaw and his right arm is stretched out along the back of Mrs. Farrow's chair.

"Not exactly," Warren shakes his head. "Just stressing a little about how things will turn out, I guess. This is my dad, Savannah."

He gestures toward the man across from him to formally introduce us, and he politely smiles at me.

"Nice to meet you," I nod.

"Call me Wade," he says.

"You've done a wonderful job with the building and getting the inventory ready, dear. We're so proud of you," Gayle chimes in, reaching across the table to cover Warren's hand with hers. "As soon as the rest is finally in place, it'll be a smashing success. Don't fret over that."

The look on her face is nothing short of adoration for her

son. Her hand squeezes his, she leans forward giving him her full attention, and the warmth she exudes is a balm to Warren's unusual nervousness.

It's fascinating, really. It's not that I've never seen an example of a caring parent in action before. I've seen plenty, and normally my knee-jerk reaction is to look away and pretend I didn't witness anything that I might consider out of the ordinary.

This time feels different. It's a nausea-inducing slow-motion torture of what I never had, five feet away from me. It's so casually given, so natural. It's everything I wish I'd had growing up. And now.

Suddenly, my food doesn't taste good anymore and I set my fork down.

"I agree," Wade says with an encouraging nod. "And you know that we're all here to help if we can."

"And what about you, Savannah? Are you enjoying your position at the law firm?" Mrs. Grant asks. She means well, and it's kind of her to include me in the conversation. I wish she wouldn't. My hips wiggle back and forth a few times in my seat, trying to get more comfortable and stalling before answering her question.

"I am. But I'm still getting the hang of things." With that statement, my eyes drift down to my plate avoiding the looks of disapproval that I expect to receive.

Next to me, Warren takes a drink of water and then clears his throat. I'm twirling my napkin under the table until his hand invades the same space and lands right above my bare knee.

"I'm fifty-four years old and I'm still getting the hang of things too," Gayle laughs.

Mrs. Grant nods in agreement while taking a sip of her drink, then looks back at me and continues. "I'm sure it's been tough having things start out the way they did."

My leg bounces and Warren squeezes to settle it.

"Doesn't matter how things started, she's in control of where she's headed. She's focused and cares a lot about her career," Warren announces in a steady and confident voice.

A stellar performance, I'll give him that. Everyone reacts with little oohs and ahhs. It's unusual how my pulse slows as his words filter through the tension in my head. I'm so starved for positive affirmation that even the little act of support that he's putting on right now brings on a wave of comfort.

Without fully facing him, I take a peek at Mr. Grant's reaction out of the corner of my eye. He seems mildly pleased with what Warren said judging by the subtle nod and relaxed set to his shoulders. This plan could crash and burn if Mr. Grant isn't buying it. Time will tell, but if Warren keeps this up and can convince him that I'm not a total fuck-up, no matter how deceiving that would be, maybe he won't fire me.

"Well, that's sweet as pie, Warren," Gayle says. "We're proud of *both* of you and so happy to have you here, Savannah."

As time passes and we move to lighter small talk, we each finish our meals. While standing from her seat and taking her empty plate with her to the kitchen sink, Gayle speaks up.

"I'm bringing breakfast to the bunkhouse on my way to the café early tomorrow morning. Do you like cinnamon rolls?" she calls over her shoulder as she rinses her plate.

Uh . . .

A panic rises in my throat wondering how to tell her that it doesn't matter whether or not I like cinnamon rolls for breakfast because I will not be at the bunkhouse in the morning. The fictitious slip about Warren and I living together is already coming back to haunt me and it hasn't even been a few hours.

I quirk an eyebrow and lean in toward Warren to whisper. "Your mom brings you breakfast?"

"It's Tripp's birthday," he whispers back.

I nervously bite my bottom lip and nod in response. That makes sense. I was about to make so much fun of him if his mom was regularly cooking and delivering his meals. I'm still pinning him as a mama's boy until further notice. Whether or not he does his own laundry or makes his own dentist appointments is still to be determined.

Something tells me that Gayle wouldn't let Warren get away with any of those things though, so we're probably in the clear.

It could be much worse when you compare it to the boys I've dated in the past, though. I have an embarrassing slew of exes that google themselves, have energy drink addictions, and claim that their love language is blow jobs. Zero out of ten, do not recommend.

Not that it matters. I'm not actually dating Warren. After the way he stood up for me today, I almost forgot that this wasn't real.

"They're the best in Texas. I'm sure she'll love them. *We'll* be there," Warren says. My head whips in his direction and he's wearing a sly smirk.

That motherfucker.

14

WARREN

"I am *not* moving in with you," Savannah grumbles as she tosses her overnight bag onto the couch in the bunkhouse living room. It's covered in blue and white flowers and lands with a heavy thud, stuffed so full I wonder if she had to sit on it to zip it up. "This is only for one night."

"Says the girl who lied and told my mom that we live together," I reply with a chuckle. Not that I'm complaining.

I tried not to laugh out loud when I realized what she'd done before I could rescue her from the conversation. I saw her uncomfortable stance from across the backyard. I should have made it to her sooner, but I was too busy staring.

It took some convincing, having her pack a bag and bringing her over to my place for the night. When I reminded her that my mom is best friends with her boss's wife though, she agreed. The truth is that I couldn't care less whether or not my mom sees her here in the morning. I just wanted to hang out with her more.

She was different around other people compared to how she was around me. She's never shied away from giving me a piece of her mind. She's been headstrong and stubborn every time I've ever talked to her and I like that. It hasn't made me want to leave her alone, if anything, it's made me want to be around her more.

But today at the Grant's something changed.

"*Accidentally*," she huffs as she slumps down into the recliner. "It just came out!"

"Mhm," I quirk up an eyebrow. "Just warn me before you blurt out that you're pregnant or we eloped or some shit."

Just as I turn toward the kitchen, a sandal flies across the room and hits me right in the middle of my back. With no one here to impress, the snarky side of her has returned and it puts a smirk on my face.

"Throw your shoe at me again, and I'll spank you with it."

"Pfft. You won't." Her arms are crossed and her face is twisted in a skeptical but curious scowl.

"The hell I won't," I say over my shoulder. She scoffs and gives a dismissive wave of her hand.

Try me, I think to myself.

Moving across the kitchen, I open the fridge and lean in, palming the tops of two cold cans of beer and pulling them out. It's early in the evening and I don't plan on going to sleep just yet. She's been somewhat reluctant to talk to me every other time I've tried, but I don't give up easily. After putting a beer in Savannah's hand, I pull my phone out and click on the group chat.

where y'all at?

TRIPP

headed back from the sale barn

stopping in town for a burger and a beer you wanna join?

I'm good.

aren't you hooked up to the trailer

HESTON

yeah and?

I laugh picturing Tripp and Heston pulling in behind the bar with a whole-ass stock trailer taking up ten parking spots. Lifting my eyes from the screen of my phone, I see Savannah taking her other shoe off and flipping up the footrest on the recliner. This is as good a chance as any to get her to talk to me.

Savannah's here

TRIPP

By choice?

funny.

Just take your time getting back

TRIPP

Why

Are you planning on lasting longer than two minutes this time?

HESTON

There's a first for everything.

middle finger emoji

I turn the screen off on my phone and toss it to the side, settling my body further into the couch and opening my beer. With a sigh, Savannah does the same with hers.

"I needed this drink after today," she sighs.

"Was it easier than you thought it would be?" I ask.

"What, pretending to like you in public?"

I nod, working to hide a grin.

She brings the beer can to her lips and I mirror her motion. Our eyes are locked and I wait for her to take a drink and swallow, then copy her moves. She narrows her gaze at me and then finally answers the question.

"Harder, actually. Nearly impossible."

I spread my legs and shake my head while running my tongue along my top row of teeth.

"I don't think you hate me as much as you *think* you do."

"Maybe. Maybe not," she shrugs, but her mouth curves into a devious smile.

I chuckle and take another drink. Like we're in a game of copy-cat, Savannah sips on her beer at the same time. I tilt my head, she tilts hers. She leans forward and purses her lips, and I place my elbows on my knees and stare right back.

I think she's testing to see if I walk away or get annoyed. See how far she can push me away before I throw in the towel and stop trying.

I hold my focus on her but look her up and down instead of right in the eyes. Her sundress, light green, makes the golden streaks in her naturally curly brown hair look brighter. She doesn't squirm when I clearly study the way her toned legs stretch across the footrest, bare and fucking beautiful enough to fantasize about how I wish I could bend them all sorts of ways.

Maybe over my shoulders. Or wrapped around my hips.

Without saying anything, she calls me out with a cocked eyebrow.

I cock mine right back and with that, I've won the stare-down because she finally rolls her eyes and takes two long gulps, finishing off her drink. I chug the rest of mine and it takes me less than a minute to fetch a few more beers for us and make it back to my seat.

"What'd your friends think when you told them you had a boyfriend?" I ask to break the silence. I could sit here and stare at her for another few hours but I expect she'd eventually tell me to fuck off and leave the room. I need to keep her talking.

The same strange air of anxiousness that I noticed earlier in the day surrounds her once again, and she begins to chew on her thumbnail instead of answering my question.

I wait, not wanting to force her to open up. When she does, I want it to be because she wanted to. Because she trusted me.

Finally, after a breath of surrender, she explains.

"I don't have friends," she laughs. Her head is leaned against the back of the chair and it's not a joyful giggle by any means. It's more self-conscious.

"Good friends are hard to come by," I reassure her.

She looks over to the fireplace. It's not lit up, being the dead of summer right now. But she pretends to admire it anyway, searching for something else to focus on.

"That's true," she agrees. "I'm not good at keeping friend-ships. Relationships. Jobs." That same laugh fills the space around us. It's meant to make light of the situation, which I'm guessing she's used to doing.

"I don't believe that."

She turns her head back to face me, eyes wide.

"I don't think you know me well enough then."

"Not for lack of trying," I say. "But I know some things about you. You're more likely to die trying than quit. You're smart, but you forget that about yourself. And I could buy a hundred acres if I had a dime for every time you stopped yourself from saying exactly what was on your mind around people that you're worried won't like you."

Her mouth drops open, just barely, but enough for me to notice.

Even I didn't realize that I knew those things about her, but they felt true coming out of my mouth. I'm pretty confident that she's easily misunderstood and not used to someone pinpointing things about her like I just did. She can come off as cold or a loose cannon judging by everything that's gone down since I've met her. But I've studied her enough over the last few weeks to know that's not the whole story.

At least part of what I said must be right on the money because she doesn't bother arguing.

"Are you buttering me up, or do you actually believe those things about me?" she asks softly.

I don't hesitate to answer. "I believe them."

She tucks a stray strand of hair behind her ear as she nods.

"When I left the city, it was because I was let go from another job. They were nice about it and used their supposed downsizing as an excuse, but I knew I hadn't been performing at the same level as some of the other attorneys there. I held myself back a little bit, I think. Fear of failure and all that. That mentality came back to bite me, I guess."

I lean forward on the couch, concentrating on her story. I want to respond, letting her know that she and I have a fear of failure in common. But I don't want her to stop talking, so I sit back and continue listening.

"My parents were already mad at me for not wanting to work for them, and losing my job made them look bad in their circle of friends. They were pissed." That self-deprecating laugh rings again, but her face falls soon after.

"Why wouldn't you want to work for your parents?"

"I don't know," she sighs. "For one, my brother works there. And he's more concerned with party drugs and making money than being nice to me. For two, I think my parents just wanted me as an in-house lawyer at their investment firm so they could keep me on a tight leash, you know? And I want to *help* people. Not sit in a skyscraper all day doing nothing but figuring out ways to keep white-collar rich businessmen with questionable ethics out of muddy water."

The last part gets a laugh out of me, and I lay back with one arm slung across the back of the couch.

"From how you describe it, I wouldn't want to work there either. But that explains a lot about your brother."

"What do you mean?"

"Well, he's dating Emma and—" I rub the side of my head, not wanting to sound like a gossip, but feeling like Savannah might want to know. "She's had a few problems in the drug department in the past too, so they have that in common. It's part of why we didn't work out."

"Oh," she whispers. "That makes so much sense now. I wondered why he was so obsessed with her."

"Yeah . . . she came over here high in the middle of the night one time. Heston's dog was going crazy barking and we found her with her hands on the hood of my truck. Claimed I hadn't called her back, and she was checking to see if my truck was hot from driving home from some other girl's house."

"No fucking way." Her expression is shocked but slightly amused and I can't help but laugh at how ridiculous that situation was.

"Dead serious. I think she's got it under control now, but I don't know. None of my business anymore." She nods and I realize that I changed the subject to my ex, which was probably a dumb move. I'd rather talk about Savannah. "Were you sad to leave?"

She shakes her head right away. "I wanted to leave. Go off and find some different scenery, new chances. Get away from my family and their expectations."

My heart sinks and I try not to immediately blurt out a multitude of more questions about her family. It makes sense now why keeping the job that she has here is so important to her. She was pretty relaxed before, but after sharing what she just told me, she's starting to bite her thumb and look away again. That's the last thing I want, so I slightly change the subject before she shuts down altogether.

"Well, I'm glad you're here," I say. "And hey, maybe next time we're around him, Henry won't be suspicious."

That gets her attention.

"Oh, god," she covers her forehead with her hand. "You noticed him being kind of skeptical too? I wasn't sure if he was buying it, to be honest. I mean, he didn't say anything but . . ."

"Yeah," I rub the side of my jaw, "I've never lied to him before. Or my parents. It's possible that he saw through it a little bit."

The click on the footrest being put down echoes around the living room, and Savannah stands, taking her drink with her. Between paces across the floor and sips of her beer, she's doing a terrible job at reining in the panic.

I just smile. When she's stressed out about something, I bet she gets over ten thousand steps in a day just from her little pacing and thinking sessions.

"Warren," she says while stopping in front of me for a moment. "This *has* to work."

I stand up from my spot on the couch and look her right in the eye so she knows I'm serious. "It's going to."

She may not know it, but at this point, I'd be willing to do anything to prevent her from getting fired after hearing what she went through with her parents and at her other job. I'd be willing to do anything to see her happy.

When her face suddenly lights up and I think she's going to give up and argue that it's not working, she drops a bomb I never could have anticipated.

"You have to kiss me again."

15

SAVANNAH

I t's the only thing that I can think of.

After we kissed at the party a few weeks ago, everyone assumed we were together. It's hard for me to wrap my brain around someone like Warren wanting to date me, but they still bought it. And that's what I need from my boss too.

He thinks the world of Warren. If he sees that Warren loves me, even if we're faking it, there's little chance he'll send me packing after the end-of-the-year performance reviews.

"It worked the first time," I shrug, not meeting his eyes. We're standing a few feet apart, but I don't care to see his adverse reaction to the idea.

Not to mention the fact that this is a welcome distraction from the previous topic of conversation. It felt good to talk about it. But I'm not sure I could have kept going much longer without him realizing that I'm more messed up than he thinks.

Thankfully, he seems to have forgotten about it for now.

"That's true," he says with one eyebrow raised.

"There's a customer appreciation event at the firm two weeks from now," I point out. "Everyone from the office will be there. It's a perfect place to do it."

The center of his forehead crinkles, deep in thought.

"A kiss might make things worse. If it's not real, it'd be easy to tell."

"Do you have a better idea?"

"I don't know," he sighs.

All this talk about kissing has my tongue wetting my lips. I stare at his facial hair wondering how it would feel against my skin again, my eyes falling half-lidded at the thought. I wasn't paying close enough attention the first time.

This is just an involuntary biological response that any warm-blooded female would have in the middle of this type of conversation. I've been drinking. He's a fucking hunk.

It's not surprising the way my body responds to that. It's basic science.

"We could practice it," he suggests. One hand rubs the top of his right thigh, and the other combs through his thick wavy hair at the nape of his neck. I like that it's a little longer in the back. It makes me want to grab it and hang on for dear life.

"Oh," I say softly, just above a whisper. It's a logical idea. Practicing might make it seem more natural and less forced. "Okay, practice. That's . . . certainly an option."

My hands meet in front of me, twisting together at my midsection. My ears feel beet red, and I'm glad that my hair is down to cover them. Warren does not need that neon sign indicating that I'm nervous.

We can kiss. In this situation, it's just remedial. Practice.

It'd be like washing the dishes or tying my shoes. A simple task.

"Like, now, or?" he asks. It's stupid that I notice how much lower his voice got with every word of that question.

To make it seem like I have full control of my composure right now, I answer quickly and in an unemotional tone of voice. "It seems like now would be a good time. The most convenient, since we might not be together again before the event."

I'm not swaying on my feet, I don't think, but the room seems to shift around me. I swipe a strand of hair off my forehead and make my best attempt at erasing all evidence of inhibition from my face before looking up at him.

Time seems to pass slower than molasses while we each wait for the other to do . . . *something*.

What should it look like? Would I reach up to pull him down or would he bend to meet me first? Would it be quick?

While I mull over the options in my head, both of his feet take one step forward. They're in my line of vision now, as I stare at the floor. Only a few inches separate my bare feet from his boots. I focus on my wine-colored toenail polish in contrast to the wear and tear of his shoes.

They're not the kind of clean and polished boots that you pull out of the back of the closet once a year for the county fair carnival. They're the kind you work in. Real, hard, dirty work. Work that makes you sweat and your muscles sore at the end of every day.

The visual shouldn't send a thrill through my bloodstream, but it does. Damn alcohol. Lusting over a man's footwear is fucking insane.

His hand moves up to lift my chin. As soon as I meet his eyes, his hand falls back to his side and we're left with a gap of space between us once again.

"First, you should look at me more. It will make you seem interested," he says.

I nod and start a mental list of things that he's telling me to do. He's taking over this lesson on how to look like you're in love when you kiss, and I'm just trying not to appear eager for his next instruction.

"And don't lock your knees and stiffen your spine like that. We're going to kiss, not give the Pledge of Allegiance."

I adjust my body language per his suggestion. I'm not the type to submit or get off on someone else telling me what to do. Or at least, I didn't think that I was. But giving up control right here, and now, burying my urge to argue, doing as he asks . . . it's a rush of relief.

I feel lighter and looser, like I'm tired of fighting him and I've had just enough to drink to test out what it's like to give in.

"Your hand could go here," he says in a low voice. It's a demand disguised as an option, giving me the tiniest semblance of control. He points to his hip, just above his belt. Slowly, I lift my hand and place it there, slightly curling my fingers into the fabric.

Although my touch is light, the body underneath the fabric feels unmistakably hard and strong. If I didn't know a single thing about him, I'd think he spends a lot of time in the gym. I know that isn't true though. Manual labor built this.

Suddenly, a wave of chills takes over the skin on my arm as Warren's finger grazes across my bicep. I hadn't realized it until now, but the motion of putting my hand on his hip must have caused one of the straps of my dress to fall off my shoulder. His finger hooks it delicately and he drags it back up into place.

Instead of retreating, his hand moves to the side of my neck, firm and cautious all at once. Instinctively, I step forward another inch.

"Good," he praises. "Now when I lean down like this," he

bends at the waist, and my hand has no choice but to slip further away from his hip, now feeling the muscles move in his lower back. "Then you know it's almost time. And that's when you close your eyes."

Without hesitation, my eyelashes flutter and my eyelids fall softly, cutting off the sight of him and replacing it with pure darkness. I bring my free hand up to rest on his pec. My sense of touch is heightened even more now, and I count his heavy breaths as his rib cage expands and contracts. Even the rapid beat of his heart vibrates through to my skin and I wonder for a second if he's really as calm and collected as he's pretending to be.

"I'm going to kiss you now," he warns.

My lips part on their own accord just as his mouth meets mine. He doesn't bother with a cute little peck to ease into it like I expected.

His tongue is inside of my mouth before I can draw a single breath.

I can't settle on one singular reaction. Shocked? Turned on? Startled? Ravenous? Yes. All of those.

If the intelligent parts of my brain that can decipher stacks of legal documents were in fully functioning form right now, I could come up with a more dignified response than opening my mouth wider for him to access and fisting his shirt so hard that it cuts off the blood flow to my fingers.

With every swipe of his tongue and desperate claw of my hand, I drift further away from all hope of common sense in the moment.

That'll do it, pull away now.

I think that's good, no need to continue.

You can't deepen the kiss any more than you already have, you feral monster. Unlatch your damn self.

I shush my brain and work harder to turn off my inner thoughts that beg me to stop. This is necessary research.

Fuck, it's a good kiss. A *great* kiss.

Maybe we're both just tipsy, but I don't care. I feel like I'm floating every time he traces the outline of my jaw with his thumb.

When he threads his fingers through my hair and sucks my bottom lip into his mouth, I know there is no point in pretending like I don't want to have a full-blown make-out session with Warren Farrow right now.

The heat of the moment turns up a few more degrees and soon, I'm pushing him backward toward the couch. When he bumps against it, he falls back and takes me right with him. Somehow I don't stumble or break the kiss for even a second while he lifts me onto his lap.

With my legs bent and knees on either side of him, he grabs a handful of my ass with both hands and presses our hips together. A moan involuntarily breaks free from my throat as his fingers dig into my flesh over the thin cotton of my dress. It's muted, seeing as how our mouths are glued together, but my eyes still snap open.

This was supposed to be for practice, not pleasure.

He searches my eyes while I clear my throat and cover my mouth with my hand. Partly to keep any more revealing sounds from coming out of it and partly to feel my swollen lips.

"That was—" Warren sits up straighter and removes his hands from my behind, "a pretty good start." He's out of breath and struggling to speak evenly and I have to admit it's kind of adorable watching a grown man put on a front of indifference. Not that I have any room to talk.

I can barely hear myself over how loud my heart is thumping.

"Yes," I nod and make an attempt at sounding analytical. "Very adequate."

I remain as still as I can, not wanting to shift my weight

or put any pressure down on him. Now that we're not kissing, it's a ridiculous position for a platonic conversation.

"We should . . ." Warren starts, but looks at me as if he wants me to finish the sentence for him.

Chug a glass of ice water? Take (separate) cold showers? Go to our (very separate) beds?

His jaw flexes and with nowhere else to put my hands, I let them rest on the tops of his muscular round shoulders.

"Try again," he finally says between quick breaths. "You know, just to make sure we've got it down."

Before he's even done with the suggestion, my head is nodding frantically, and both of my hands inch closer to his neck.

"I agree. We should be thorough. You can never be too prepar—"

He cuts me off by slamming his lips back onto mine.

I let out a tiny squeal from the force of his arms circling my waist and dragging me against him.

It feels wild, not fighting him for once. Despite our arrangement, I've been constantly reminding myself to keep him at arm's length to protect myself. On the surface, it's because of the drama surrounding our first date, borderline mortifying as it was. But what's my excuse now that we've put that behind us?

On a deeper level, it's because he scares me. All potential relationships scare me. But especially this one because of the way he disables my urge to hide.

Even more alarming is the feeling of being wholly seen and still desired. Hell, just the fact that he makes me feel anything at all strikes fear in me. I've been so guarded over the years that I haven't even allowed myself the luxury of *feeling* at all. He's already broken through that, even with my defenses up.

He might be carried away in this moment, consumed by

the way our bodies move so well together. An emotional discovery for me if I'm honest. Because even as great as we feel together right now, if he came to know the real me, he'd lose interest like everyone else. I'd disappoint him.

That's not a new revelation. I've known this to be true all along. And I know that my chronic fear of failure clouds my judgment at times—another moan rumbling through my chest while his grip tightens being a perfect example of that.

For the next few minutes though, I'll live in this blissful state of delusion where I don't have to worry that any of those things matter. I'll kiss him to pretend the darkest parts of me don't exist.

I mean, *practice* kissing him to keep my job.

Except, Warren's lips have left my mouth, now roaming over my cheek as his hand skims my bare shoulder blade. It's so euphoric, that I can't help but want more, so I arch into his touch and tilt my head back.

As his mouth moves down and his tongue darts out to taste the sensitive skin on my neck, I know we're beyond just a practice kiss. Hell, it's moving beyond a kiss in general. My hips rock forward, and I realize that behind the zipper of his jeans, he's rock-hard.

The last time I was buzzed off a few beers and dry-humping a guy sporting a boner under his jeans was under the bleachers during my senior year of boarding school. It was fun then, and it's fun now, but also, how the hell did we get here?

One more intentionally placed roll of my hips causes Warren to suck in a sharp breath against my skin. All movement from him stills, save his ragged breaths. I'm panting too, but I can't bring myself to back away. My eyes roll into the back of my head and I push down harder, savoring the addicting tingles that shoot all the way to the tips of my fingers.

The pressure of him right between my legs, right where my body is begging for release, is deliciously intense. I could almost . . .

"*Shit*," he whispers with his head buried in the crook of my neck. "If you keep doing that, this isn't going to end in a fucking kiss, sweetheart."

16

SAVANNAH

My brain heard his warning, but my body wasn't listening. I move back and forth again, this time bringing my head forward to recapture his lips. I have to. It feels *too* good.

He must be on the same page, or extremely committed to making sure that our public kiss at the event coming up is sensational. That's probably no longer on his mind though, because I doubt we'll be dry humping in public any time soon.

He leans back and pulls me with him, our bodies glued together from our mouths to our chests to our waists. Waves of almost unbearable heat are building in my core, and I do absolutely nothing to put out the fire.

I could stop myself if I wanted to. I know this. But I can't seem to find a single fuck to give at the moment.

The growling coming from the back of his throat isn't helping either. My hips take the sound as encouragement, grinding down harder in a desperate search for more.

The way he responds each time with a kiss or moan or the movement of his hips tells me that he wants me. This man, who goes out of his way to spend time with me, listen to me, help me any time that I've asked him to . . . *wants* me. And that right there is enough for me to say *fuck my protective walls.*

Right now? I want him too.

And I want his damn shirt off. Mental images of seeing him without it on aren't enough anymore. When I lift the hem of it up and clumsily tug it over his head, I only get a chance to admire what's finally in front of me for a second before his mouth moves to mine again.

He tugs at my bottom lip first, then travels back to the spot on my neck just underneath my ear. I arch into him, unable to fight the addictive rush of tingles every time he plants those open-mouthed kisses over my skin.

"Tell me to stop," he growls as both of his hands move up my thighs, pushing up the hem of my dress. He pauses right before he reaches the apex, waiting for me to take him up on his offer to put this to an end if I wanted to.

"I can't," I whisper.

His rugged hands dig deep into my skin, and I gasp from the mix of pain and blinding pleasure. Like they have a mind of their own, my hips tilt forward, begging for contact.

Without warning, the pad of his thumb meets the center of my opening through the thin material of my thong, which I know for a fact is already soaking wet. For some reason, it doesn't embarrass me like it normally would. The thought of him feeling the evidence of what he's doing to me is thrilling and erotic.

He presses firmly and moves his thumb up until it swipes right over my clit. I gasp for air and claw at the back of his neck.

"Warren. You're gonna make me come," I moan.

I've never been so close to the edge this quickly before. And I've never been so forthcoming with my words. Smothering my thoughts in anticipation of someone not liking what I have to say is usually more my speed. This time, with how safe I feel against his body and pleasure coursing through me, my typical reluctance is nonexistent.

He fists the back of my hair to bring my mouth back to his, diving his tongue in to devour me while the relentless pressure of his thumb threatens to end me within the next minute.

My head falls forward and I practically cry into the side of his neck when he finally pulls my underwear to the side and his callused fingers dip down to my core.

"*Yes* right—*there*."

Just as his middle two fingers tease at my entrance and my legs begin to shake, he yanks his hand out.

"What—" I breathe out in shock.

"I want to see," he growls.

In a matter of seconds, my dress is flung over my head and tossed to the floor. My back hits the couch and I don't even have time to lift my hips for him before my thong is yanked down my legs. Everything feels like a blur, so I could be mistaken, but I could have sworn he stuffed them into the back pocket of his jeans.

With one hand, he slides his hand behind my back. I lift off the couch slightly to give him room, and he snaps open the clasp of my bra with one twist of his fingers. As soon as he grabs it and flings it over the back of the couch, he stares down at me with a flexed jaw. The air conditioning vent that's right above us hits my nipples and they harden instantly under his gaze.

His eyes close momentarily, sucking a deep breath through his nose, and I arch off the couch expecting him to give attention to my exposed breasts first.

But he proves too impatient for that.

I wasn't prepared for him to lay down at my feet, hook his

arms around my thighs, and haul me toward him with such force. He's not usually so commanding. But I'm beginning to think in situations like this, Warren doesn't understand the concept of slow and steady or delicate and tender. And I am *not* complaining.

"Last chance," his deep voice vibrates inches away from my pulsing clit. "Tell. Me. To. Stop."

I couldn't even if I wanted to. I stare down at him—all broad shoulders and messy pushed-back hair. I'm panting through my nose and not voicing a single word of protest.

Without breaking eye contact, his mouth opens and he drops his chin. The moment he latches on to my clit and pulls it into his mouth in one ruthless suck, my head falls back and my eyes slam shut.

"Fucking hell, Warren."

I relish each swipe of his tongue. But the way my skin feels under the aggressive squeezes and rubs of his fingers adds a whole new sensation. Usually, I'm grappling just to reach an orgasm with a man. This time, I'm fighting for my life not to finish too soon. I guess soft hands just don't do it for me. I crave his roughness.

I want this to last longer, but I'm not the one in control here.

"Are you still going to be fighting me every day after you come on my mouth?" Warren asks between brutal licks. One of his hands releases my thigh and he thrusts two of his fingers right into me with no sense of caution. In tandem with his curling fingers, his tongue finds its way back to my clit.

"Hmm?" he hums with his lips around me, sending what feels like an electrical current through every inch of my body.

My brain is barely functioning, but a quick thought

enters my mind when I see him lift his head and smirk in reaction to how I'm writhing beneath him right now.

Before his head disappears between my thighs again, I clench a handful of his hair and pull hard, forcing his hungry gaze to mine to make sure he's listening.

"What if I *do* keep fighting you?"

When he doesn't respond right away, I let go of his hair and bring my hand up to my brow, half wiping the sweat away and half covering my eyes from staring at him between my legs.

For a moment, we're silent. But after he kisses me on the inner thigh and I can't help my traitorous body from melting under his touch, I look back down at him.

"Keep hiding all you want, Savvy girl. Push me away. I'm a patient man. I'll earn you."

He places another kiss against my skin, this time on my other inner thigh. I realize that I'm smiling. And slowly losing the last shred of my ability to resist his charm.

"Not before I suck this orgasm out of you and then blow all over your stomach, though," he clarifies with an aggressive growl.

It's his filthy promises, a curl of his fingers, and one strong pull of my clit into his mouth that does me in. I know he feels it because he groans and his hand that's not currently finger fucking me goes straight down to his belt.

I thought that by the time he shoved his pants down and rose to his knees, I'd be coming down from it, but the pulsing current through every nerve ending in my body surges on and refuses to stop. Even when I force my eyes open to see one set of fingers still buried inside of me and the other stroking his thick cock.

It's not humanly possible. It's biologically unfeasible to be that fucking sexy. I ride out the final waves of my orgasm while staring in awe at the deep valleys of hard muscle on either side of his hard length.

With only a few more strokes, ropes of his cum paint my bare stomach. The sight is salacious and mesmerizing and I can't help but lift the small of my back from the couch, arching into every last drop.

"*Fuck*," he groans, finally taking a second to catch his breath and slow his movements. "Look at you." His tongue rolls over his bottom lip. Is he still tasting me?

I sit up slightly, putting my weight on my elbows. It's then I realize that his fingers are still inside of me. As he slowly and carefully pulls them out, I wince. Not from pain. But from the clouds disappearing in my head.

In sobering awareness, I stare at his fingers coated in my wet arousal and then at the evidence of his across my body.

Oh . . . oh *god*.

I collapse back to the couch and cover my eyes with the nearest pillow.

"Hey." The cushions shift beneath us, and it sounds like he's pulling his jeans back on. "Don't freak out—"

"Okay," I mumble into the fabric of the pillow.

And how exactly am I supposed to not do that after the most gripping and violent orgasm I've ever had? I feel stripped bare to my core, lying here suffering through my internal thoughts and desperately plotting how to rebuild the force field around myself that this man just obliterated.

I squeeze my thighs together, willing them to stop shaking.

Slowly, he grabs the pillow on my face and removes it from my grasp. Then without another thought, he touches me at the base of my neck and trails his fingers over my chest, the valley between my breasts, and through every streak of his cum on my naked body.

He's swirling it around like it's a damn finger-painting art project. It tickles and my mouth opens in a wide grin. He did what I think he was trying to, which is break up the war going on in my head and remind me he's not letting me fight that battle right now. Not after what we just did.

"You're fucking sexy, Savvy."

He bites his lip and I start giggling when his fingers dust over the sensitive spot next to my hip bone.

"Don't smile and laugh like that when you're covered in my cum," he smirks. "Or I might start to think you like it."

17

WARREN

"Lucky!" I yell from the doorway in the barn, followed by a loud whistle.

Heston's heeler comes bounding around a tree at a full sprint. His legs and belly are soaking wet, and he shakes back and forth the second he stops in front of me, sending a spray of wet dog water straight into my face.

I wipe the drops from my cheek with the hem of my shirt and laugh. "Stop taking a dip in the stock tank before your breakfast, you old dog. At least wait until the sun's up."

Heston had plans last night. I don't know where or what it was for, but I always take care of Lucky whenever he's gone overnight. I set down the black rubber bowl of dog food and scratch behind his ears before walking out of the barn and toward the farm truck. I wish the familiar morning routine did anything to quiet the thoughts in my head.

After what happened on the couch, Savannah climbed into my bed last night. Even though we'd cleared things up about our first date and I had just felt her come right on my fingers, I still expected her to shack up in the loft or maybe even Gage's old room. She wanted a fake boyfriend, not a real one with enough drama attached for a trailer park reality dating show.

I had zero objections and it took me a little while to stop smiling when she wanted to stay with me instead.

I didn't want to push my luck with her just yet and risk her pulling away from me again, so I held back as much as I could. I kissed her, chanced some touches here and there, stole a few glances while she slept, and lay awake over-thinking how much I wanted her to trust me and how to make that happen.

It was almost impossible for me to avoid pulling her into my arms when I woke up next to her, so I was out the door and getting an early head start on chores.

The plan was to avoid smothering her and try to stop thinking about last night. I see now that was a lofty goal because even an hour into my day, the image just won't leave me, and I think I'd need a full brain transplant to erase the memory. Even then, every cell in my body would remember.

Dust from grain and soil flies inside the cab when I slam the door and start up the engine. The County Ag Report starts through the speakers as the radio comes to life, and I listen to the news.

It's a weekly radio broadcast every Monday morning, one I rarely miss. Sometimes they talk about market prices, land management, or the weather and how it could affect the upcoming days. But I like to hear the interviews and local stories they feature from the people themselves more than anything.

Growing up in a small rural community, this way of life is second nature to me. But it's the people in it that were the reason why I wanted to start my business. There was a need for an accessible and affordable dealership and service center that I wanted to fill.

That might not sound like a very big deal to most people, but to me it is. My dad and I used to spend hours working on trucks and other equipment when I was younger. He taught me everything I know, and I think if circumstances were different for him when he was my age, he might have tried to do something like what I'm doing now.

I want this business of mine to be a success. Not just for me and to prove to myself that I'm more than just a simple country boy who can get paid to drive a tractor or stack hay for someone else, but for my parents to feel proud of me too. They'd argue until the sun goes down that they're already proud of me, and I believe they are. It's different when you feel like you did something to garner that other than just being the lucky son of two great parents, though.

The chances of things going well business-wise aren't far-fetched. The farmers and ranchers around here know me well and trust me. They're aware that I'm good at what I do and that I always have their best interest in mind. But it's still going to be up to me to not fuck things up.

The truck rumbles back and forth as I drive over a cattle guard and into the first pasture. It's just a routine morning check since the grass is holding nicely and we've stopped putting out hay. I look over the water supply, do a few head counts, and replace the empty vitamin tubs.

Between me, Gage, Tripp, and Heston, it still takes hours to keep this ranch running smoothly. With this many acres and cattle, it's normally a sixty-hour week for all of us even with a few part-time guys on the side. A small sinking guilt settles in my chest. One I've been feeling a lot lately.

I still put in work on the ranch in the early mornings and late evenings. Mainly because I love being here and I need the extra cash. I haven't been able to help as much as I usually do while trying to get my business up and running, though.

The grand opening is coming up fast, so I soak up whatever time I have left here whenever I can.

The truth is that I don't know that I ever want to leave this ranch completely behind. These guys are my best friends and there's no greater peace than spending time in a place I know so well. But it's not *mine*, and it's not my dream. I can make a greater impact in the community elsewhere, and that's what I'm going to do.

Gage is supportive of it, of course. He gave me this job and a place to live when I had nothing but the shirt on my back and a beat-up truck that barely ran. I wouldn't expect him to be mad about me eventually leaving my job here just because I have bigger plans for myself now. Still, it doesn't make it any easier.

There's something else out there for me, and I can't ignore the hunch that it's more than just a new career. It's a whole life. Working here, living with my buddies, partying on the weekends—it's great. But at thirty-two, it still feels like something is missing.

I cover the rest of the pastures on the east side of the ranch over the next hour, and by the time I make it back to the barn, the unrelenting summer sun is farther up the horizon and finally above the fence line. Lifting the bottom of my t-shirt, I wipe the sweat from my forehead.

My face twists when I see the door to the feed room swinging wide open. I always close that door. It's an unbreakable habit now after getting my ass chewed way too many times growing up for leaving a gate or a barn door open.

A minute later, I'm walking into the feed room to investigate when a fizzy spray of lukewarm shook-up beer hits me straight in the chest.

"HAPPY BIRTHDAY, MOTHERFUCKER!" Gage shouts,

holding the now empty beer bottle in the air. "Oh shit," he laughs, "I thought you were Tripp."

I hold my arms out on either side of me and look down at my soaked shirt. "What the *fuck* are you doing dude," I say, slightly annoyed.

First, I'm doused in wet dog, and now this. I smell like a mix of old well water and a stale barrel of hops.

"Sorry," Gage laughs harder, covering his mouth with his fist. "I thought you were inside with your mom and it was Tripp pulling up in the feed truck."

"My mom's here already?" I figured I had until at least seven. I pull my phone out of my pocket, that's luckily still dry somehow, and see that it's already past that time.

"Yeah, I saw her car out front when I got here."

I turn quickly to walk out toward the bunkhouse, and Gage follows and closes the door behind us.

"So, does your mom know?" he asks as we make our way across the gravel.

"That Savannah and I aren't really together? Nah," I shake my head. "Not sure how long that's going to last though."

"How long before your mom figures out, or how long you're going to last pretending to date a girl you have feelings for?" Gage asks.

"Both," I sigh. "I don't like lying to my parents about it though, I can tell you that."

"I'm telling you man, just date her for real."

"Easy for you to say. They don't all fall at my feet on day two."

"I'm a lucky bastard," he grins, and I shove his shoulder hard enough that he stumbles to the side but it just makes him laugh again.

The Gage I knew when I first started working here didn't use to laugh and smile this much. He was a grumpy son of a bitch before he met Blythe.

I never understood why some guys make a big fuss about their best friend falling for their sister. If you don't think she's a grown woman capable of making her own decisions, or that your friends are shitty enough that you don't want them near your sister, just say that.

They're happy, so I'm happy about it too. Plain and simple.

Doesn't mean I'm not a little jealous of what they have.

We walk into the kitchen from the back door and within seconds I read the state of nervousness on Savannah's face. Fuck, she's beautiful. I'm staring like an idiot and doing nothing to hide it.

Leave it to me to be obsessed with a girl who isn't exactly jumping at the chance to be with me outside of a fake relationship.

"Happy birth—" Mama starts to say from her spot next to the oven, but stops short when she sees Tripp isn't with Gage and me. "Where is he?!"

"No clue," I answer as I make my way to Savannah. I stand behind her chair, placing my hands on the counter on either side of her body. Her hair, smelling like a sweet and fresh bouquet of flowers overpowers my senses and I lean in closer without thinking.

"Was there an early morning wet T-shirt contest I wasn't aware of?" she asks with a quirked brow and crinkled-up nose.

I look down at my water and beer-soaked shirt and then step toward her to close the last bit of distance between us so that I'm pressed up against her back. She squeals and tries to push me away, but I laugh and keep her caged in.

"You're going to ruin my outfit, get that nasty shirt away from me, it smells terrible," she squirms and giggles. She wants to pretend that she's grossed out, but the grin on her face says differently.

It might take longer than I'd like for Savannah to fully give in to me. But I think seeing her smile like this is enough to hold me over.

I see it the moment it happens—when she realizes that her guard is down and this side of her comes out. It's the same girl I met that first night.

In a flash, she straightens her face. Her heel-clad legs uncross and she sweeps a handful of curls behind her ear, effectively reinstating her protective exterior.

She thinks it'll get me to stop.

But I grab her chin between my fingers, turn her head, and plant a kiss on her lips anyway.

"Mornin', Savvy."

I spot my mom wearing a soft smile and peeking at us over her lashes while she pulls a stainless steel bowl off the stand-up mixer. No doubt, she'll be gushing about us to Mrs. Grant within the hour.

No surprise, Savannah wasn't expecting that, and her breath catches, her eyes popping open.

Unable to help myself, I kiss her again for good measure and to cover up her shocked expression.

When I move to take the seat next to her, Blythe and Gage are staring at me with identical faces that say *you're pathetic*. As soon as Mama turns around to get something out of the fridge, I flip them both off and sit down.

The entire bunkhouse smells like cinnamon, sugar, and fresh dough. I should probably change and take a shower before having breakfast, but I'm too hungry to wait.

"Your blazer is so cute," Blythe says while cupping her mug of hot tea in both hands.

"Mine?" Savannah asks, pointing to herself and looking down at her clothes. I'm not a women's clothing expert, but even I know that she has good taste. She always looks like she's about to walk the runway during fashion week and then give a speech at the capitol building on the same day. It wouldn't matter to me what she wore, but I think it makes her feel good to dress the way that she does. I work to not bite my bottom lip while my eyes roam over her.

"Yes, silly," Blythe laughs. "I don't have to work this weekend. We should go shopping!"

Savannah opens her mouth to reply but then swallows hard and closes her lips. I noticed her doing the exact same thing at the Grant's yesterday. It's like she never lets out the first thing that comes to her mind.

"I mostly shop online," she finally replies. "But . . . we could go. I'd love to go." A tentative smile spreads across her face.

"Here, put your number in my phone," Blythe says as she holds her phone across the counter toward Savannah.

After typing in her number, Blythe takes it back and she must have called her because Savannah's phone rings instantly.

"Now you have mine too! I'm putting your name in as S." Blythe types on her phone with a laugh. "S and B," she points between her and Savannah. "Too perfect."

I'm confused, but the girls both giggle. Judging by the look on Gage's face, he doesn't understand either.

"I was worried you had never watched Gossip Girl and wouldn't get that reference," Blythe laughs again, still smiling from ear to ear. Savannah relaxes into her seat, matching her grin and typing on her phone to add the new contact.

Mama pulls out a stack of plates and places a spatula in the cinnamon roll pan when a door slams down the hallway. A few seconds later, a girl who still looks half-drunk from the night before comes stumbling out. She's wearing a tank top over men's pajama pants with the waistband rolled over several times and is holding a pair of shoes and a handful of clothes in her arms. I've never seen her before.

"Hey," she mumbles with a shrug. No one has time to reply to her, because she scurries across the room to the front door and slips out without another word.

As soon as the door closes, Gage and I look at each other with knowing smirks.

He takes a sip of coffee and then counts down. "3. . . 2 . . . 1—"

"What a beautiful day, am I right?" Tripp comes strutting into the kitchen with one hand rubbing his bare chest.

I snort and Mama side-eyes him and points with the fork in her hand. "You're trouble."

"And you spoil me anyway," he says as he walks around the island to give her a bear hug.

Steam pipes off the freshly baked cinnamon rolls next to a bowl of made-from-scratch whipped icing and a plate of fruit. Tripp makes two plates and passes them to Blythe and Savannah. "Ladies first," he croons. I roll my eyes and get up to make a drink.

"Well, I have lots to do today, so I'm heading out. You kids have fun! Happy birthday, Tripp," Mama says as she gives Tripp a motherly kiss on the cheek and a hug to the rest of us, even Savannah. Especially Savannah. She holds the hug a few seconds long and promises to stop by sometime this weekend so that she can teach her how to make her famous lemonade that she liked so much yesterday.

For a few minutes, we all fall silent, with our mouths too full of Mom's delicious food to speak. It isn't until Savannah speaks, staring at the ink on Tripp's bicep that she breaks the silence.

"What does that say?" she asks with squinted eyes, trying to make out the shitty design.

His face lights up when he realizes she noticed his arm full of tattoos.

"This one?" He points to the half-heart shape just above

141

the crook of his elbow. Savannah nods and Gage and I both burst out laughing. The word on the tattoo is barely legible, looking more like chicken scratch than anything.

"It says *Best*," Blythe says, shaking her head.

"So, we're tanked at the bar one night, right?" Tripp starts with the same story that he loves to tell about this awful tattoo. "It was a few weeks after Heston started working here." After a dramatic pause, he drops his voice. "He saved my life that night."

Gage rolls his eyes, but Savannah scoots to the edge of her seat in interest. You'd think by the way her mouth opens slightly and her brows rise that she was about to hear something groundbreaking.

"Heston caught Tripp when he fell off the damn stage trying to hit on a girl in the band in the middle of her set," Blythe leans toward Savannah and mumbles the realistic explanation.

"I could have hit my head," Tripp snaps. "And that was the moment I knew Heston and I needed matching tattoos. It only took a few more shots for me to make him do it. His is the other half of the heart and it says *friends*," he says proudly.

"Wow. That's—" Savannah struggles to find the right reaction, but can't help but smile.

"Dumb as hell," I laugh. "They didn't even spell friends right. There's no 'i' in it."

"I don't think it's dumb. It's a great story. If I had someone that saved me and then got a friendship tattoo with me in the same night," she stops to think, shaking her head in wonder, "I'd brag about it too."

"Thank you. Exactly," Tripp exclaims with his hand stretched out toward Savannah. "Are you two love birds still messing around for shits and giggles by the way?" Tripp asks through a mouthful of food.

Savannah whips her head around to check the front door

and make sure my mom wasn't lurking around before answering, even though she's been gone for a while already.

"What do you mean for shits and giggles?" she says while clearing her throat, attempting to not look horrified.

"Heston told me it was all for show for your boss or something," Tripp says with a straight face like it's no big deal.

I look straight to Blythe because she and Tripp gossip like a few middle-aged divorcees at the hair salon.

"I told Heston," Blythe chimes in to confess.

Then, it's Savannah's turn to make an accusatory glare, and I'm on the receiving end of it.

"I told Gage and Blythe," I admit. "Can't hide much around here."

Savannah's cheeks turn bright red and I feel a little bit guilty seeing the nervousness in her expression.

After one more small bit and a quick sip of her drink, her fork clangs against her plate as she gathers up her dishes and brings them to the sink. There's a pretty good chance she's going to chew my ass for making our arrangement common knowledge around the ranch. I put my dishes up as well, hoping to talk to her before she has a chance to bolt out of here.

"I better go, I have a meeting," she says right on cue.

"Savannah," Blythe stops her by standing from her seat and blocking her way out of the kitchen. "We won't tell anyone else. Promise."

She nods and smiles, quickly turning to sling her bag over her shoulder and leave. Before she closes the door, I catch it with one hand and follow her outside to her car.

"I'm not mad, you can stop following me," she says without turning to face me. Her heels dig into the gravel with determination, each step quick and hard against the ground.

"Look," I say with a deep breath once I catch up to her. How is it, I'm always chasing after this girl? "I might be able to pull it off around my parents and other people, but I can't lie to my sister or my friends," I explain.

"Yes, Warren. I know that. It's okay," she seethes through her teeth as she practically jumps into the front seat of her SUV.

Not mad, my ass.

Again, I stop the door from closing by catching it with my hand.

"You can trust them if that's what you're worried about."

"That's the problem, isn't it?" she stares out the windshield with both hands on the steering wheel. She's frustrated, and laughs in a way that's more out of hysterical realization than humor.

"Your friends are all funny and *nice* and seem more than trustworthy. You're honest with each other. I can't be mad about that. And your sister, well, she's only the most gorgeous and kind human being I've ever met. Your mother," her hands are animated and waving around her face as she rambles on, "she's—she's downright delightful. It's maddening!"

I bend my body toward her and get closer to eye level, trying to understand what she's getting at and why she's acting the way she is. I never tire of trying to figure her out, but it still drives me insane when I can't.

Slowly, her head finally turns in my direction, and I search for what emotion she's fighting off this time.

"I'm envious, okay?" she whispers. "That's a terrible thing to feel, I'm sorry, I just . . ."

My face falls. I can't imagine that was easy to admit, but she's being open with me right now. I don't want to break that new and fragile line of trust.

"You can feel that way. You can feel any way you want, and you don't have to apologize to me."

She leans back against the headrest and lets out a long, frustrated breath.

"I think if I had friends like that, parents like that . . ." she trails off, deep in thought. "I'd be different. I don't like being jealous or constantly struggling like this. I just don't know if my life will ever feel easy."

"It might not get easier, but you'll get stronger."

A tiny smirk threatens to break out on her face as she thinks about what I said.

"And I wouldn't want you to be any different anyway," I add. "A world without the Savannah Chase that I know? Boring as hell."

Her head swivels to face me and she narrows her eyes. "You say that like it'd be a bad thing. Some people want that. Maybe I'd like a boring life."

"Maybe," I shrug. But I can't picture her trapped inside a dull existence forever. She thinks that boring means less pain, which might be true part of the time. But less pain can mean less love too. "I don't see it. You're too bright to be boring."

Her lips purse while hiding a smile.

"That's cheesy," she laughs. "But you have a way of saying things that make sense and leave me feeling better about myself."

The second part of what she said wasn't an easy flowing sentence. It sounded like something she'd normally hold back from saying, but forced herself to voice out loud this time.

Before I have the chance to respond, she lifts her hand to run her fingers through the hair just above my temple.

"What are you doing?" I chuckle.

"Just looking for any distinguished gray hairs to match the wisdom that you insist on spewing out whenever I'm around." Her eyes are squinted as she leans forward and focuses intensely on my hair which is most definitely not gray.

"If you keep driving me crazy, I wouldn't be surprised if a few silver strands started popping up," I joke.

"When this is over," she contemplates, hand still in my hair and eyes roaming over anything but my eyes, "you won't have to worry about that anymore."

Fat fucking chance. The idea of *this* being over is what drives me so mad in the first place. I bite down on my molars, flexing my jaw.

I don't mean to lean in toward her—it was pure instinct. I don't think she notices though, because her hand is already falling away from the side of my head. Her attention switches to the steering wheel in front of her while I inch closer to her. I almost fall forward before jerking back like a dumbass.

"Now go take off that ruined shirt that smells like roadkill and then get in the shower," she scolds me with a scrunched-up nose. Her foot presses on the brake while she presses the start button, bringing her SUV's engine to life. With both hands on the wheel, she looks over at me still holding her door open and keeping her from leaving.

"Or you could take it off for me," I say in a low voice with one arm hanging over the top of the door, and one braced against the roof of the car. "Right after we talk about last night."

At first, she subtly bites her lip and readjusts the chain on her gold necklace. Then, she pulls her phone out of her purse and flashes the screen toward me.

"Would you look at the time!"

I roll my eyes and lean into the car. "Later, then?"

"Okay. Later."

When she's out of sight down the driveway and I drag my feet back inside to clean myself up, a smirk tilts up one corner of my mouth. Sitting on the edge of my tall bed is Savvy's overnight bag. I think I'll conveniently be "unable" to bring it to her later. Then she'll have to come back here herself.

18

SAVANNAH

Leaning over the counter toward the mirror, I dip the applicator back into the tube of nude lip gloss and swipe it across my lips. The bathroom at the office has terrible fluorescent lighting, and I would normally never do my makeup in here. But this is just a little touch-up after having breakfast at the bunkhouse this morning before coming into work.

From the amount of times that I've touched my lips with visions of last night, I've already had to fix my makeup twice. Since I woke up, I've been teetering on the edge of madness trying to focus on anything but mental snapshots of Warren's body, the way he spoke to me, the way he touched me . . . no luck blocking it out so far.

Hopefully, this morning's meeting will do the trick and serve as a distraction.

Mrs. Powell insists on this "gathering of the minds", as she calls it, at the beginning of every week. I am still determined to continue impressing her and Mr. Grant, so I've done everything that I can to prepare mentally to contribute and learn. Even though most of the senior attorneys do all the talking, I make it a point to listen and take copious notes.

I know I don't have a high-ranking position at the office yet, being both an inexperienced attorney and a new hire. One on probation, no less. I need to be content to earn my place here and work on cases mainly in a supportive role for now. That's research, brief drafting, and due diligence for the most part.

If I'm going to be less average and more successful here, or anywhere for that matter, I need to do those things perfectly.

Keep my emotions in check. Stay prepared. Act the part.

As I walk into the conference room with straight shoulders, there are only a few people who have made it here before me. Mr. Grant gives a nod in my direction, a full greeting by his standards. A couple of other attorneys smile at me. No cringing in my direction or ignoring me altogether. I don't know if it has anything to do with the fact that they all believe I'm dating the nicest and most popular guy in town, but it's probably not a coincidence.

Pretending to date Warren to gain a little favor from my boss and everyone else around here might just be working. I could lie and say that fact surprised me, but after getting to know Warren more, I get it. Winning people over seems to be his special talent.

I quietly jot down a few notes while the rest of the employees trickle in over the next few minutes. By the time Mrs. Powell fires up the screen and pulls up her meeting agenda for all to see, Emma walks in and sits down in the seat next to me.

"You've got to try this, it's to *die* for," she whispers with a wildly big smile. She pushes a smoothie toward me, and I gladly take it.

Offices should really come up with something other than

coffee and donuts to serve in the mornings. They're not awful and most people love them, but they're not my favorite. I'm always thirsty and hungry after these things.

It's weird as hell knowing that three different versions of Emma are working against each other when I'm interacting with her. Is she going to act like my brother's girlfriend, my coworker, or my fake boyfriend's ex? There's no winning for me no matter which flavor she is.

So I stick with the safest option—indifferently pleasant and cordial.

I take a sip, noticing right away how overly sweet it is. I squint and purse my lips, but it's not too bad so I take a few more drinks. Maybe the extra sugar rush will boost my energy a bit for the long day of work ahead.

"Thank you," I whisper back. "You didn't have to do that."

Normally, I'd complain that it's not very good, but that's what the old me would have done. The new me is more likable and keeps her job for longer than a month.

"I don't mind at all," she beams.

A throat clearing turns our attention to the front of the room.

"This will be a brief meeting, as I have already emailed you all a detailed document of what you'll each be working on specifically until further notice," Mrs. Powell starts. Her cream pantsuit with a simple black top underneath is stunning against her black hair and she stands tall with an air of confidence that would strike fear in anyone who dares question her.

I've always admired her for that. As I watch her lead the meeting, I picture myself in her shoes, being able to do that myself one day.

"If you have any questions about a case, please feel free to communicate those to me either right now or at any time during the day as I will be in the office for the entirety of the week. Mr. Grant will be at trial until Thursday. Contact his assistant during that time."

Under the table, I cross one ankle behind the other and fiddle with my pen. While a few employees raise their hands to ask questions, I sit quietly and listen.

When conversations wrap up, Mrs. Powell shuts her laptop and people begin to stand from their seats. I stand as well but stop short when I hear my name being called from the far end of the table.

"Savannah, a moment?" Mr. Grant says.

"Of course," I reply. I gather my things in a rush but walk over to him steadily so as not to seem too eager.

"Great job on the timeline you submitted for the Ashwood case last week. I had a chance to look it over and it was very thorough." He's looking at a piece of paper while he talks to me but then looks up once he's finished speaking.

"Thank you," I say.

"We have a monster to tackle with that one. You're well versed on the research so far, so I need you on the team with me if you're up for it."

The team he's referring to are the senior attorneys and partners who are normally the only ones who work directly with the clients. For someone so new to the firm, I stay in the background. I'm okay with that, but what he's proposing is a rare opportunity. If Henry feels I could help in a bigger capacity on such a significant case, I'm all in.

"That would be amazing, Mr. Grant," I say with more conviction than I feel.

"Good. You can meet the Ashwoods at the client appreciation event coming up, then. Is Warren coming along with you?"

"Yes," I say with a smile. "He'll definitely be there."

I haven't felt this good about how my job is going in, well, *ever*. It's a struggle not to bypass my desk and head straight for the storage closet for a private celebratory dance party.

Instead of doing that, I fall into the chair at my desk and pull my phone out to type out a text.

> You wouldn't believe what just happened at work. I'm on a client team for a big case!

As soon as the whooshing sound pings through the phone and my text bubble turns blue, a knot of regret forms in my stomach. Why the hell did I just text Warren out of the blue to tell him good news?

We've never done that sort of thing.

He's going to think it's weird. Hell, I think it's weird. Since when is he the first person I think of when I have good news? I don't usually *have* good news though, so I don't know who that person would be in the first place.

After a few hours of sweating, shaking my head, and chastising myself for sending that stupid text, with no reply from him I might add, I finally stopped checking my phone and stuffed it in my bag to leave for lunch.

Since I didn't stay at my house last night, I didn't pack a meal or even a snack to bring with me today. I feel like I'm going to pass out if I don't eat soon.

Waving to the secretary at the front desk in the lobby, I hurry toward the double glass doors on a mission to find the nearest chicken strip basket. With a few steps to go, a tall figure steps toward the entrance from the outside and pulls open one of the doors.

He takes off his cowboy hat and runs a hand through his hair which has no business being that thick and grabbable. Delight flashes across his face as the glare of the sun reflects off the closing glass door behind him.

"Warren Farrow, what on earth are you doing here? This is a pleasant surprise!" the secretary beams.

"Just stopping by to pick up my girl, Donna. Have a good afternoon," he winks at her and scoops one arm around my waist, pulling me toward him. "We're celebrating. You hungry?"

"Very," I manage to squeak out despite my shock at seeing him here.

"Good," he nods with a devastating smile.

After kissing me on the forehead and grabbing my hand, he leads me outside and down the sidewalk of downtown Westridge.

"My girl?" I giggle, giving him shit for that line in the lobby.

"Felt right," he says without slowing his quick pace as he pulls me along.

"I wasn't expecting that after you ghosted me and never texted me back."

He laughs and I find myself wearing a big smile, helpless to fight off his contagious excitement.

"When you're proud of someone, you don't reply with a lame *congratulations* over text. You pick them up and take them out to lunch," he states. This time, he looks over his shoulder at me, and my cheeks heat up realizing how thoughtful he is.

I keep up with him the best I can while we pass under several hanging flower pots and little shops with hand-drawn signs out front. Just when I'm about to protest that these heels were not made for walking, he takes us inside the quaint diner nestled on the corner of the street. It's bustling with people, but he snags a freshly cleared-off booth in the back by the window and slides into one side.

Relieved, I sigh and sink into the spot opposite him. As

soon as I lift my hand to pick up a menu though, I freeze. A sudden sick feeling rolls around in my stomach, and a few deep breaths and rapid blinks do nothing to send it away.

When Warren looks up and sees my face, his brow furrows.

"Are you alright?"

I touch my hand to my forehead. It's clammy and warm.

Maybe it's anxiety. Getting sick for that reason wouldn't be far-fetched for me, and I was feeling queasy with regret after sending that text to Warren, not knowing how he'd react. And more importantly, wrestling with the fact that he was the first person that I thought of when I had good news to share in the first place.

This doesn't feel like that type of sickness, but I've been wrong plenty of times before.

Not wanting to ruin our lunch, I fake a soft smile.

"I'm fine," I lie. "I just need to eat something?" It comes out more like a question than I meant it to. "I'll just have whatever you're having, can you order it for me? I'll—be right back."

It starts the second I stand and turn away from the table. Nausea rises like smoke from the pit of my stomach, and I run as fast as I can into the single-stall bathroom down the hall. Despite my urgency, I barely make it inside fast enough before I'm clutching my midsection and heaving straight over the toilet.

It makes sense that I'm currently emptying the contents of my stomach in a public bathroom. It was only a matter of time before this day, which was going far too well, took a turn for the worse.

I squeeze my eyes shut, trying to force the relentless nausea away and pretend that I'm not kneeling in a public fucking bathroom right now. After a minute, my stomach seems good and emptied, and I feel brave enough to stand.

A knock echoes around the small space, and I hurry to flush the toilet, wash my hands, and rinse out my mouth. The skin on my face is splotchy as I glance at myself in the mirror, splattered with patches of cherry red and sickly beige.

"Savannah," a deep voice rumbles on the other side of the door along with two more knocks. "Open the door."

"Just a minute," I say, but it sounds weaker and more humiliating than I intended.

I cover my face with a damp paper towel, willing the lingering dizziness away. By some miracle, I do start to feel better and after another minute of deep breaths, the sickness starts to lift. Freshening up the best I can without a toothbrush or a breath mint, I finally open the door.

"Hey," Warren says with a concerned frown.

"Sorry, I wasn't feeling good for a second," I laugh haphazardly. "Would it be alright if we took something to go? I need to get back to the office soon."

"Sure, but . . . are you sick? I can take you home if—"

"No, it's okay. I'll wait outside if you don't mind ordering something. I just need some fresh air."

He takes my hand and gently pulls me toward him. I try not to lean into his touch too much when his hand roams over the side of my face, feeling for a fever. It hits me that I may be embarrassed, but if anyone is going to see me like this and then quiz me about whether or not I'm alright, I'm glad it's him.

In the middle of that thought, my body inches forward to press against his. Strong arms wrap around my shoulders and back. It's enough contact and pressure for comfort but not so much that it makes me need to turn right back around and hurl in the bathroom again.

"I'll get some food," he says into my hair.

A few minutes later, Warren walks outside the diner with

several plastic bags full of to-go boxes in both hands. From my spot on the bench, I laugh and stand to take a few from him.

"What'd you do? Order one of everything?"

"Maybe," he grins.

We walk back down the sidewalk and his eyes are on me every few seconds. I don't miss the way he slows down to keep my pace.

"You look a little better already," he suggests.

I nod and focus on putting one foot in front of the other without falling. I don't feel like I'm going to spontaneously blow chunks anymore, so it's not a complete lie. Now I just feel like the wind has been knocked out of my sails and I could lay down for a twenty-four hour nap.

"Congratulations. About the case," he says and we continue walking.

"I probably shouldn't have been so excited, I was just really surprised," I say. It's disturbingly easy to say exactly what I feel around Warren when I don't have the mental capacity to talk myself out of it. It slips out of my mouth before I even have a chance to come up with something more upbeat or self-assured. "I thought I had ruined my chances at working on a big case ever again after what happened when I was sent to help at the courthouse last time."

He thinks for a moment in silence while I mentally curse my inability to time travel and say something different.

"You're awfully hard on yourself," he finally says. "It seems like they're excited about your work. You should feel proud."

I huff so loud that a stranger passing by does a double take.

"Proud of myself," I mumble. "Right."

As we approach the front doors of the office, he turns to face me, blocking me from going in just yet.

"This is what you wanted, remember? Another shot? I'm proud of you."

I look up at him, straight in the eyes to avoid the dimple in his left cheek and the few little freckles that have become more noticeable over the summer. They're too distracting and I want to know if he's serious or blowing smoke up my ass.

"You are?"

There's no shifting of his gaze or hard swallowing. He's telling the truth. I try to remember the last time someone told me to my face that they were *proud* of me and meant it. I try so hard that my eyes close trying to recollect those words being said out loud to me.

"Yes, I am," he confirms, breaking the silence. "Now hand me your phone."

My eyes shoot back open as I'm jolted back to reality.

"Why?" I'm not sure why I asked, because I'm already lifting my hand and placing my phone in his palm like he requested.

"Because you're sick but won't admit it or let me take you home. I'm not dumb enough to argue with you about it but I'm sharing your location with me."

His fingers fly across the screen, swiping and clicking until he looks satisfied and hands it back to me along with one more of the bags of food he's holding. "If you don't reply when I check in with you later to make sure that you're okay, I'm going to assume that you passed out or something and I'm coming to find you."

Maybe I should reconsider going home after all. I think I need a dry change of underwear after hearing those words out of his mouth.

"That's ridiculous," I lie. It's hot as hell.

"Maybe," he shrugs, as he opens the door. "Don't care."

Isn't this the part where I quip back with something

snarky to protect myself? Roll my eyes? Maybe lecture him about how I don't need him to take care of me?

"Bye, Warren," I say with a stupid fucking grin. "Thank you for lunch."

"Anytime, Savvy girl."

19

SAVANNAH

"Do you have it in pink?" Blythe asks the employee at the boutique. Other than antique shops and a hardware store, there isn't much as far as shopping goes in Westridge, so we drove a few towns over to try and find some cute clothes.

"I don't think so, I'm sorry," the girl answers.

"That's okay. Thank you," Blythe says as she hangs the top back on the rack.

I laugh under my breath because she's already set aside several pink items to buy but is still on the hunt for more.

I didn't bail on our weekend shopping trip, even after a stressful week at work, because I found myself excited to go with Blythe. Being around her settles me just knowing how honest yet positive she always is. When she showed up to my house this morning with two iced refreshers and a smile, I practically skipped down the walkway to her car.

Pop music plays throughout the store that's filled to the brim with bright summer colors. I stroll past the jewelry table, stopping to pick up a pair of earrings that catch my eye.

"These would be cute for work, right?" I ask while holding up the gold knot stud earrings.

Blythe glances over her shoulder. "Ooo, yes! Very chic. Very Savannah," she laughs. "Hey, speaking of your job, how's everything going there?"

I shrug at first and place the earrings in the basket I'm carrying. Then I think twice about downplaying it. "I don't think I've ever worked so hard."

Blythe's face lights up and she stops searching through the sea of clothes to fully face me. "Yeah?" She really wants to know. There's an earnestness about the Farrows that throws me off.

I've been existing all this time, afraid of people like that, always wondering if it was nothing more than a front to mask their malicious intent. Now I find myself wanting to surround myself with their brand of genuine personalities rather than running, no matter how foreign that feeling is.

"There's a big case coming up that I've been helping with," I add. "I'm pretty excited about it."

"That's amazing, Sav! What about the firm in general though? Do you like it there?"

I think about her question, grazing my fingers over a long floral skirt hanging in front of me. A soft smile breaks over my cheeks. "It's everything I've ever imagined, B. My work feels meaningful and I'm starting to remember why I went into this career field in the first place. I used to think it was so that I could challenge myself and prove to my brother and my parents that I could achieve something beyond their expectations of me. But now, I know that an even bigger reason was so I could make a difference."

The honest confession about my work came out easier than I thought it would, and it feels amazing to say these things out loud instead of harboring them in my mind. My job means a lot to me, and I know that Blythe is very career driven too, so it feels amazing to have a friend who gets it. Someone who understands.

My heart buzzes with the sweet realization that Blythe *is* my friend, and it has little to do with the fact that we were once beer pong partners or that I've been carrying on with her brother in a fake relationship.

"I see why he likes you so much," she mutters with a smirk.

"Who?"

She rolls her eyes and huffs. "Who? Drop it, girl. You know exactly who I'm talking about and if you keep finding a way to only see him once a week he's going to roll over and die."

"We've both been busy," I throw out the excuse. I can't lie though, I would rather see him more than once a week too. I find myself wishing the customer appreciation event was this Friday instead of next.

"Yeah, that's true. He works around the clock these days it seems like. I think it's just to distract himself and not smother you, though," she laughs. "Oh my god. Look at *this*."

I look up from the rack of skirts that I was continuing to browse through, scrunching my nose up at the tiny thing that she's holding up.

"Can you even call that a shirt? It's basically lingerie." It's gorgeous, but it's nothing more than a tiny scrap of lace.

"Okay it's a little skimpy. But you would rock it," she laughs. "At least try it on."

Picturing myself in the top she's holding up, that's nowhere near my usual style, has me mirroring her laugh and envisioning the look on Warren's face if he saw me in it. I reach my hand out and sigh.

Add *shopping for clothes* to the list of things that I can't manage to do without thinking about him.

Shaking my head to clear my spinning thoughts, I reach my hand out. "I could try it on, I guess."

She squeals and puts the hanger in my hand. "Take pics. I'm going to look at shoes."

I clutch the hanger in my hand while Blythe walks over to the shoe display. After finding an open dressing room and then locking the door behind me, I slip off the cropped cotton t-shirt and light blue bralette that I wore in.

My fingers dance across the lace as I pull the bodysuit off the hanger. It doesn't fit over my head at first, but then I realize that there's a small zipper on the side. Once it's finally situated, I tuck the bottom into my high-waisted jean shorts and pull the side zipper back up.

It's . . . very tight.

My boobs are closer to my neck than I think they've ever been. I pull on the built-in cups that do almost nothing to hide my nipples, attempting to tame the girls at least a little bit. The center is low cut, dipping down just above my belly button.

Do girls wear this out? I feel next to naked, honestly. My eyes narrow and I run my hands over the material as I look at myself in the full-length mirror.

I can't stop my next thought wondering what Warren would say if he saw me in this. As soon as it enters my head, my phone vibrates. My hand flies to the back pocket of my shorts, reaching for it. Like I manifested it in my mind, it's a text from Warren.

WARREN

Still shopping?

I cock a hip and smile while staring down at the screen.

I'm with B, what do you think?

WARREN

haha figured.

> Office or ranch today? Or did you decide to take the weekend off for once

WARREN

Office.

Just a little paperwork nothing major. Are you going back to your house after shopping?

> I think so. I have a lot of reading to do before a meeting on Monday.

The incoming text bubbles pop up and disappear again for a minute as they tend to do when we text. I watch them and wonder what he wants to say but never does. Why is it so hard for me to kick down the barrier and ask him if he wants to hang out even if my boss isn't around to see us together? Why is it so hard for me to believe that I could be loved?

My stubbornness rears its ugly head and I'm running out of reasons why I shouldn't try harder to shut it down.

Vulnerability takes time for me, but Warren has been patient. I'm not sure how much longer I can pretend that I don't adore that about him. Continuing to mask my feelings with insecurity while he so openly cares about me doesn't feel as necessary as it once did.

Resisting him started out as an imperative safeguard. And maybe not much time has passed, but time alone is not the only path to understanding your own feelings. Right now, my objection to the idea of us feels like I'm betraying my own heart by pointlessly protecting myself from something that I've realized won't actually hurt me.

Acknowledging all of that to myself is the first step. And a much easier one than confessing it to Warren. Would he suddenly lose interest because the thrill of the chase would be gone?

Before texting him back, I look at myself in the mirror one more time. I should probably get a move on and get back out there, so I switch over to the camera on my phone so I can take a picture to show Blythe.

I'm not a model, but I know what my flattering angles are, so I turn slightly and lean one shoulder forward to snap a few pics. Clicking on them to see how they look, a slow smile makes its way to my lips and I cover it with my hand.

Damn. I wasn't expecting it to look *that* cute. Blythe is a genius because I don't think I've ever looked or felt this confident in such a skimpy piece of clothing. It hugs my body perfectly and I am *so* buying this.

In a rush, I click on the messaging app and send her the picture. After swiping away from our text thread though, my finger pauses over Warren's name.

I smirk and sway my hips back and forth with the phone still in my hand. What a shame it'd be if I *accidentally* sent it to him too.

Before overthinking about how immature it is to bait his reaction, I send him the picture for a little theory test.

"Oops," I say with a satisfied shrug.

I take a quick cleansing breath, then set my phone down to try and figure out how the hell I'm going to peel this thing off without ripping the delicate fabric.

After trying and failing to get the side zipper down, my phone buzzes violently on the bench. I lean over to look at the screen without picking it up and see three unread messages from Warren.

WARREN

Holy shit.

That's the hottest fucking thing I've ever seen.

Show me more.

I swipe the phone from the bench, working to not giggle out loud.

INCOMING FACETIME WARREN

Fucking hell. That wasn't part of the plan. I know better than to ignore it, he'll just keep calling until I pick up.

I think about throwing my t-shirt on before answering, but what would be the point? He's obviously already seen what I have on.

The low timbre of his voice fills the space in the dressing room as soon as I hit the green accept call button.

"Savvy."

I swipe the curls out of my face, revealing my flushed cheeks. "Hi."

"Hi, yourself. What are you trying to do? Kill me?"

I let out a breathy laugh and fiddle with one of the body-suit straps nervously. "I'm sorry. I must have sent that to you by mistake," I tease.

Warren is sitting at his desk wearing a gray t-shirt and his typical straw cowboy hat. It's sitting back on his head and is tilted slightly to the side as if he pulled it off to run a hand through his disheveled hair before calling. I bite my lip while waiting for him to respond, trying not to focus on how badly I want to steal that shirt he's wearing and sleep in it later.

He stiffens and leans forward in his seat the longer he processes my apology.

"Who the fuck did you mean to send it to?"

My lips part hearing his agitated tone. Is he . . . jealous? I feel the warmth from that realization all the way down to my toes, which I know is silly. I shouldn't feel giddy about Warren looking like he could strangle someone thinking I'd taken that picture for someone else.

Even so, I smirk with amusement and shrug. And maybe lower the camera angle a bit.

He arches an eyebrow and then blows out a breath. "Don't play with me."

"I was sending it to your sister for approval," I admit.

He clears his throat. "Oh. Right. Okay."

I laugh and sit down on the bench, leaning my back against the wall. "Did you think I was sending it to some guy?"

"No," he scoffs.

"Liar," I whisper with a teasing smile.

His dimples make an appearance right along with a subtle blush on the apples of his cheeks while he shakes his head. We stare at each other for a moment until he lowers his voice to break the silence. "Move the phone farther away."

I don't know what I was thinking, following his command so effortlessly, but my arm stretches out in front of me.

"*Jesus*," he mutters as he scrubs a hand down his face. "Now pull the top down."

"Warren!" I whisper. "I'm in public."

"Is the door locked?"

"Yes."

My eyes flick between the phone screen and the door. I can hear the low rumblings of a few shoppers blending in with the music being played over the speakers. They'd be none the wiser if I just . . .

I lock eyes with him and suddenly lose all train of thought. It's not like he hasn't seen me naked before. But he looks like he's about to come completely unraveled on the other end of the phone anyway, tracking my every movement. Unable to resist his request any longer, my middle finger trails along the bare skin between my breasts.

I keep my eyes on Warren's as my fingers dance along the lace and finally grasp the top of the fabric that sits barely an inch above my nipple. Slowly, I pull it down.

"*Fuck*," he growls. A hand runs through the hair on the side of his head while he leans back in his seat and looks at the ceiling. "I'm coming to get you right now."

I shake my head and giggle softly so that no one on the other side of the door suspects anything. "Don't do that, we're almost done shopping anyway."

My hand moves to the other breast so that both sides are pulled down.

His expression is one that I've seen before. I've spent too many nights dreaming about the same look during what we did after that first kiss. His tongue, his fingers . . . my eyes close just thinking about it and my finger starts circling a nipple.

"I want my mouth right there so fucking bad," he growls.

My tongue darts out to pull in my bottom lip just thinking about it. "Or you could put it here—" I trail my hand down my stomach. Until the banging on the door starts, that is.

"Are you on the phone? Let's go. I'm almost to that point in the shopping trip where I want to race home and lay on my back in a quiet dark room by myself for a few hours." Blythe's voice jolts me out of my trance, and I instantly pull up the top of the bodysuit and sit up straight.

"Don't hang up."

"I'm hanging up," I whisper as fiercely yet quietly as I can. "Be right there!"

I change clothes as quickly as I can and rush out of the dressing room.

"I'm ready to be done," Blythe sighs when I sidle up next to her at the register.

"Same," I say, trying to keep my voice even and not sounding like I just did sprints up and down every aisle of this store.

"Snacks and music on the way home?"

I nod as she loops her arm through mine. "Perfect."

20

SAVANNAH

"Are you pregnant?"

I choke on the bite of cheese and cracker in my mouth and place my hand around the base of my throat. From her spot next to me, Emma outstretches her hand and slaps me on the back a little too hard. I stumble forward on my high heels and grimace in her direction.

"Jesus, calm down, it's just a question," she says while I right myself and take a sip of water.

"*No*, I'm not pregnant," I hiss. "Don't ask people that." The glass of water in front of me is covered in condensation from the heat despite the sun still being an hour from setting. I wipe it with a napkin and take another drink.

If I was still a glutton for self-sabotage, I'd join most everyone else here tonight who is indulging in something stronger.

Directly behind the row of businesses on the street where the firm's office is located, is an open grassy area. It's a well-groomed park with a lush public garden, some large shade trees, and a stone fountain in the middle. Once a year, the law offices of Powell and Grant transform the space into a party for a customer appreciation event like the one tonight.

"It's important that we nurture the relationships that we have with our clients," Mariana always says.

The decorated cocktail tables, hanging twinkle lights, and smells of BBQ are all lovely and inviting. The social interaction aspect though? Not something I've been looking forward to. I don't exactly thrive in environments like this, or at least I haven't in the past. But I'm intent on working through it the best I can without any big mess-ups.

I wish that Warren would hurry up and get here. He mentioned he had to drop something off for his dad at his job, so he's not technically late. But I'd be lying if I said I wasn't excited to see him after not crossing paths all week.

When we first agreed to pretend we were dating, his main job was to help me win over the people in the town, especially my bosses. But in a short time, my expectation of him has morphed into something more personal and I started wanting him around because of the way that he makes me feel. I'm more comfortable when he's around. He's kind to me and I don't find myself having to worry about what I might say or do when I know that he's there to bail me out— figuratively *and* literally.

"I was just wondering," Emma whispers back to me with some snark in her tone. "You're the only one not drinking champagne."

"This is a casual evening work event, not a New Year's Eve party," I defend myself while trying to hide my annoyance. She eyes me with skepticism like she doesn't believe my reasoning. "Stop looking at me like that, I am *not* knocked up. That'd be impossible."

"Ohhh," she draws out the word and tries to hide a smile. "I see. So, you and Warren aren't sleeping together."

I'd rather not discuss my sex life with Warren's nosy ex-girlfriend. I'd rather not picture letting Warren have his way with me either, but it's impossible to stop the visual now that she brought it up. I've already done enough of that this week and I'm running out of reasons to push him away.

"We're—" I shake my head, "It's none of your business, Emma."

And why do you even care?

I realize how rude I sounded even without the last part I wanted to add, and instantly wish I could take the sentence back.

At the table next to us, Mr. Grant approaches a group of clients with a smile and engages in conversation. It's a reminder that part of this job is being good with people, even if you don't like them.

"I mean, I just keep those things private is all." I tack on a closed-mouth smile for effect. "We should mingle," I suggest, hoping she takes the hint and either goes away or changes the subject.

"Of course," she leans toward me and places her hand over mine. "But if you ever need someone to talk to about your relationship issues, I'm here for support. I happen to know a thing or two about Warren if you know what I mean."

Yes, I think I know what you mean.

And I'd also like to cunt punt you into the next dimension right now.

Where does she get off thinking—

My thoughts get cut off when I see my brother perusing the open bar. Everyone is allowed a plus one, so I suspected that Emma might invite him. Even if I expected his attendance though, I still recoil. He's more of an asshole when he's drinking, and he loves to torment me at any given opportunity. If anyone is going to ruin this event, it might not be me after all. It'll be him.

I continue ignoring Emma while I watch Spencer walk away from the bar and straight up to Mrs. Powell. I lean to the side, peeking around the floral centerpiece in the middle of the table. His face lights up in a way that tells me he is about to say something off-handed or sarcastic, and I dig my fingers into the palm of my hand.

Suddenly, my rule of no drinking tonight is no longer in place, and I snatch the bottle that Emma brought to the table.

"What the—" Emma snarls when my elbow bumps her in the process of reaching for an empty cup, filling it with a generous pour, and downing it in two swigs. I'd like to slam the cup on the table and storm out of here like a coward, but I can't. This event has barely even started and I need to be here.

As much as I would rather avoid it, I need to intervene before Spencer's conversation with my boss turns into a Savannah Chase roast session.

"I'll talk to you later," I say to Emma. She lifts a finger from the stem of her champagne flute in less than enthusiastic acknowledgment and I head straight through the crowd of people to break up whatever my brother is up to.

"Here she is," Mrs. Powell smiles and steps to the side to make room for me once I reach them. "You didn't mention that your brother would be in attendance today."

"I—didn't know he would be here," I answer carefully.

With a fake and slightly buzzed smile, Spencer puts the attention back on him.

"She's only teasing," he says to Mrs. Powell without so much as looking in my direction. "She knows that I'm here with Emma Brooks, my girlfriend. One of your brightest associates I understand."

I hate how formal and proper he is in public.

"Emma has had her fair share of achievement, yes," Mrs.

Powell agrees, but with a straight face. "She has certainly made an impression."

I narrow my eyes when I detect a hint of derision when she says the word impression.

"And bonus! She has a clean record," Spencer howls while placing a hand on my shoulder to keep himself from falling over in fits of laughter.

His joke didn't hit the way he'd hoped it would though, because I'm far from laughing and Mariana remains emotionless.

"The charges were dropped," I say through clenched teeth.

"Well, in any case," he sighs trying to regain some composure after his joke fell flat. "I'm sure you'll catch up eventually, sis. The finance world has been great for me. I'm an executive at our family's investment firm," he clarifies for Mrs. Powell as if she's a child. Probably for the best since his words are slurred and difficult to understand anyway.

He brings a drink to his lips and his eyes meet mine in a devious stare that says he has no intention of behaving nicely even if he's talking to *my* boss.

My bottom lip stings as I dig my teeth into it, and I momentarily close my eyes to avoid scowling or glaring at my brother. It's one thing for him to constantly give me shit when we cross paths, but it's another thing entirely to try humiliating me in front of my boss.

A waiter passes us carrying a tray of drinks, and Spencer stops him to reach out and curl his fingers around another tumbler of amber-colored liquor.

"The company is thriving right now," he continues despite both Mariana and I looking less than interested. "Target the struggling small businesses," he points to his temple like he's just revealed some sort of insider tip.

"They're cheap and vulnerable. Perfect for acquisitions. It's simple, really."

He looks toward Mrs. Powell and winks while taking another swig.

"Riveting," she mutters dryly. She's not usually one to hold back her opinions, but judging by the look on her face, it seems like she's fighting the urge to call him a douche canoe right to his face. I don't want to make her feel obligated to stand here and listen to my brother spew dense business jargon for the next thirty minutes, so I offer her an out.

"Sorry to keep you, I know there are a handful of people you wanted to speak with tonight."

"Ah, yes," she replies, her eyes lighting. "It was nice to meet you, Mr. Chase. Sorry to end our conversation so prematurely, but I do have business to attend to. You understand."

My chest deflates as he curtly nods, and she returns to the crowd behind us.

"Well, you've embarrassed me just like always," he seethes when she's finally out of earshot. "You completely bombarded our conversation and then made her leave."

"She's busy," I say softly to avoid making a scene if possible. "And anyway, you're the embarrassing one. Making jokes about me in front of my boss? *Real* classy, Spencer."

"First time hearing classy and Spencer in the same sentence," a husky voice sounds from behind me. It instantly soothes my brewing irritation, and I turn just in time for him to step right up next to me, one arm wrapping around my waist.

My shoulders relax and I want to scream because of how happy I am to see him. Feel him. Not just because I'm no longer fighting a losing battle alone against my asshole brother, but because we haven't seen each other in almost two weeks. Unless you count the dressing room Facetime, and I don't. In person is infinitely better.

Sure, we've randomly texted most days. But our busy schedules have kept us both glued to our jobs that are so important to us right now. Subconsciously, I wasn't brave enough to put myself out there and ask him to spend time with me outside of our arrangement. Knowing him, he might have been worried that if he was the one to ask, I'd turn it down.

Before I have a chance to overthink myself into an early grave, he leans down, tilts my chin up with his index finger, and presses his lips to mine. It takes the edge off my interaction with my brother, and I lean forward on my tiptoes to make it last longer.

It doesn't feel like the show-off kiss that we originally planned for. It's more along the lines of *I missed you and I don't even care if your boss is watching or not.*

"Seriously?" Spencer mumbles.

Impulsively, I pull away from the kiss and lean into Warren's body, feeling the safe warmth of his chest against the side of my face. His reaction is to squeeze my hip and I look up only to find that he's glaring a hole straight through my brother.

Spencer looks disgusted and twists his face at the sight of Warren.

"Shouldn't you be chewing on straw in a pair of overalls," he spits.

"Don't stereotype farmers, darling," Emma says as she places a hand on Spencer's chest and flips her hair over her shoulder.

Convenient timing, her showing up right after Warren did.

Her cleavage looks less subtle than I remember it being when I first got here, and she's fluttering her eyelashes at

Warren. I think she's trying to look sexy, but she's overdoing it and from my point of view she looks more like she has something stuck in her eye.

Spencer grabs a handful of her ass and makes a revolting growling noise as he kisses the side of her neck.

Gross. I refrain from rolling my eyes and shift my weight to stand closer to Warren.

"I'm not a farmer," Warren says. "Closest I come to farming is cutting hay on the ranch in the summer."

Emma purses her lips in annoyance knowing that Warren had to correct her. I follow her eyes as she studies his hand on my hip, then up to where I'm leaning against him. Unable to help myself, I raise my eyebrows and give her a vapid smile.

"Who cares?" Spencer says with an eye roll.

This could easily turn into a pissing match, but Warren's body language remains calm and indifferent. I try to do the same, but I'm still uncomfortable.

"Can you just act nice for once?" I plead while trying to ignore the sick feeling starting in my stomach.

"Why, so I don't make you look bad? You've been making our family look bad for years. And this little party is fucking stupid anyway," Spencer seethes. "Why you'd want to live or work in this dump of a town instead of in the city is beyond me. As soon as Emma agrees to leave and work for me, I won't be back."

My family's definition of *making them look bad* is a lack of an Ivy League degree, a penthouse, and a position at a Fortune 500 company. My bad grades and suspension at boarding school or the public arrest probably didn't help, either. But that doesn't change the fact that their standards are impossibly high.

Westridge is small and looks a hell of a lot different from his rich lifestyle, but it's far from a dump and I like living and working here. I don't voice that defense though, because I'm not sure how to word it in a way that doesn't remind him that I haven't conformed to the family's ideal image.

"I wouldn't expect you to understand me," is the best answer I can come up with.

"Well, you're not exactly an open book Savannah," Emma points out. Spencer nods in smug agreement with her.

Warren's chest begins to rumble with light laughter, a contradiction to my brother's tense attitude.

"Something funny?" Spencer asks with an accusing glare.

"It wouldn't matter if she was an open book or not," Warren says. "You're still an emotionally illiterate ass who wouldn't know how to treat your sister if it was spelled out for you in a large print manual."

My brother releases his arm that was around Emma's waist and aggressively steps up to Warren with fury in his eyes.

"What are you going to do? Punch me?" Warren laughs. "You're pathetic, dude."

He might, I think to myself.

Spencer thrives on chaos. Craves it, even. If there isn't some sort of drama or conflict happening, he creates it. And I'm always in the line of fire.

My eyes scan the party still happening around us, hoping no one is intently listening or watching this play out. When my gaze locks on Mr. Grant narrowing his eyes in our direction, I swallow the lump in my throat and grip Warren's shirt. My vision goes hazy and if this conversation keeps going in the direction that it is, I think I'm going to be sick.

At his side, Spencer clenches and releases his hand several times. The veins on his palm are visibly pulsating.

With a tight-lipped and red-painted smile, Emma steps forward and rests a hand on Warren's forearm. "Maybe we should go get a drink and let them hash this out in private."

"No thanks," Warren replies without a glance in her direction.

With a huff, she whips her head in Spencer's direction to get his attention, but it doesn't work. He's focused on Warren, red-faced and practically bouncing off the ground in anticipation. I wouldn't be shocked if this came to blows, but luckily Warren still seems less bothered. In fact, he seems amused.

"Who ties your shoes?" Warren asks Spencer as he looks down at him.

To my surprise, Emma snickers at that jab, but I wince knowing it's just going to piss him off more than he already is. I cover my mouth and sway on my feet as a familiar bout of nausea rises.

There's no smart reply from my brother, so Warren keeps going.

"Stop disrespecting Savannah or fuck off."

He says it with enough volume and authority that several people standing near us turn their heads.

"Or what?" Spencer challenges.

I don't catch what Warren says next, because I can't hold it together for another second. With a hand over my mouth, I turn and run through the party for the nearest bathroom.

21

WARREN

I planned on giving Spencer a piece of my mind until his face turned blue, but when Savannah ran off toward the office located behind the party, I followed her immediately. Before stepping inside the door to the building, I glance over to the parking lot and see Spencer and Emma getting into their cars, parked next to each other.

I understand now how everything that Savannah believes about herself has been filtered in a negative light. It's no wonder she doesn't easily buy into every feeling that I've tried confessing to her. She's used to people putting her down, even those closest to her. I don't know if her parents are exactly like Spencer is around her, but if they are, I have half a mind to never let her be alone with any of them again if I can help it.

The lights are off inside the office space, except for an exit sign and a few desk lamps. I pass several cubicles on my way to the hall and scan each door looking for the bathroom. Before I find it, Savvy comes striding down the hall with a washed-out complexion and a napkin in her hand.

Tears gather in the corners of her eyes as she looks up at

me. Without asking questions, I take her hand and lead her back toward the desks.

"Is your purse in here?" I ask.

She nods and points to a particularly organized desk not far from where we're standing, complete with a line of perfectly spaced pens and exactly zero family photos. I spot her purse underneath and grab it, heading straight for the door.

We walk the short distance to my truck in silence, and I glance over at her a few times to check that she's okay. She seemed to be holding up even with the Spencer and Emma interaction, but seeing her now, I realize she must have been feeling sick again.

After I open the passenger door, she steps inside my truck with no protest, and I set her purse gently on her lap. I like it when she lets me do things for her, but right now it worries me. If she was feeling fine, she probably would have put up a bit of a fight and insisted that she didn't need me to drive her anywhere.

"Thank you," she says quietly.

"Do you want me to take you home?"

I wish she'd say no so that I could take her back to my place.

But she nods. I make my way to the driver's seat and take off reluctantly in the direction of her house.

When Westridge is finally starting to disappear in the rearview mirror, I reach my hand across the center console. A burst of warmth blooms in my chest when she takes it into hers so effortlessly. I clear my throat while tightening my grip on her hand before asking her a question.

"Did you get sick in the office?"

"Yes. I don't know what's wrong with me, it's like every few days I puke my guts up."

Her head is leaned back against the seat, but she covers it with her free hand for a moment.

"Sorry, that's gross," she says. "Pretend I didn't just tell you that."

"I work on a ranch," I reassure her. "I've seen and heard a lot worse, trust me."

"Right," she laughs softly. It sounds weak and I really don't want her to stay alone tonight. If she lets me, maybe I can convince her to let me stay with her.

Ten minutes later, I'm about to turn into her driveway, but stop the truck before driving toward the house.

"Is—that your mailbox?"

I squint my eyes and lean forward in my seat. Savannah sits up in her seat to look out the windshield and her mouth falls open in shock.

"You're kidding me," she huffs. "Who would do that?"

The white mailbox with hand-painted floral designs on the outside is lying on its side, a few inches from falling into the ditch on the side of the road. Tire tracks surround it and I realize what most likely happened.

"Didn't realize kids these days still went around backroading," I say. I'm not proud of it, but I used to do it all the time with my buddies. Back when our frontal lobes were half the size of the tab on a beer can. It's dumb and reckless, and I've replaced my fair share of mailboxes after an ass-chewing from my dad. But it was fun at the time.

"Damn," she whispers.

"I'll help you fix it," I say and I drive past it and turn toward the house.

"Warren!"

I jump in my seat when Savannah shouts my name, not realizing what she's yelling about. Then, I see it. The two flower beds that run the entire length of the front of the house are completely dug up.

Her mouth slowly gapes and she releases my hand to place it over her chest. I check each direction, hoping to see a car or sign of whoever did this, but there's no one.

"No," she cries. "It was so beautiful. Mesa loved those flowers so much. She's going to be so upset."

After fumbling with her seat belt in a rush, she reaches for the door, but I hook her elbow and pull her back into her seat.

"Stay in here while I check things."

She starts to argue, but I give her a look that says I'm not fucking around. With a defeated sigh, she nods and I step out of the truck. I do a quick scan of the property but realize pretty quickly that with it being so dark out, and being generally unfamiliar with the place, it's not going to do me much good.

Stepping through the beam of the truck headlights, I walk closer to the house. The entire front lawn is covered in dead blooms that were dug up and thrown out of the flower beds, and the stone walkway is sprinkled with soil.

Based on the mailbox, and the thorough hack job of this amount of flowers, I'd say this wasn't a fun prank by a tipsy group of dumbasses passing by. This was intentional.

I make my way up the steps and try the front door. Still locked. Neither of the front windows are broken, but several pots and random decor has been knocked over on the porch like someone might have been looking for a hidden house key.

Without wasting any more time, I pull out my phone to dial Justin's number and he answers after the second ring.

"What's up, man?"

"Hey, you on duty?" I ask.

"I'm at the station, but I haven't started my shift yet. Everything good?"

"It might be nothing. But someone came and vandalized

Savannah's yard. Well, the yard at the house that she's renting." I let out a deep breath and nudge a knocked-over flower pot with my boot. "It doesn't look like they got in the house, but I don't know for sure."

"Is she safe?" he asks. His question has me thinking of all of the worst possible scenarios that could have happened if I hadn't driven her home or if she had been here when whoever did this showed up.

"Yes. I'm here with her. I don't know the exact address but I can ask her real quick."

"Just drop me a pin. I'll leave right now."

My next instinct is to shoot a quick text in the group chat, and I think Gage could definitely help with some security measures. But knowing him, he'd open the gun safe the second I told him what happened and go hunt the motherfuckers down. Literally. Tripp and Heston would be along for the ride without question, so it's probably best to just ask for their help fixing the place up tomorrow instead of riling them up tonight.

A truck door slams, and I look up from my phone to see Savannah walking toward the house. Her mouth is covered with her hand as she takes in the damage as I walk down the steps.

"I called the police. They'll be here soon," I say, trying to keep my voice at least somewhat soothing.

She nods but continues to walk through the ruined plants and flowers.

"I was supposed to take care of these. They were special to her," she says as she sniffs back tears. "None of them can be saved."

I shake my head. I don't know much about flowers, but even I can tell that there's no salvaging them.

"I was kind of hoping we might become friends," she breathes out a frustrated laugh. "Not likely now, I guess."

"If she gets mad at you for something that was out of your control, then she wouldn't have been a good friend anyway," I say honestly. "This wasn't your fault, Savvy."

"You're right," she sighs.

I think my heart almost stops when she takes the three steps of distance between us. Her hands slowly slide over my hips and then loop around my lower back. Her chin tucks down and she leans her cheek against my chest, right between my pecs.

"We'll take care of the police report and then you can worry about calling her in the morning," I say as she melts further into me. I hold the back of her head with my hand and wrap my other arm around her body. "Do you want to grab a few things so you can stay with me for the weekend?"

It's bold to ask her to stay at the bunkhouse for more than a night like she has once before. But I wouldn't sleep a wink with her staying here, and maybe this is selfish thinking after the night she's had, but I'm fucking desperate to have her in my bed again.

She nods, making her nose burrow into my chest.

"Warren?" she whispers.

"Yeah, baby?"

"I'm so tired."

"I know," I say as I kiss the top of her head.

"Savannah?" I whisper.

"Hmm?" she answers without opening her eyes.

She managed to take a shower and gave in to letting me put her into comfortable clothes. I dug for the biggest and softest T-shirt that I could find in my drawer. With a sleepy look on her face, she stood in front of me with her arms up and I gently pulled it over her head. I hugged her and tried to gauge her temperature at the same time, thinking she probably had the flu.

After that, she insisted on 'hanging out' on the couch for a little bit instead of going to bed, but it took all of five minutes for her to fall asleep. That was two hours ago.

It didn't take long for her to mistake me for her pillow, either.

I've been sitting here with her head on my shoulder the entire time trying not to blink too hard or breathe too loudly. Answering emails and dealing with some business stuff on my phone has barely distracted me enough to not think too much about how one of her arms is stretched around my waist and her breath dancing across my neck every few seconds.

"It's pretty late," I say.

No answer.

"Savannah." I lean in closer this time.

"What," she whispers.

"Time for bed."

"I'm already sleeping," she mumbles in a slur of disoriented speech.

Carefully, I lift my arm that's been trapped under her this whole time, but when I do, she flops right down into my lap.

"*Jesus,*" I grunt, lifting her back up to a sitting position. Her head flops to one side and her eyes remain closed. "What the?" I grab her by the shoulders and give her a gentle shake. It's enough to make her heavy eyelids lift up and down a few times.

"Stop it," she demands, once again slurring her words. "Go back to sleep."

She places one hand on each of my pecs and pushes me down. I land flat on my back, now stretched out on the couch cushions. I'm not complaining, but I'm shocked when she scoots down and lays right next to me, trapping me behind her.

I could probably get up now and carry her to bed. But she snuggles closer to me, and I don't think I would move now for anything.

As if her new position wasn't comfortable enough, her body turns to face me, and she wiggles in close. My eyes go wide as her right leg hooks over my waist, and she rubs her head back and forth until she's perfectly satisfied with its position on my chest.

"I like it when you hold me."

There's no way she doesn't feel my heart trying to violently beat its way out of my body right now. Time stands still and I commit her words to memory. I've imagined her saying something like that to me so many times, but it sounds even better in real-time.

Slowly, I curl the arm that's underneath her up and around her waist. My hand rests near her hip bone—a respectfully neutral zone. Not too low. Not too high.

I can't help baiting her, pathetically, to say it again or reassure me that it's true.

"You do?" I ask. It wouldn't shock me if she lightly slapped me and laughed like it was a joke and she was kidding all along.

"Mmhmm," she breathes sleepily through her nose and nuzzles against the fabric of my shirt. My skin is going to melt off if she pushes her hips against my leg again like that. "But you're going to get sick too now since we're touching."

"Don't care."

"I like—" she says through a yawn. Her hand trails up the middle of my abs and lands just above my belly button, "you."

Not even a second later, she's softly snoring.

My arm around her tightens while I stare up at the ceiling with a face-splitting grin.

"About time, Savvy girl."

2 2

SAVANNAH

"Should we wait on him?" an amused voice whispers.

My eyes are already closed, but I scrunch them together harder to will myself back to sleep. The blazing migraine that is currently splitting my brain in two is hallucinating voices and I'd very much like to go back to my cave of silent darkness for a little longer.

"We're supposed to be there by seven," a different voice whispers.

"He looks a little preoccupied," the first voice chuckles.

"Kick his foot."

"You do it."

Okay, those voices sound closer and more real than I thought they were. I don't think I'm imagining things. Slowly, I open one eye halfway. The world is blurry at first, so I blink a few times.

A few pairs of jean-clad legs stand directly in my line of sight. My head lifts slightly and when I look up, two men who seem freakishly large from this angle are staring down at me.

188

What the hell?

"Mornin', sunshine," the happier-looking one croons.

My vision is still spotty as I fight to come out of my deep sleep, rubbing the corners of my eyes. One of them pulls the brim of his cowboy hat down and smiles in a way that I finally recognize. What is Tripp doing in my room? The other guy looks like someone already ruined his day, but judging by the lack of light coming in through the window behind them, the sun's not even up. That'd be Heston.

I close my eyes again and groan from the pain lancing through my head. When I try to move to sit up though, I'm pinned down.

"Go away," a deep gravelly voice behind me mumbles.

The sensation of lips and breath against my neck sends a shiver through my entire body. I screech and launch myself upright as quickly as I can when I recognize it as Warren's voice. His lips on my skin. His arms around me.

"What the hell is—" I scramble for words, looking around to find myself not in my room at all, but on a couch in the bunkhouse living room with Warren while Tripp and Heston look down at us.

My memory is slow and fuzzy, and I have never felt a headache this paralyzing. But slowly, the events from last night start to come back to me. With a groan, I close my eyes again and stretch my tight back muscles that weren't graced with a mattress last night.

"What time is it?" Warren asks. The couch cushion shifts underneath us as he sits up next to me.

"Time to go," Heston growls. "You told us not to be late, so get your ass up."

Tripp and Heston exchange looks—one of amusement and the other of annoyance—and leave the living room.

While I rub my temples with my thumb and forefinger

trying to ease the throbbing pain, Warren's hand slips under my arm and around my waist to pull me back until I'm pressed against his front. It feels nice to lean against him because another minute of sitting up on my own and I think I might have fallen over. His other hand moves my hair off to one side as he leans in to press his lips against the shell of my ear.

"Why are we on the couch?" I ask while tilting my head to the side to give him better access.

"Because when I tried to move us to the bed last night, you were already half asleep and basically shoved me down on my back and I couldn't move," he laughs.

"Right. Sorry, I was a little loopy last night. Actually… I still feel kind of out of it."

He pulls away from me slightly and I look at him over my shoulder. Something in his face changes from an early morning sleepy expression to one of concern.

"What do you mean?" he asks.

"It's like I rode ten roller coasters in a row and then chugged a jar of moonshine," I try to explain. I've had hangovers before, but never this strong. And as far as I can remember, I only had one drink of champagne at the firm's customer appreciation party. Okay, a few chugs. But still, in the grand scheme of things it wasn't nearly enough to make me feel like shit the next day.

"I'm texting my sister," Warren declares as he maneuvers around me to get up from the couch. His phone is sitting on the rustic log wood coffee table, and he swoops it up and unlocks the screen before I have a chance to protest. I hate the idea of ruining her morning just so that she can come over here and check on me.

But I don't have the energy right now to object.

"There," he says as he tosses the phone. "She should be here soon. Want some breakfast?"

"Sure," I reply with a soft smile. Some food and then maybe a nap might help. Thank god it's the weekend and I don't have to go into the office.

A shower always makes me feel better, too. But I honestly don't feel like standing for that long. Instead of a full morning routine, I settle for heading to the bathroom to at least brush my teeth and change into some real clothes.

When I picture a guest bathroom of a bunkhouse on a fully functioning ranch, it's a lot messier than this one. Calculate in the fact that three grown men all live here, four at one point, you'd think it'd look more like a bathroom in a frat house than a girl's apartment.

Based on the fruit-scented products on the shelf in the shower and the clean hand towel, it's normally frequented by women. It only stings a little bit when I wonder if any girls who have stayed over with Warren in the past have used this bathroom just like I am right now.

I've had my fair share of hookups in the past too, so it shouldn't make me feel territorial knowing that Warren has most likely shared a night or two with plenty of girls here previous to our arrangement. Things have felt more complicated and different between us lately though. I don't hate it, in fact, I like how it feels. It's still weird to admit to myself though, seeing as how we haven't exactly talked about it. At first, the timeline of our fake dating depended on me keeping my job. Now I don't know where the faking ends and the real feelings step in.

Of course, I look like I died overnight and rose from the dead standing in the bathroom that a dozen or more other girls have stood in while thinking about this. I toss my hairbrush back into the bag that I brought in here with me and then try wiping the last bit of sleep from my eyes.

By the time I make it back into the kitchen twenty minutes later, it smells like bacon and Blythe is sitting at one of the bar stools at the large island. I drag my feet, take a seat next to her, and rest my elbows in front of me on the stained butcher block counter.

"You seem bright and chipper this morning," Blythe says between sips. There's a tiny tag attached to a white string hanging out of the side of her steaming mug.

"It's a good thing you're a doctor and not a lawyer because that's a load of bullshit and I don't buy it for second," I tease with a sigh.

"Fine, you look like ass."

"Under the weather would have sufficed," I laugh while self-consciously running a hand over my clammy forehead.

Blythe gently pushes my hand away and feels the temperature of my skin for herself, then purses her lips. From where he's standing by the stovetop, Warren looks over his shoulder and watches as she checks me over.

"This isn't necessary, I'm sorry that he made you come over here," I say.

"Shush, you know I don't mind. What kind of symptoms have you been feeling?"

"Umm . . . just random nausea. One minute I'm fine, and then the next I'm dizzy and feeling awful. Last time it went away quickly, but this time it lasted a lot longer."

"That's unusual. Possibly Norovirus, but it's not typically sporadic like you're describing."

"An English explanation would be good," Warren scoffs.

"Stomach bug," she clarifies with a laugh.

"Doesn't that only last a few days though?" I ask.

"Usually, yes. But in some cases, it can hang around for up to 10 days," Blythe explains. "Have *you* been sick, Warren? It's pretty contagious. Other than lovesick, I mean."

A blush creeps over my cheeks, but Warren just smirks.

"No, I feel fine," he says.

"Hmm," Blythe stops to think and holds her fist to her

chin. Even with her brow furrowed in concentration, her eyes are kind. I think if I ever needed anything, I could call her and she would come without question, not unlike her brother.

"I have to get going," Warren says from behind me. I hadn't realized that he walked over to me, but his arm stretches around my body, and he places a hot plate full of breakfast right in front of me and then braces his hand on the counter. Bending down, his lips graze the hair on the side of my head. "Eat. Then lay down. I'll be back soon," he says in a lowered voice.

I cross my legs, ignoring the chills making their way up my spine, while he moves toward the door to slip his feet into his boots. A second later, he's out the door and Blythe tilts her chin down and quirks an eyebrow up at me.

"What?" I squeak.

"What?!" she throws her head back and laughs. "I thought you were going to melt into the damn floor just now."

"It's nothing," I lie. Trying to brush it off was pointless though, because if Warren calling his sister to check on me while he cooked and served me food wasn't enough, my inability to rein in my reactions to him practically whispering in my ear like that is a dead giveaway that things between us don't seem as fake as they once were.

"Oh, come on," she draws out dramatically. "He's so whipped over you. And you're eating it right up."

"He is not," I giggle. But as I search for evidence to prove her wrong, I come up short. I tilt my head in thought and turn to face Blythe for this topic of conversation. "Is he?"

"You already know the answer, you're just not ready to admit it yet," she says in a snappy tone while taking another sip out of her mug.

"You're so sure, huh?"

"Definitely. If he wasn't, he wouldn't be on his way to

LAINEY LAWSON

cleaning up, replacing the flowers, and putting up security cameras at the house you're staying at right now. That's crazy what happened last night by the way. Are you okay?" Her gentle hand lands on my shoulder. "Besides how sick you've been feeling, I mean. I'm so glad you weren't there when it happened."

"I'm fine," I mutter, but I'm still stuck on the first thing that she said. "That's where Warren was off to? To do . . . all of that? How do you know about what happened?" The questions spill out fast and unfiltered. Unable to hold it back, tiny pools of water gather in the corners of my eyes.

"He sent it in the guy's group chat last night and asked them all to show up this morning to help fix it. Gage told me, of course. He knows I'll kick his ass and enjoy it if he doesn't tell me everything," she laughs. "He left our house before dawn to go pick up the cameras, but he said they'd be done with it by lunch."

My knee-jerk reaction is to be surprised. Because who have I ever had in my life that would stop everything that they're doing to help fix up a mess that I'm in? But that emotion doesn't last long because if I'm being honest with myself, it's not unexpected anymore that Warren would do that.

"My brother is a pretty straightforward guy," Blythe interrupts my thoughts. "You don't have to overanalyze it, girl. He likes you. A lot."

"Yeah. I think he does," I admit in a whisper. It's a conscious effort to *let* myself believe what has already been in front of my eyes the whole time.

Blythe smiles while I take a bite of my food. It does little to help the still lingering headache, but at least it's not making it worse.

"I don't know what's going to happen," I sigh. "When I've made friends or had relationships in the past, I always ruined them somehow. I was afraid to get hurt that I'd put an end to it before that had the chance to happen, you know?"

She nods and tilts her head while she listens to my embarrassing confession. Why I decided to vent to Warren's *sister* of all people is a mystery, but I trust Blythe and it feels good to get it out.

"I feel like I'm always the broken one who also cares too much, so I get out to protect myself. I don't know if that even makes sense," I mumble and shake my head.

Self-reflection is just another way to invite shame in my experience. But with the way Blythe is looking back at me, more understanding and less judging, a side of me feels relieved instead.

"It does make sense and I completely understand what you're saying. But Savvy, you don't care too much. You care deeply and it shows that your heart is good. Look at me," she demands, and I turn to stop avoiding her gaze. "*You are good.*"

"Thank you," I whisper, narrowly escaping the urge to argue. She has nothing to gain by lying to me, and I force myself to accept her kind words instead of leaning into the delusion that there's something wrong with me.

I am good, I repeat to myself inside my head.

As if she sensed what I was doing, she smiles and nods several times.

"Will you text me if you don't feel better in the morning?"

"Okay," I nod.

"Good," she beams and then stands to put her empty mug in the sink, "because we're going to the river tomorrow if you're up for it."

"I probably won't be much fun, but sure I'll go."

She shuffles toward me and after feeling my forehead one last time, wraps me in a warm hug.

"You don't have to worry about being fun. I want you there either way," she says before releasing me.

As soon as the front door shuts and I hear the engine of her car start up, the waterworks start. The tears don't scorch my skin as they trickle down my cheeks. They're cool and healing.

I suppose loving yourself isn't as hard as I thought it would be when you have others helping you do it.

23

WARREN

"That's the last one," Gage says as he nudges a bit of mulch to spread it out around the flowers that he just planted. He dusts his hands off and then places them on his hips, sighing with satisfaction.

I lean on the shovel in my hand, surveying the front yard of the house where Savannah's been staying. It's nothing like the immaculate landscaping that was there before, but the damage has been cleared out and we added back as much as we could with what little skill in gardening that we have.

It was an absolute mess when we started, but at least now it looks less like a construction zone and more like the inviting yard that it was before. I may have FaceTimed my mom a few times with questions so I didn't mess anything up, but we figured it out on our own for the most part.

"You know that this isn't a *half-naked men doing yard work* calendar shoot, right?" I say to Tripp as he picks up his shirt that was long since hung over the porch railing.

He flips me off and wipes away the sweat on his forehead with the shirt.

"It's hot as shit here, you can't expect me to be fully clothed," Tripp quips back.

Gage is swiping across his phone and then flips his screen to show me.

"Cameras are working. If whoever came and did this decides to come back, we'll know who it is."

The screen on his phone is of a security app, showing a grid of several camera angles each pointed in a different direction. Unless they were completely decked out in black from head to toe and covered their license plate, we should be able to identify anyone who sets foot anywhere on this property.

It's a small sense of relief for me, but it doesn't completely erase the worry. It's possible that this was a one-off, but they didn't steal anything. Either way, I'd rather Savannah stay at the bunkhouse for a while until I know that it's completely safe here.

"Once I ask Savannah if it's okay, send me the login so I can keep an eye on things," I say. "Thanks."

Gage nods and pockets his phone, then picks up a garden rake from the lawn. "Think of it as your going away present."

"Wait, you're not moving out, are you?" Heston all but panics. "You can't leave me alone with him." His thumb juts out pointing to Tripp.

I don't *have* to live there anymore—except for the fact that my savings are currently empty, so I can't afford my own place just yet.

A chapter of my life is ending. No longer working at the ranch after over a decade there is going to be a huge adjustment. I'm good with the decision so that I can move on to bigger and better things for myself in my life, but I'll still miss it.

What I don't want is to move out right away and miss my friends every single day too.

Not yet, anyway.

"And not come home to your pretty face every night?" I over-dramatically twist my expression and shake my head with pursed lips. "Not a chance."

"I knew you loved my face," Tripp says with a smug grin.

"I was talking about Heston."

"Right," he huffs.

Gage interrupts Tripp's pouting, changing the subject. "Maybe the girl that owns the place has a few enemies in the area that she failed to mention."

"Maybe," I nod as we walk back to where we parked. I grew up here and have never met or heard of anyone named Mesa, so I know she's not from Westridge. But skeletons in your closet will follow you no matter where you go, so it wouldn't surprise me if this was a hit against her personally. "I don't know if she's bad news, but I'm going to have to find out. She's living in Savannah's apartment in the city right now."

"They traded houses?" Heston asks from behind me in a confused tone.

"That's wild," Tripp laughs.

I shrug and flip up the tailgate after everything is loaded up. "Savannah seems to like her. I don't know the whole story. Just that Mesa had asked her to take care of the plants and flowers."

"I know a guy that could look into her and get back with you by tonight," Gage chimes in.

That seems invasive and probably unnecessary. But if there's something there, I want to know about it if Savannah is going to be living here. "I'll ask Savvy and see what she wants to do," I say.

"Alright. Just let me know," he nods. "I'm headed back to my house. See y'all tomorrow."

Twenty minutes later, I drive past the front entrance of

my business on the edge of town and pull up next to the door out back that leads to the service shop. It's a massive building, built to accommodate large equipment. At the moment, it's nothing but inventory on the inside. But with it opening for business soon and harvest around the corner, it'll be full of all kinds of projects that need fixing or tuning up before I know it.

Heston, Tripp, and I walk through the shop and into my office that's just to the left after you enter the showroom.

"Place looks good," Heston says, sinking into the chair across from my desk.

"Yeah, these chairs are nice," Tripp adds as he runs his hands along the sides of the leather chair identical to the one Heston's sitting in.

"You can thank Blythe for those. Pretty sure she did some damage on Gage's credit card because something new from her shows up in a delivery truck every other day," I laugh.

"Did she hang that picture too?" he asks, referring to the black and white photo in a barn wood frame sitting on the corner of my desk.

The picture was taken not long after Heston had moved in and started working on the ranch. We'd just finished gutting out a few stock trailers when my mom showed up to drop off something I'd left in Dad's Blazer. Laughing about how rough we looked, she pulled out her phone to snap a picture.

In the photo, straight-faced Heston is leaning against the side of a trailer with a foot propped up on one of the tires. His dog, Lucky, is lying on the ground in front of him, unamused. Tripp is smirking toward the camera wearing a holey cut off with his bare arms crossed. Standing next to him, Gage has his hat pulled down and a hand in his pocket. And in the middle, there's me. There's less scruff on my face and meat on my bones since it was taken so long ago, but I look just as happy to be there as I've always been.

The clarity of the photo isn't great with the dust kicking up in the dry breeze, but you can still see the evidence of sweat on our skin and dirt on our jeans and boots. Funny, I never remember how strenuous and sometimes miserable those workdays were. I only recalled how lucky I was to have a good job, a place to live, and to be around my best friends 24/7.

We've always had a hell of a time together and I wish I wouldn't have taken it for granted. Things are going to look a whole lot different soon with me around even less than I've already been.

"Good times," Tripp says with a sigh, picking the picture up to get a closer look.

"The best," I agree.

"Are y'all going to hold hands and trade friendship bracelets now, or can we get back to the ranch?" Heston asks.

"Yeah sorry, I just need to find—"

I ruffle through the stacks of various billing statements and papers on my desk, looking for the one I need.

"Got it," I say holding up a crumpled piece of yellow paper torn from a legal pad. It's covered in spontaneous scribbled notes that I'll have to work to make sense of, but I fold it and put it in my back pocket to look at later.

"What is it?" Tripp asks.

"Some notes," I answer. "Just some stuff I'm working on for the opening party."

I've done the groundwork to get this business ready since the day the idea popped into my head. Aside from using my savings that I'd been piling up for nearly a decade, I did whatever it took to get the rest of the necessary funds and support. From the loans to the investors, the permits, and even the employees, all my ducks are in a row.

At this point, all that's left is to cut the ribbon and celebrate the opening.

Going into this, I thought that the early stages of getting everything squared away and ready to go would be the hardest part. Instead, the biggest challenge has been all mental for me. I've tried not to worry about how monumental of a failure it could be if a business of this scale doesn't perform according to plan once it's open.

I'm a damn hard worker and I'm good at what I do. At least, I've been told. But in business, not everything is in your control—and that's what keeps me up at night.

"Are y'all going to be there?"

Heston nods twice.

"Does Dolly Parton sleep on her back?" Tripp asks.

I smirk and flick off the lights as I walk out of the room.

"It won't be a huge deal, just a little kick-off," I say.

Maybe I'm downplaying it in case not many people show up. It's a busy time of year for a lot of people, and I don't anticipate everyone in town to drop everything that they're doing just for some free burgers and a little tour of the dealership and service center.

If I let my expectations get too high, the chances of disappointment are more likely and I can't let that get to my head before I even have the chance to get things off on the right foot.

Tripp and Heston follow me as we pass the parts counter, sales desks, and lobby. Every surface is clean, every bit of merchandise is organized, and even the neon open sign hangs in the window waiting to be plugged in and turned on. I try to picture the space buzzing with customers and employees and fear of it all failing creeps back in.

"Is it too late to sell it all and stay on the ranch?" I joke with a half-hearted laugh.

It's a backup plan if things here go south, at least.

"I'd say so," Heston mutters.

Leaving the office and lobby area, our footsteps echo off the walls as we walk on the concrete floor back through the shop.

"Everyone that supports you is going to be there, man. Don't worry," Tripp pats me on the shoulder as I hold the back door open. He's right, of course.

Every time I picture it though, I see Savannah there with me. And I'm not sure if he factored her into the *'everyone'* that he was talking about. I smirk remembering that she's probably in my room right now.

When Tripp and Heston both walk through the door, I turn to close it and lock up. I'd hoped we'd be done by lunch but after things taking longer than expected at Savannah's place and then having to stop by here, the hottest part of the day has already passed and I'm hungry for dinner.

"Are we having a party tonight?" Tripp asks as I back up the truck and pull onto the street.

"No," Heston and I say in unison.

I have zero intentions of hanging out with more than one person tonight.

2 4

SAVANNAH

Music plays softly from my phone while I take my sweet time with my nighttime skincare routine. I hum along to the song as I take a sip of water and then readjust my headband.

In the middle of finishing applying my serum, I pause, hearing footsteps in the hall. A moment later, I hear the creak of the bedroom door that belongs to Warren.

Instantly, I smile and tap my phone screen to pause the music. In a rush, I finish my routine with some moisturizer and then stash everything away in my bag.

Before walking out of the guest bathroom and going into his room, I tighten the silk belt on my robe. It probably wasn't necessary to double-check my reflection in the mirror or swipe on a little bit of tinted lip balm either, but it couldn't hurt, right?

The door to his room is open when I finally step into the hall. The last bit of soft sunlight from the day filters in through the thin curtains on his west-facing window. I stop before walking all the way in, crossing my arms and leaning against the door frame when I see him.

"Hi," he smiles.

He's relaxed in the middle of the bed on top of the comforter with a t-shirt and a pair of athletic shorts on. I'm guessing he took a quick shower and changed clothes because his hair is darker, slightly damp, and pushed back. The whole space smells fresh and masculine and suddenly I want to steal his soap so that I can smell it all the time. I take a deep breath and smile back at him.

"Hi," I reply.

My eyes rake over his long body and then his strong arms that are relaxed behind his head. *God*, he looks good. It should be a crime, really, and if I was feeling 100% today there's no way I'd have the self-control to not pounce on him.

"What were you up to today?" I ask, still not moving from my spot in the doorway.

I enjoyed the day to myself here at the bunkhouse if I'm being honest. Being alone is usually my favorite thing to do because I don't have to say anything or make any decisions that someone else might not like. But now that it's nearly evening, I have to admit that I'm happy to see Warren.

I never wish I was alone when he's around.

"Not much," he replies. But my eyebrow quirks up and he gives me a knowing smirk.

"That's not what I heard."

"We might have cleaned up a little and put up some security cameras," he admits.

My lips press together as I keep my gaze locked on his. "Thank you," I whisper.

"You don't have to thank me. I just want you to be safe. I'm going to put the security app on your phone and you can have access to it. You can send it to Mesa too and make sure she's cool with it. It's just a precaution. We won't check them unless there's an emergency."

"Okay. I called her earlier to tell her what happened, but I'll send her a text about the cameras tomorrow."

"Good. Now come here."

Slowly, I shake my head just to see what he'll do. It's the same game that we've played before. A stare down to see who gives in first. In a way, it's satisfying for me, because I've tested his patience plenty of times and he still has yet to give up.

"At least open your robe if you're just going to stand there," he suggests with a gleam of lust in his eye.

I try with all my might to fight it and appear unfazed, but I can feel the flush in my cheeks. He remains in the same comfortable position but doesn't take his eyes off of me.

"Stop playing and come here," he growls. "Or I'll pull this rope off my bedpost and make you."

My eyes flick to the rope hanging on the corner of his bed. It's faded and worn, but I have no doubt that it would do the trick. With one flick of his wrist, I'd be wrapped up in it and pulled where he wanted me. But he's only joking, of course.

I'm proven wrong in the next moment. With a devilish grin, he bends his leg and leans his body to the side reaching for the rope. I don't waste any time calling his bluff as I jump forward, giggling.

"No!" I squeal. "Don't you dare."

He falls to his back, laughing.

"Fine," he mumbles as my knees hit the mattress and I crawl toward him. "There's always next time."

As I approach, he sits up and scoots back, then pats the spot on the bed that's between his legs. I sit back on my knees when I'm facing him in the spot that he patted, but apparently, he had other ideas, because he places his hands on my shoulders and turns me away.

In one fell swoop, he wraps an arm around my waist and

pulls me so that my back is against his front. With the feel of his warm body, the pillowy bedding, and the lights in the room down low . . . there isn't a single shred of question or fight left in me. I exhale deeply, letting my full weight settle on top of his.

I turn my head to the side, and my cheek brushes against his shirt. It's clean and soft, and my eyes close on their own accord from the comfort. His one arm remains around my waist and holds me tight enough that I wouldn't be able to get up if I wanted to, but tender enough for me to breathe deeply into a state of calm.

When he demanded I come to bed, I envisioned him ripping my clothes off, a messy but tantalizing kiss, and maybe some more of those filthy words of his that I've missed. This is entirely different.

He's content to hold me, and my weary mind and body drink in the feeling. But my heart is loving it even more.

In true form to ruin the moment, my unfiltered thoughts seep out without warning.

"Is it customary to be this intimate with your fake boyfriend?" I ask.

The deep rumble in his chest vibrates through my entire body as he laughs, and it puts me at ease. It didn't anger him or ruin the moment, in fact, he brings his hand up to push the curls out of my face.

"It is now," he says in a low voice, making chills run up my arms. "How are you feeling?"

"Still tired even though I did take a nap earlier," I say, keeping my eyes closed and focusing on the light touch of his hand still running through my hair. "I'm not going to throw up right now if that's what you mean."

"Alright good," he chuckles. "Because you're one sick day away from me taking you to the hospital."

"Ugh. Please don't, I'm fine," I protest. "It's still pretty early, what did you want to do tonight?"

"Listen to you tell me about your day while I kiss your neck," he says into my hair.

Sold.

"There's not much to tell. Sleeping, a little case research, dodging calls from my mom," I say in nothing more than a whisper because it's difficult to catch a significant breath while his lips graze my skin.

At the mention of my mom, he pauses his open-mouthed kisses on my neck and leans forward to rest his chin on my shoulder.

"Your mom's been calling you?" he asks.

"Yes," I sigh. "I never feel good about myself after conversations with her, so I haven't answered. I can guess what it's about without having to hear her say it. I probably shouldn't be so avoidant, but she stresses me the hell out."

I hadn't realized that with the subject change, I'd tensed up a bit. Warren notices though, and he lifts a hand to knead the spot between my neck and shoulder. My head rolls to the side and I moan when he massages a particularly tight spot.

"It's not bad to avoid something that doesn't make you happy. That's healthy," he says while circling his thumb to a different spot.

It's not easy focusing on a conversation when I'm literally laying on top of him and he's giving me the best massage of my life. But it's distracting enough for me to speak honestly.

"So . . . what am I supposed to do? Just never speak to my parents again? Ignore my brother for the rest of our lives?" I laugh.

"Maybe," he huffs. "Family is everything at the end of the day, I've always believed that. But family is more than just who you're blood-related to, it's who loves you how you deserve. From what you've told me, I don't like how they treat you. You can set some boundaries with them and if they can't respect you and are still making you feel terrible about yourself, then we need to figure something else out."

He said we.

He said *we* and my fucking eyes are stinging.

"You don't make me feel terrible about myself," I whisper as I snuggle deeper into his hold. "I've been fighting you every step of the way, and you just keep showing up. I don't know what I did to deserve it."

"Wherever you want me, wherever you need me, I'm going to be there. You're worth showing up for. If you can't understand that about yourself, then I'm going to believe it for you."

My heart rate slows to a steady thud, soothed by his words and his big warm hands that are still massaging me.

Without replying, I sit up and turn toward him. The comforter catches underneath him when I attempt to pull it down, but he quickly understands what I'm trying to do. He shifts his body so that he's under the covers, and I slip into bed next to him.

I wrap my arms around his neck while his hand smooths over my lower back, tugging me toward him. One of his legs hooks over mine and I laugh because as much as he's trying, I don't think we can get any closer.

My chin tilts up and I look at him for at least a minute. I study his strong features, tan skin, kind eyes . . . and I kiss him. It's tender and deep in a way that makes me wonder what the hell I'm doing spending any time worrying about things that don't serve me when I could be feeling this every day instead.

When he finally pulls away, I tuck my head down into his broad chest.

"You're getting a little too good at your role of a fake boyfriend," I mumble, drawing attention to the elephant in the room that we have yet to fully address.

"Hmm," he hums and pretends to look perplexed. "Fake boyfriend? Forgot all about that."

25

SAVANNAH

This morning I was woken up by deafening music from the living room.

How I was able to take a nap yesterday and sleep well last night, yet still feel aches in my body and fatigue weighing me down today is frustrating. But I suck it up and after dragging my feet to the shower and changing clothes, I walk out into the bunkhouse hallway to find out why on earth there's an 8 a.m. rager happening.

I was hoping to see Warren. I even pick up speed so that I can run into his arms and kiss him good morning.

But as I round the corner to the kitchen, I find the true culprit. Tripp is standing in front of the open refrigerator door wearing an apron with no shirt underneath. He's singing something about fishing in the dark at an astronomical volume better suited for pregaming after dark instead of while making breakfast. When he spots me, he shuts the fridge door and grins.

"Scrambled?" He yells over the music while holding up a carton of eggs.

I nod and shrug, laughing at how exuberant he is even early in the day.

Blythe comes striding in a second later, wearing the largest sunglasses I've ever seen and carrying way too many grocery bags. She and Tripp sing along to the words of the song like they've done this a million times before. It may be early in the day but it seems second nature to them, so I guess this is the norm around here.

I wait for that old but familiar out-of-place feeling to hit me. It doesn't come.

"Oh good, you're up. Put these in that cooler," Blythe says to me as she lays a few bags of ice down at my feet and then sets the rest of what she brought on the counter.

Heston walks by and kicks the lid of the cooler open with the heel of his boot before grabbing one of the bags and dumping the ice in. I pick up the other one, dump it into the cooler, and then he takes the empty bag from me and throws it away without saying a word.

In the pantry doorway, Blythe is dancing while she fills a big bag with various snacks. She's wearing jean shorts and a baby blue bikini top, and her shoulders are white from what I'm assuming is a generous amount of sunscreen.

Heston is sitting at the kitchen island now, and when I step toward the chair next to him, he pulls it out for me. I take a seat and watch as Tripp and Blythe put on their own version of a kitchen karaoke dance party. A few times, Heston looks over at them from his phone and shakes his head.

I tried to be sneaky looking behind me and around the open space of the bunkhouse for Warren. I think Heston notices though, because he leans toward me and speaks over the loud music.

"He's in the hay field," he explains.

I miss him.

I miss him and I'm not panicking while admitting that to myself.

I can't put my finger on the exact moment my inner hesitancy evaporated. Everything he said to me last night, the way I feel when he's not here, a combination of every little moment we've shared . . . I have half a mind to leave this kitchen and go find him and *tell* Warren instead of sitting with it in my head.

"Bon Appé Titties," Tripp shouts from the other side of the island. As if he's a bartender in an old saloon, he slides two plates across the counter and Heston catches them before they fall off the edge.

I look down at the plate and laugh at how much shredded cheese he put on the scrambled eggs. Right next to the eggs is a biscuit that looks like it was made from scratch and three sausage links.

Can all of them cook? I mean, other than red meat, of course. This is not the first time a man has made me breakfast in this place and I'm starting to think I don't ever want to leave again.

After a few bites of his food, Heston gives his review.

"Six out of ten," he declares in a sure tone.

Tripp is standing at the sink, and with a dish towel in one hand and a soapy pan in the other, he whips around to face Heston with a scowl.

"You're kidding me," he pouts.

"You *know* his system," Blythe says while grabbing a plate of food for herself and sitting next to me. "Major deduction for no gravy."

"I like butter on my biscuits," I say to Tripp with a casual shrug to make him feel better.

"'That's what she said," he replies, pointing the dish towel at me with a smirk.

213

"Mm," Blythe moans while she tries her food. "Well seasoned. A solid eight out of ten."

Tripp rinses the pan and puts it on the drying rack, turns around to lean his hips against the sink, and folds his arms. I realize after a moment that he's staring at me like he's waiting for my score. Blythe and Heston both look in my direction as well. This must be a game they play, rating each other's food. And they want me to do it too.

They're just having fun, but to me, this feels like my initiation to the friend group. I smile and laugh nervously while putting a perfect bite—a combination of all three items on the plate into my mouth.

The eggs taste like cheese and green chile and the sausage is a little well done, but I like it that way. The buttery biscuit is fluffy but still has a subtle crunch to the crust.

They continue watching me, waiting for the verdict. I swallow, place my fork down next to my plate, and clear my throat.

"Nine out of ten," I say confidently.

Tripp howls with enthusiasm and throws the dish towel in the air. Blythe catches it, laughs, and then digs back into her food. Heston turns his hat backwards and shakes his head mumbling something about the travesty of biscuits with no gravy.

Just then, the music from the jukebox cuts off and we all turn to see Gage standing next to it across the room.

"Thought you weren't going to start without me," he says, walking straight toward Blythe for a kiss. He stands behind her, leaning over her shoulder. After they kiss, she lifts her fork to put a bite of food from her plate into his mouth. It's sweet and I realize that I'm staring, so I turn my focus back to my food before they notice.

I used to think that love was devastating in the worst way. Friends can lie and stab you in the back. Parents fight.

Boyfriends break your heart. But if love is so devastating, then why is everyone here so happy?

Maybe in the past, I wasn't loving the right people. I'm not going to push it all away this time just to try and protect myself.

"Mm," he nods. "Ten out of ten. Where's Warren?" Gage asks while reaching for a water bottle on the counter.

"I'm assuming he left out early trying to get the last bit of hay done before it's supposed to rain a little this afternoon. I think I saw the tractor in the field when I pulled in," Blythe answers.

I can hear my phone ringing from the other room, but I ignore it assuming it's one of my parents. After a second of silence though, it rings again and I decide to go check and see who's calling me back to back. I don't want to miss it if it happens to be one of my bosses who is probably working right now even though it's the weekend.

"Be right back," I say as I stand from my seat and pad across the floor back to Warren's bedroom.

On the nightstand, the phone buzzes with a lit-up screen and I pick it up.

WARREN CALLING

"Hello?"

"Hi," Warren's voice comes through the line.

"Hey," I say with a smile. "Everyone's asking about you."

"Oh yeah?" he chuckles. "I got a weather notification about rain this morning and decided to run out here real quick and load the rest of the bales I left out the other day. Thought I'd be back by now, sorry."

"It's okay." I sit on the edge of the bed, biting the corner of my thumbnail and swinging my legs like a teenage girl talking to her crush on the phone. "Are you almost done?"

"Yep. Wanna come get me? This old thing quit on me and

I'll have to bring a few parts out to fix it before I can drive it back."

"I—sure. Where are you?"

"Take the ditch road behind the barn. Just a few fields down, you'll see the tractor. See you in a minute?"

"Okay," I answer with a ridiculously large smile.

Hanging up, I hop up from my spot on the bed and smooth down the front of my sundress. Not sure it's appropriate for a hay field, but I decided to leave it on because it's cute.

Okay, it's hot as hell and makes my tits look good. I wouldn't hate it if it made Warren sweat a little bit.

T he back of my hand swipes across my cheek as I stare at the spectacle in front of me as I approach the tractor. Warren is working on the back of it, and I stop in my tracks, fixated on the way his muscles ripple with each turn of the wrench in his hand.

I don't need foreplay. I need a muscled-up and half-naked working man covered in sweat.

I never considered how attractive it is when a person knows exactly what they're doing until now. If it were me, I'd be shamelessly searching for tutorial videos online or calling an expert and paying them to fix something for me. But Warren doesn't need to ask questions or call for someone else to do it for him.

And fuck, that shouldn't turn me on as much as it does. From where I'm standing, I squeeze my thighs together. But it does nothing to dull the ache between my legs while I watch him work.

There's sweat on the back of his tan neck, his hands are

positively filthy, and when he finally finishes what he's working on, he pulls his shirt off to wipe his face with it.

I clear my throat and turn my face, but keep my eyes on him as he tosses his t-shirt over the baler hitch. When he finally turns around and sees me, I can't stop myself from licking my lips.

"Hey," he says, looking between me and the tractor. "I think I fixed it."

"Oh, great! So, you didn't need me after all," I narrow my eyes and playfully smile.

"No, I do," he deadpans. We stare at each other for a minute. My breaths pick up speed as I wonder what he really means by that. I know what I *want* him to mean.

He has the audacity to stand in front of me shirtless and all but tell me he needs me and then not expect me to climb him like a tree for fuck's sake? I'm not strong enough for this. My insides are screaming for me to stop thinking and *do* something.

In a split second, I make a decision.

"Well, you should probably test it out. Can I ride along?" I say looking up at him and trying not to appear too eager.

The corner of his mouth quirks up as a bead of sweat rolls down the side of his face. "There's only one seat."

I shrug and bite my bottom lip.

His jaw flexes and he widens his eyes as he turns to climb the steps to the cab. He gripped one side of the railing and skipped the middle steps, so it was more of a leap than climbing, I suppose.

I walk toward the tractor mentally preparing myself for what I'm about to try and do. When I'm at the bottom of the steps, he leans down toward me.

26

WARREN

My hand reaches out to grab Savannah's as she climbs the steps to the tractor cab rumbling beneath us.

"There are a lot more screens and buttons in here than I expected," she laughs while scanning the small space.

It's nothing too fancy and could use a good cleaning. We take good care of our equipment, but there is still a decent amount of dust and dirt covering the ground and surfaces. That's inevitable when you're in the hay fields long enough.

The driver's seat creaks as I sit down and release her hand. With the sun where it is in the sky right now, deep orange rays pass through the windows creating a glow of light around her as she stands in front of the door. Her hands tangle together in front of her like she isn't sure what to do, so I place my hands on her hips and spin her around so that she's facing away from me.

There's not enough room between my seat and the steering wheel for her to sit on my lap straight on, so I spread my legs and pull her back to sit on my left leg. As soon as she lands with a huff, I loop my arm around her middle and scoot her ass back toward my hip.

"*Jesus.* Are you incapable of being gentle?" She laughs, balancing herself with a hand on my knee while she straddles my leg.

I laugh and rub my thumb along her rib cage. "I can be gentle. Is that what you want?"

My grip on her remains tight while I adjust the knobs on the air conditioner. There's an optional buddy seat right next to me that flips down and acts as a spot for an extra passenger, but I keep that detail conveniently to myself.

"No," she murmurs. "Not right now."

She leans back when my left foot moves toward the clutch, but I stop short before pressing on it.

"Savvy . . ." I say into the shell of her ear while she arches her back and runs the tips of her fingers over my arm wrapped around her middle. "What are you doing?"

"Nothing," she hums. But she's smirking as her head falls back onto my shoulder. The heat between her legs is impossible for me to ignore. I can feel it straight through my jeans. "Did you *have* to remove your shirt out there, or were you just trying to show off?"

I don't answer, because the truth is borderline embarrassing. Those posed pictures of shirtless farmers throwing a hay bale onto a trailer floating around the internet? Give me a fucking break. The most unrealistic shit I've ever seen. So, no, I didn't *have* to take my shirt off. In my defense, it was hot as hell and I didn't have anything else to wipe the sweat off my face.

Alright, maybe I knew Savannah was behind me and the material was just begging to be stripped from my body.

I look down at my bare chest with her back pressed against it and it reminds me of last night. I lean forward and kiss her at the base of her neck. Her dress has thin straps and is made of a light airy cotton material. It's a pale yellow and covered in tiny cream-colored flowers, almost as soft as her perfectly smooth skin. My tongue darts out to pull my bottom lip into my mouth and I wish dragging my teeth over it did anything to distract me from the thought of having other parts of her in my mouth instead.

I can't stop the rumble in my chest from turning into a growl when she rolls her hips, grinding down on my thigh.

And here I thought we'd just be taking a quick little ride in the tractor. It seems Savannah had different plans.

Who am I kidding? I pulled her onto my lap just looking for an excuse to hold her, feel her, maybe even kiss her. Anything. It's all I could think about.

She covers my hand with hers and slowly slides it down the front of her dress. I don't protest or take the lead, letting her use me however she wants. The tips of my fingers drag lower and lower, desperate to get the layer of fabric from her dress out of the way.

When my hand is finally positioned right at her center, her hips roll once more, all but begging me to give her what she wants.

"What's gotten into you, hmm?" I say in a low voice. My head is turned toward her now and my lips trail over the side of her neck. "Are you needy for it?"

I yank up the bottom of her dress when she responds with a nod. Her eyes close and she pushes into my hand even harder when I yank the bottom of her dress up and smooth my fingers over her clit and then lower toward her opening. Even through her panties, I can feel how wet she is and I almost pass out right then and there from all of the blood in my body rushing straight to my cock.

Savvy has always turned me on in a way that I've never been able to explain, let alone control. But when she's grinding on me like this, moving my hands, practically begging for it with her body? I'm completely lost in her and the thought of giving her what she wants. What we both want.

And I want her so fucking bad it hurts. I have for a long time and I rarely sleep without dreaming about her finally giving in to me.

While my fingers dance over her throbbing clit and she writhes on top of me, I stare at how beautiful she is. The full wavy hair, her curves moving like soft and slow waves, the way her lips are parted and she moans with every back and forth movement of my hand. I couldn't look away even if I tried.

"*More*," she moans.

For a split second, the part of my brain that controls my common sense takes over. I'd do anything this woman says. Anything she wants. It's not just *this* that I crave, it's *all* of her. The parts she hasn't been willing to give me yet.

I swallow hard trying to silence the annoying little voice in my head that reminds me it might mean something different to her than it does to me.

To me, it's everything.

"*Please*, Warren."

Her pleading words pull me out of my head and I'm thankful for the distraction before blurting out exactly what I want to say to her.

I'm about to push her underwear to the side when I finally look down and stop moving altogether.

"Shit," I curse under my breath. Little streaks of black cover the skin on her lower abdomen, the front of her panties, and even the edges of her dress. I lift my hand to see the grease and dirt on my palm and fingers, evidence of fixing the tractor earlier.

She looks down and instead of gasping in horror and demanding that I go wash my hands, she grins mischievously.

"Sorry, I—"

I stop short of my apology when she stands up in front of me, pulls the dress off her body entirely, and places her hands on my shoulders. The breath in my lungs feels heavy and stuck when she sinks down onto my lap, facing me with her legs bent on either side of my hips.

She leans in close, stealing every bit of restraint I had just a moment ago by leaving a trail of open-mouthed kisses along my jaw.

"Don't be sorry," she says between kisses. "It's not your fingers that I wanted inside of me anyway."

27

SAVANNAH

I'm practically naked on Warren's lap, moments after pretty much telling him that I wanted him to fuck me, and the look on his face is like he's trying to figure out a confusing math problem during a stressful exam.

Not exactly the reaction that I was going for.

Despite the hesitance on his face, one of his hands pulls me toward him by the back of my neck and he kisses me on the lips.

My eyes close and I press my body into his. I know he wants me too, I can feel his hard length through his jeans beneath me. My hands squeeze the top of his shoulders, feeling every ripple of solid muscle. The combination of his grip, the throbbing between my legs, and the vibration of the rumbling tractor that we're in is almost a sensory overload.

But it feels *so damn good*.

My past sexual partners have all been somewhat satisfactory, I suppose. Nothing to write home about though, unfortunately. And it was never a given that I'd be wildly turned on or have to hold myself back from exploding just from his touch.

With Warren though, it's an eruption of sparks behind my eyes before we even get past second base, and I want to know what it feels like to have all of him. I *need* to know.

Something about his body language, the way he's moving, tells me that he's thinking extremely hard. I'm not a mind reader, but somewhere behind the lusty haze in his eyes, he's spinning. Wondering. Trying to figure me out again.

"Just ask the question, whatever it is," I say while kissing the underside of his ear.

"I'm wondering exactly what's going through that pretty head of yours," he groans.

His rich husky voice sounds somehow assertive and nervous at the same time. His words feel like they're vibrating off the walls, sending chills across every surface of my skin.

"Well, I was wondering what's going through yours," I laugh.

It scares me to be unreserved and honest, even though I've been more comfortable in that state with him lately. I'm still learning to let go of my inhibitions and just tell him what's on the tip of my tongue. I get the feeling that's exactly what he wants from me right now, though.

"You already know how I feel about you, Savvy. You go first," he growls in my ear.

While the options of responding roll around in my head, my hands continue to move, now slightly tugging down the top of his pants. He lifts his hips in a show of mutual insanity. When they're around his ankles and I've resumed my spot directly on top of him, he holds my hips still with a powerful grip.

I cover his ear with my mouth, trying to kiss and speak and avoid his eyes all at the same time. "I tried so hard at first, fighting how much I wanted you. I don't have it in me anymore to act like I'm not aching for more of you. All the parts of you that you're willing to give to me, I want them. Every single one."

"Fuck, baby. You mean that?" His lips drop to my collarbone after I nod. Then his ragged breath teases across my sensitive skin and it's all I can do not to spontaneously combust from the sensation.

I grab a hold of his briefs and frantically yank them down. Just enough. When he springs free and I'm reminded of the glorious bare sight of him, the inside of my mouth starts to salivate. If we were anywhere else, I'd take him in my mouth before he could say another word or move another inch. I bet he tastes even better than he looks.

To distract myself, I have to slam my eyes shut and use his forehead against mine for balance.

"Kiss me," I breathe out. "Put your dirty hands all over me and—"

He cuts me off when my hips begin to roll and grind down on him again, this time with only the flimsy bit of my underwear keeping me from dropping down and letting him fill me.

A snap sounds from behind me and my bra falls into his lap in front of me. Breaking the kiss, he ducks his head and leans me back, taking my right nipple into his mouth. His thumb flutters over the other one and I gasp for air, blinking up at the ceiling.

I almost collapse into the steering wheel when his mouth takes the place of his finger on my left breast, this time biting down enough to send a thunderbolt of pleasure straight through me. I whimper when his lips and tongue trail over it then, perfectly light and soothing.

"Don't move," he growls as he leans forward slightly, reaching one hand down to his jeans. I pant, impatiently, but I follow his order and stay still while he rummages through his pockets.

Finally, after a minute and a few curses, he's pulling a condom out of his wallet, ripping it open with his teeth, and sliding it over his hard length.

Everything happens in slow motion after that. Our lips meet and my soft body melts against his. He rips off my underwear with an alarming lack of effort. Then, like one end of a match lighting the other, his hips rise to mine. I brace my hands against his chest and slightly lower myself on top of him, feeling his tip teasing at my entrance.

Before he's finally inside me, that solid grip of his stills my hips once again. I groan in frustration, begging him with sweet torture in my eyes.

"I'm not going to fuck you—" he starts.

I hold my breath and roll my lips into my mouth, biting them fiercely and closing my eyes.

"Unless you're mine. *Really* mine. No fake bullshit. *Mine.*"

My gaze snaps open. His jaw is flexed as we stare at each other. I count three quick breaths before speaking.

I had no backup plan going into this. Maybe the reason for that was because failing once again was not a viable option for me. Or maybe the reason was because unconsciously, I knew it would work. That *we* would work.

"Put me out of my misery, baby," he whispers.

When this first started, I pretended to hate Warren because I liked him so much that it scared me. I pushed him away, but he never left. Not once.

I press my forehead against his and my thighs begin to burn from holding myself up and not sinking down on him completely yet. It's a sizzling tension that's pleading for me to move.

"I'm yours," I continue. "I've *been* yours. Getting hurt doesn't scare me anymore."

"I would never do anything to hurt you."

"I know," I whisper. "Warren?"

"What, baby?"

"Please fuck me now. I want to feel all of you inside me. *Please*."

In the next second, his hips flex up and he pulls my hips down at the same time. No slow build, no hesitation, and no further thought.

I suck in a sharp breath and hold my open lips over his. His fingers dig into me when I clench around him. It's a delicious burn, and I don't dare move. Not before I memorize the feeling.

Clearly, Warren does not have the same plan, because after a few moments, his strong hands are lifting my ass and slamming me right back down.

"Oh, *god*," I scream.

A blaze of heat surges through my body, leaving a tingly yet numb feeling all the way to my curled toes. I bite down hard on the top of his shoulder every time I rise up, then come crashing down on him once again.

"Can you feel what you do to me?" he growls into the side of my hair while gripping it with his fist. "You feel so perfect, Savvy. So tight. I want to lay you down and fuck you into the goddamn floor."

"Yes," I moan into the crook of his neck. "Do it."

He can fuck me into the floor. Into the wall. The mattress. The freaking hay itself, for all I care. Right now, I'm nearly finished and already greedy for more. *More*.

I'm surprised by our smooth rhythm, despite the lack of space and my borderline frenzied response every time he pumps harder and faster into me.

When I flip my hair over to one side and drag my nails across his upper back, I lean forward and lick a trail along the tan line that creates a perfect ring around the bottom of his neck. His neck and the better part of his arms are all much tanner than his chest and abdomen. And god, it's the most unexpected turn-on I've ever had.

There are many things about Warren that I find sexy, but this one takes the cake for me. Tell me there's something sexier than a rough and hard-muscled working man with a farmer's tan and I'll call you a dirty rotten liar.

I feel every part of his brute strength as he drives into me again and again. When I feel the pad of his thumb on my clit, my motions still, and an explosion of pleasure makes its way from my core to every other part of my currently helpless body.

My cheeks feel flushed, my brain buzzes, I can barely hear the roar of the tractor engine, and I curl my body into Warren's.

"Oh my—god, ah—" My voice is a shaky and high-pitched cry.

While the aftershocks of the orgasm continue to rock me, I lift my head to lock eyes with Warren while his relentless thrusts become harder but slower. The moment I feel him pulse inside me, he lets go of my hips and grabs either side of my face, smashing our lips together.

I'm practically panting trying to catch my breath when he finally pulls our mouths apart. Cool air from the vent above us brushes over the sweat on my temple when he smooths the hair out of my face and behind my ear. Our foreheads meet once again and as if the high of our climax wasn't enough, he starts whispering in between open-mouthed kisses all over my face and neck.

"Do you have any idea how gorgeous you are when you come on top of me?"

My eyes drift shut and I tilt my head to give him better access to my neck.

"I've thought about how good it would feel to have you

like this so many times, but it was even better than I imagined."

"It felt amazing," I agree with a contented sigh.

"I don't mean the sex. I mean having *you*. All of you."

Maybe it's from the high of an orgasm, maybe it's the emotions at hearing his words. But my eyes tear up and I close them before any have a chance to escape and make me look like a crybaby who can't keep it together.

"This is it, isn't it, babe? You and me now?" he asks while his hands roam over my body.

I nod and I don't even have to think twice about it. This is it.

A soft smile spreads across my face and his mouth moves back up to trail kisses along my jaw.

"But the sex—yeah. Fucking better than I imagined it too," he says and kisses me again. "Do you want to do that again as bad as I do?"

With my arms around his shoulders, I stare out of the now foggy back window of the tractor as he makes sure not a single sliver of the skin on my neck has been untouched by his mouth. The bright summer sun shines down on the field around us and I bite my lower lip in thought.

If I thought I could walk away from this without giving every part of me over to him, I was wrong. And I don't regret it a single bit.

Mine. His words echo in my mind and warmth blooms in my chest.

It doesn't take me more than five more seconds of thinking to nod and say yes. I want to do that again a million times. More than he knows.

28

SAVANNAH

"I feel bad that they're all waiting for us right now," I laugh.

My back is leaning against my SUV and Warren is standing in front of me, one hand braced on the roof of the car above my head. He leans down slightly and twists a strand of my hair through his fingers.

"We could ditch them and fuck in bed all day instead," he suggests with a straight face.

"Blythe never gets weekends off and they're our friends. We should go, it'll be fun," I protest. But he puffs his lip out and I cover it with a kiss. "Then you can have your way with me in bed all night."

Our friends. It sounds right when I hear it out loud coming out of my mouth.

"Deal."

Warren slaps the roof of the car once, then shuffles me to the side to open my door for me.

"I'll drive the rig back and park it then meet you in the bunkhouse and we can go, " he says.

I step into the car and buckle my seat belt, but then look

down at my dress that's dirty from the grease on Warren's hands. My head falls back on the seat and I realize that I don't have anything to change into that I could wear to the river.

"Ugh," I sigh.

"What?"

"I need a swimsuit."

"Borrow one from B. She has tons of them," Warren says.

I shake my head, picturing trying to fit my hips into a pink string bikini and laugh. "No, it's okay. I'd rather wear mine. I'll just go grab it real quick. I could grab a few more things so I can stay with you this week if you want," I add with a smirk.

The edges of his eyes crinkle up from his smile hearing that recommendation.

"I can take you as soon as I'm done here."

"It's fine," I argue with a casual wave of my hand. "You don't have to do that, I'm a big girl. I'll be quick I promise."

He thinks for a moment, rubbing his jaw and looking behind him at the tractor and trailer full of hay that needs to be put away.

"Alright," he sighs. "Drive safe and come right back."

He leans into the car and curls his left hand around the side of my face. It's meant to be a quick goodbye kiss at first, but I hook my hand around his elbow and pull him back in for another one. He moans against my lips and I finally pull away before the inside of my car becomes the next place I scream his name.

He kisses the tip of my nose, closes the driver's side door, and walks back to the tractor. I stared at his ass in those jeans while he walked away, but then shook my head remembering that I should stop being distracted by him and get going. There will be plenty of time for me to ogle him later. Preferably with no clothes at all this time.

G ravel crunches under the tires of my SUV as I pull into the driveway of Mesa's cottage. My brain understands that the main reason that I'm here is to pick up my swimsuit, a towel, and a few other things so I can go to the river this afternoon with everyone. But my heart wanted to see the work that Warren did on the flower beds and the front of the house too.

It won't take me long to get my things from inside. After grabbing my phone and keys, I step out and close the driver's side door. At the sight in front of me, I can't stop the massive grin that creeps onto my face.

Right below the front porch, fresh mulch covers the ground on either side of the walkway framed by smooth gray stones. While slightly more sparse and less manicured, the new flowers are vibrant and evenly spaced. For the most part, the colors match the ones that were there before and that small detail makes me bring a hand to my chest.

I never asked Warren to drop everything and come fix all of this up. I especially never expected him to recruit his friends to aid in the process, either. But he did it anyway.

I'm learning that I can be a powerful and vulnerable woman at the same time. I needed someone to care for me while I was starting a new path in life and struggling to be kind to myself. I'm not so stubborn anymore that I can't admit that.

I'm lucky to have him, I think to myself. It's an empowering thought that solidifies what I already knew in my heart—he is mine and all of the bumps in the road to get here were worth it to have him.

Remembering that everyone at the bunkhouse is still waiting on me, I stop staring at the flowers and jog toward the arched front door. I look down at the key ring in my hand, trying to find the correct one.

Before I have the chance to position the right key between my fingers, the door swings open in a rush and I stumble back a few steps, gasping. My foot catches on a flowerpot and I'm sent flying back, landing on my ass several feet from the door.

"Took you long enough," Emma says with a sinister scowl. "I have been waiting for hours and was about to give up and wait until tomorrow."

"What the hell are you doing here? And how did you get inside?!" I demand. My hand is at the base of my throat as I work to regain the breath that was knocked out of me.

"It's a simple lock to pick," she shrugs.

"Wh-Why would you—"

"No more questions," she seethes. Her hand raises from behind her back and she's holding a gun. I remain perfectly still with it pointed straight at my face, sucking a shaky breath through my nose.

Is this all over Warren? Does she really want him that badly?

My heart sinks and even though I don't feel empathy for her at all right now, I know firsthand how strong Warren's effect can be. His power to bring out the best in people is special and I'd probably fight for that too if I lost it.

I damn sure wouldn't hold anyone at fucking gunpoint, though. There's got to be more at play here.

"Don't look so scared and confused. It annoys me like you wouldn't believe," she says and rolls her eyes. "This will be over quickly and we can all go back to how things were before *you* showed up and ruined everything."

There's a crazed flare in her eye that makes me nod. I don't dare flick my gaze toward the various cameras around the front of the house. She may have already seen them and simply doesn't give a shit that they're there. Either that or she's already attempted to disable them. Silently, I pray that isn't the case.

My backside is sore and throbbing from my rough landing, and I shift my weight. That was a mistake.

"Stay. Right. There," Emma spits. "Was anyone following you?"

"No," I shake my head. "I came to pick up a few things and then go back to the ranch."

In hindsight, that was a stupid thing to say because her face is instantly inflamed.

"You won't be going anywhere. Where is your phone?"

I look to my right, realizing I had dropped it when I fell. Slowly, I point to where it lays face down on the cobblestone-style porch flooring.

She waves the gun in her hand toward the phone and then back to me.

"Pick it up."

I tentatively crawl toward the phone, turning it over in my hand only to see that the screen is cracked. It's not shattered, and it still lights up, so at least it isn't completely damaged.

"Now unlock it and hand it to me," Emma demands with her hand outstretched toward me, waiting for me to do as she says.

I look up at her realizing what she's about to make me do. I'm desperate to change her mind but she's clearly manic and determined. With a gun pointed in my face, I'm not sure I have any option other than to follow her directions.

The Face ID isn't working, so I manually type in my passcode, revealing the home screen. My eyes slam shut as I hold it out in her direction, hoping whatever she plans to do with it has nothing to do with Warren.

Without lowering her hand with the gun in it, she yanks

the phone out of my hand and begins furiously scrolling and tapping on the screen. She hisses as the broken glass cuts her finger. The recognizable sound of letters being typed in a text message chimes through the space.

The phone buzzes, but she stabs at the screen as if she's declining a call.

Several more minutes pass by with her splitting her attention between keeping me on the ground and typing on my phone.

Finally, with a satisfied grin, she stuffs it in her back pocket and walks out of the doorway to stand behind me.

"Now get up and walk through the house. Slowly. Don't even think about trying anything or I won't hesitate to shoot."

A part of me doubts that threat, because her voice subtly trembles.

Does she even know how to use that thing? I can't comprehend the current situation, but I'm not sure it's worth the risk of finding out whether or not she'd put a bullet in my foot for not listening. Or worse.

As I bend my knees and lean forward to stand, my eyes lift to the tiny camera in the top corner next to the doorframe. I'm not sure if it's working, but in case it is, I plaster on the strongest expression that I can manage at the moment so that whoever might be watching knows that I'm okay. For now.

With light steps, I walk through the small cottage. Instinctively, I scan the space for something that I might be able to swipe and use as a weapon, but the barrel of a gun sticking in my back reminds me not to be reckless right now.

The back door slams closed behind us and we walk out into the yard. Barely visible behind the large oak tree and the greenhouse, I spot Emma's silver Mercedes.

"Stand by the trunk," she snarls.

I stop behind the car just as the trunk pops open. Emma pulls out a bag of zip ties with her free hand. For a moment she doesn't move or say anything, but she eventually places the gun down in the trunk while keeping her eyes trained on me.

"I'm going to restrain you now, but the gun is *right* here, so don't move."

I nod, but note the tremor in her hands and the redness that rims the edges of her eyes. Her hair is frazzled and damp and her movements are jerky.

"You don't have to do this, Emma," I plead softly.

"Shut up!" she screams, startling me.

She grabs both of my hands and twists them behind my back, but the zip tie that she was holding falls to the ground. The moment that she bends to pick it up, I bolt.

I take off in the direction of the small shed next to the greenhouse, knowing that there's a shovel leaning against it. My abdomen clenches as I sprint across the lawn, pumping my arms as hard and fast as I possibly can.

"Stop!" Emma yells from behind me, but my chest heaves and I barrel ahead.

When the pop of a gunshot tears through the air, I lunge forward and fall to the ground with a thud.

29

WARREN

"Give me one good reason why we can't buy a golf cart," Tripp says. He's standing by the door wearing nothing but a straw cowboy hat and swim trunks.

Gage stares at him from his spot in the recliner in the bunkhouse living room.

I laugh and shake my head picturing Tripp installing a sound system and off-road tires on a damn golf cart then zipping it around the ranch.

"What the hell are you going to do with a golf cart that you can't do with a four-wheeler?" I ask.

"It's more comfortable," Tripp explains. "And electric. Environmentally friendly."

"Not enough power," Heston says.

B is sitting on top of the cooler in the middle of the living room with a drink in her hand and the rest of us have been arguing over fucking golf carts due to boredom. I look down and mindlessly scroll through my phone for a few minutes, waiting for Savannah to show back up.

My brows draw together as I try to calculate how long she's been gone. She said she'd hurry back, but maybe she decided to change there or she couldn't find what she was looking for at her house.

I'm about to call her and check-in when a text notification pops up at the top of my screen.

> SAVANNAH
>
> I'm not feeling up to anything and would rather be alone, so I'm going to stay here instead.

"What the fuck?" I say under my breath while trying to make sense of her text. Why wouldn't she have mentioned that before she left? Or called to tell me that? She seemed like she was excited to hang out at the river this afternoon but maybe she was putting on an act.

A painful sting resonates in my chest when I think about what happened in the tractor. I didn't want to take things to that level with her without being honest about how I felt. Everything that she said and did in response to that felt genuine. She could have been lying. Did I scare her off?

Fuck. Even with the possibility of her running in the opposite direction, I don't regret telling her how I feel. I could give her some space, but I really don't fucking want to. I click on her name and put my phone to my ear.

It rings several times with no answer and eventually goes to voicemail.

I try again with the same result.

Standing from the couch, I type out a text to her in case she's just ignoring me and doesn't want to talk on the phone.

> We can stay in instead of going to the river if you want. Talk to me.

> SAVANNAH
>
> No thank you

Alright, what the hell changed in the last half an hour? My mind races with the possibilities, but I can't wrap my head around it. This doesn't seem right.

I try calling again, which probably makes me seem like a psycho, but I don't care. Again, there's no answer. I can't control whether or not she tries to walk away out of fear after what we did and everything that was said today. But I'm not going to sit back and let it happen without at least a damn conversation.

I'm coming over

SAVANNAH

No!

If you even respect me you give me space when I aks for it! I want to be alone!

Whats mean to be will always be.

heart emoji

I've never let out such a heavy breath in my life. Is she being serious right now or is this some sort of prank? A test? I doubt she'd say those things to me just to test me. We've played back and forth for too long and I straight up told her exactly how I felt about us.

I study the text again and my brows pull together. Savannah is a stickler for grammar, and I cringe at the spelling mistakes. That's not like her at all, and she must be pretty flustered. The random emoji at the end is somehow the most confusing part.

And I *do* respect her. She damn well knows that and so do I.

This is so out of left field that I have no idea how to respond or what to do.

"The hell's got your panties in a bunch?" Tripp asks.

I don't bother lifting my gaze from my phone.

"Nothing," I reply and shake my head. But I'm sure they can read straight through my pained expression. It doesn't feel right talking to everyone else about it if Savannah wants space from me. I'm not sure I could get the words out anyway, so I give them half of the truth. "I don't think Savannah's feeling too good. Y'all can go ahead."

"What?" Blythe stands from where she was sitting on the cooler. "Is she okay? I think maybe she needs to have some tests run at the doctor, Warren. I'm really starting to worry about how often she's been sick lately."

"Me too," I nod. "I'll make sure that she's alright."

"She seemed fine this morning," Gage adds. "Something else going on?"

Everyone in the room faces me and waits for me to speak. I open my mouth, but there's a lump in my throat and no words come out.

I made her mine and now she wants me to leave her alone.

Heston must read the hesitation on my face because he stands from the couch, takes a casual drink of his beer, and comes to stand next to me.

"Catch y'all later then," he says to me and then turns to walk toward the door. "Let's go."

Thankfully, they all follow him, even with curious looks in my direction. Once they're gone I take advantage of the silence, trying to slow down my racing thoughts. I'm overthinking this, right? So, she needs a little space. I can give her that.

I think.

In a moment of insanity, I check her location. Something felt off about her texts and the way she wouldn't answer my phone calls and I thought that seeing if she made it to her house and if she was still there would make me feel better.

When her location shows up at her house, I sigh. But it didn't put me at ease at all like I thought it might. In fact, it makes me feel overbearing and like I'm betraying her trust somehow by checking to see where she is. That's not the kind of man I am.

My hand runs through my hair and my shoulders feel tight.

Remembering we agreed that the cameras were set up for her safety, I pull up the security camera app. We didn't set any up on the inside, but I click on the view all tab that will show me the entire exterior of the house.

Nothing looks out of the ordinary and her car is parked out front. The sight is enough to stop my veins from their panicked throbbing.

I hate to be paranoid, but after what we went through with my sister at the end of last year, I'm not taking any chances.

The only thing that's kept me from going over to her house is the fact that she suggested that if I respected her, I would give her the space that she's asking for. I re-read that text for what seems like the hundredth time. I'd be taking ten steps backward with her if I showed up and demanded she stop avoiding me.

Every bit of my instinct tells me to keep calling until I can at least hear her voice, so I try her a few more times.

She'll come back, I tell myself every time it reaches voicemail.

"Hey, Savvy . . ." I speak into my phone while it records my message. I should try to avoid any long pauses while I choose my words carefully, but I can't help it. I don't want to say the wrong thing and make it worse. "I don't feel right not being able to talk to you. This is—I—" My words fumble over each other as I grapple with how to sound less desperate. "I want you to be happy. I want that more than anything in the world. If you could just call me back—"

I move the phone away from my ear and hold my free hand over my eyes for a moment, then put the phone back up to my ear.

"I didn't mean to scare you off if that's what this is. But I did mean everything that I said to you today. Every bit of it. If you feel differently then I—"

A beeping sound comes through the phone and I look down at the screen to see that my time has run out and the call has ended.

I slump onto the couch and begin to go over every touch, every word, every breath between us today. Where did I go wrong?

30

SAVANNAH

My estimation may be off since I've been trying not to cry while counting in my head, but I think that we've already been driving for more than twenty minutes. Based on the speed of her car, we're on the highway now and any hope that I initially had about staying in Westridge so that someone could find me quickly is beginning to dwindle.

When Emma shot her gun as I tried to run away from her, I was shocked. I didn't think she'd actually do it. She missed, but I could have easily been hit and now I know for sure that she isn't afraid to pull the trigger.

I had no choice but to do as she said after that if I didn't want a bullet painfully buried somewhere among my internal organs. Which is why I'm currently curled up in the trunk of her car with a busted interior latch desperately trying to remember every detail that might help me figure out where we're going. Or at the very least have a rough idea of where we are once we get there.

Thankfully, after I feigned cooperation to avoid any further trigger pulls, she gave up on trying to bind my hands together and then threw a bottle of Gatorade at me before I was stuffed in here.

I waited helplessly in her trunk for a while, presumably to clean up evidence, before she finally got in and started driving.

My legs curl up toward my chest and I rub the sore red spots on my knees from where I fell to the ground. The pain isn't unbearable, but I still wince and suck in a breath from the sting.

Other than the drink and myself, there's nothing in the trunk that I can use as a weapon or to help me pry open the trunk.

"*Shit*," I whisper, realizing that I've forgotten to keep track of time.

Maybe wherever we're going will have a landmark that I can identify. In frustration, I try to kick the latch that opens the trunk, but there's barely enough room for me to move my leg. I'm not a strong person to begin with, so it's probably no use.

Warren's face flashes in my mind the moment I feel like giving up. He wouldn't like that I was talking to myself like that. He'd remind me that I am too hard on myself, and that gives me the strength that I need to take a deep breath and recalibrate my inner thoughts.

You are strong, he'd tell me if he were here instead of only in my head.

You're going to get out of this.

My body sways back and forth from random swerving every few minutes. Emma is most likely weaving in and out of traffic and changing lanes on the highway. A couple of times, I thought I heard a muffled voice coming through the speakers as if she was on a phone call. It sounded like a male voice, but it wasn't loud or clear enough for me to understand what was being said or who it was.

By the time that we finally slowed to a speed that was more synonymous with driving on a two-lane road or residential area, I'd come up with a few different options as a plan of attack.

Option A was thrown right out the window when Emma finally stopped the car, then opened the trunk door with the barrel of her gun pointed straight at my face. When I heard her get out of the driver's seat and walk toward the back of the car, I braced myself to throw a fist into her stomach. Unfortunately, I had to stay down and stare at the Glock in her hand instead.

Option B is biding my time until I can catch her off guard again. I'll be faster next time if I get the opportunity.

Carefully, I take in the surroundings while she orders me to step out and walk toward the house she parked in front of. My eyes sparkle when I see the familiar skyline of the city I know so well. We're on the outskirts in what looks to be an undeveloped suburb. There are houses on either side of the one we're at, but they are merely in-progress wooden frames with no sign of people or any vehicles around them.

I step slowly toward the house while Emma slams the trunk closed and walks behind me. There's no grass in front of the house, just dirt. The sidewalk is finished, but rough around the edges like it was done quickly. We approach the entrance and I reach for the handle of the front door, but quickly bring my hand back to my side when Emma jabs the gun into my lower back.

I step to the side, and she reaches around me to open it. Inside, there isn't a single piece of decoration. It's a large house with cathedral ceilings and a spacious layout, but there are no light fixtures or furniture either. Clear plastic sheets and industrial-sized paint cans line the baseboards.

I stop in the center of the foyer, continuing to scan the

space with my eyes, but not being too obvious by craning my neck or turning my head.

"Keep walking," Emma demands. She sniffs violently several times and her voice sounds shaky. "Down the hall to that white door."

I let out a long breath, but follow her directions without a verbal reply or protest. The white door that she's referring to has a hole in it instead of a doorknob and is already swung open into the hall. I swallow hard and bite down on the inside of my cheek when I see that there are steps leading to a basement.

The steps look stable, but it's dark at the bottom and I *really* don't want to go down there. Could I spin quickly and knock the gun out of her hand? If I did, then what? We're evenly matched in terms of height and build, but I'm not fully confident that I could take her in a physical fight. I'm not sure it's worth the risk.

Reluctantly, I walk down the stairs and immediately scrunch my nose at the stench. It's not dirty smelling, but more chemical. Like strong adhesives, paint, and cleaning agents. There's an egress window on the far wall letting in a sliver of muted sunlight, but other than that, there is no other light source.

In the corner, there's a bathroom with no walls around it and a kitchenette with bare and unstained cabinets and missing fixtures.

I stop in my tracks and my spine goes rigid when I see a metal pole in the middle of the room with a chain attached to it.

"*Hell no,*" I say under my breath.

"Sit down." Emma seethes and points to a spot on the dusty concrete floor next to the beam. I can't imagine how I'd get myself out of being chained to a fucking load-bearing immovable beam. In response to my hesitation, she aggressively jabs the gun into my back again, successfully reminding me of my lack of choices here.

Fastened to the end of the chain is a pair of handcuffs, and I eye them wearily as I finally sit where she asked me to.

"Put your wrists in the handcuffs."

"Emma. This is outrageous. Why are you doing this?" I ask in the most soothing tone that I can muster. I don't *want* to plead with her or appear pathetic, but I don't want to piss her off either. So I keep my voice as soft as I can.

"You're getting in the way and I can't have that anymore," she explains angrily. She grits her teeth and moves closer to me, tracing my cheekbone with the tip of the gun in her hand. "Now put on the handcuffs now, or I'll have to bury you under the foundation next door instead."

Why not just kill me now then? Seems a lot easier than all of this. But I don't voice that observation out loud. This is premeditated, based on the chain attached to handcuffs. But, I am not sure she has thought this all the way through. And that might work to my advantage.

My thought process must have been written all over my face though, because she offers up an explanation.

"You took what was *mine* and now I get to watch you suffer as I take it right back." Her smile is crazed and laced with sinister satisfaction.

I realize she's talking about Warren and my stomach turns. I inhale through my nose to steady my emotions and try to come up with something that will convince her to keep talking to me instead of chaining me up.

"You don't have to do this. Let's just talk about it," I try to negotiate.

"But, I do! I *do* have to do this! Because I love him and—" she screeches. "Nothing else was working and I am running out of time."

I study her unhinged expression while rolling over possible responses in my mind.

"Emma," I whisper. "What on earth are you talking about? Please. Just reconsider this for a second. I thought we were friends." It's a lie. We have never truly been friendly with each other. "What do you mean nothing else was working?"

She grinds her teeth and pulls at the stringy ends of her mussed hair. It's then I notice her sunk-in cheeks and deep dark circles under her eyes.

"You'd think the arrest set-up would have been enough to get you fired and make you leave, but nooooo," she draws out her words dramatically and waves the gun around, throwing her arms out in irritation.

Did she set me up that day in the courthouse? How? My eyes narrow and I press my lips together so that I don't blurt out any curses that could get me killed.

"Was it not enough to destroy your job, your house, and fucking poison you? I mean for *fuck's* sake. You're a nightmare, Savannah. You have no idea how bad I want you *gone*." She spits her last words and tiny bits of saliva land on my arm.

The word poison catches my attention and I think back to all of the times that I felt sick after being around her. I never thought for a second that she would do something so menacing and reckless. My hand wraps around my middle as I realize that I drank almost half of the bottle of Gatorade that she threw at me when we left the house.

I thought I'd need to be hydrated if I was going to fight my way through this, but I was aiding her process instead. Slow waves of nausea begin to drift up my chest and to my throat, but I close my eyes and will them away as much as I can.

The pieces of this big mysterious puzzle start to fit together in my mind. It's been more than the universe working against me lately. Emma's been sabotaging me within an inch of my life.

She stomps her foot and waves toward the handcuffs with the gun, then pointing it back at me furiously. With her red face and the fact that it looks like she's about to abandon her plans and end me right now, I reach for the chain.

I place my wrists in the handcuffs the best that I can, but she still has to lean down and tighten them. She pulls on them, then the chain, testing their effectiveness. Pleased with their sturdiness, she spins on her heel and walks toward the unfinished bathroom.

"I don't want to clean up after you," she mutters with disgust. "There's enough water in this bucket to drink and pour into the back of the toilet for a few flushes. Ration accordingly."

Without another word, she stomps toward the stairs and climbs back up to the main level of the house.

"Wait!" I yell. I pull my hands apart, having already forgotten that they were restrained. The chain clangs against them and the rattle echoes through the nearly empty basement. "How long am I supposed to stay down here?!"

There is no answer. She climbs the rest of the stairs without so much as a glance in my direction. My eyes shoot to the ceiling where exposed pipes jut out in every direction. Her footsteps travel across the floor above and I follow their sound.

In the next minute, the front door to the house opens and closes, her car engine roars to life, and her tires screech on the pavement.

31

WARREN

I slept all of one hour last night. Maybe not even that long, if I'm being honest.

It took everything in me to stay in this bunkhouse as long as I did, walking around and practically pulling my hair out. I'd convinced myself to calm down one moment, trying to believe that this wasn't as big of a deal as I was making it. The next, I was going over the worst-case scenarios.

Gage was the most apprehensive about her not coming back to the bunkhouse. We both checked the cameras in front of her house again, but each time her car was still out front. It's driving me insane, but at least we know she's there.

I left to do chores before the sun was up. Busying myself didn't help at all. I went into my office at the business and checked off everything on my to-do list that I could with what little focus I had left.

Now the sun is almost directly overhead, and I'm driving across town to catch Savannah on her lunch break. I'm trying my best to be respectful. But if she claims that she wasn't given enough time to think things through, then I'm hauling her over my damn shoulder and parking her ass in the passenger seat of my truck until she talks to me.

There's a ding overhead when I open the glass doors to the law firm. I probably should have changed out of my work clothes, dirty as they are, but I couldn't be bothered to care at the moment. I lift the brim of my straw hat when Donna greets me from the front desk.

"Warren? I'm surprised to see you here today," she says while tilting her head.

"I was hoping to catch Savannah before she left for lunch. Is she still at her desk?"

She purses her lips and gives me a confused look.

"Savannah isn't here today," she says.

It's rude to walk away, but I don't give it a thought. I walk straight out of the lobby and toward the offices. I don't stop when I see that her desk is empty, heading for Henry's door.

Without knocking, I open it and see him shuffling a stack of papers. His head snaps up when he hears me, and he instantly smiles.

"Good, I'm glad you're here. Have you heard from Savannah? I've been trying to get a hold of her since she missed an important meeting this morning. Emma stepped in and everything was fine. But be a champ and have her get back to me if you don't mind. I need her on that case."

My jaw flexes and I bite down on my molars.

I'm not a genius at sniffing out sketchy situations. But in this moment, I finally let the bad thoughts win. I knew in my gut that something wasn't right and I should have listened to it. *Fuck*. I should have gone over to her house. I should have questioned this whole situation more than I did and never given her space.

Savannah cares about this job as much as anything in the world. If she was alright, she never would have not shown up without a simple communication to her boss that she risked everything to impress.

Maybe nothing's wrong, but I refuse to ignore my instincts any longer.

"Warren? Are you okay?"

Sharp breaths force their way in and out my nose while my hand fists at my side.

"I'll let you know if I hear from her," I say. "Please call me if she comes in or calls the office."

"Is everything okay?" Henry stands from his desk and his expression turns concerned.

"I'm not sure," I admit through gritted teeth. "Can you just call if—"

"Of course," he blurts out, no doubt noticing that I'm losing my ability to stay calm.

I nod and spin on the heel of my boot, leaving his office in a rush. As I take long strides past the sea of cubicles, Emma steps in front of me. She smiles and flutters her lashes, tucking a strand of hair behind her ear and popping out a hip.

"Are you busy for lunch today?" she asks. "I'm craving—"

I don't let her get another word in edgewise.

"Have you seen or heard from Savannah?"

She drops her pleasant expression and replaces it with annoyance.

"No, not at all," she replies with a straight face. "You two having a rough patch? Ugh, Spencer and I are too. You and I could—"

"Just call me if you hear from her," I demand and start walking away toward the front lobby.

"You want me to call you?" she asks with a raised voice laced with optimism.

"If you find out where Savannah is, then yes," I call over my shoulder.

The driver's side door to my truck slams shut and I barely wait enough time for it to start up before throwing it in reverse and calling Gage.

The call rings out with no answer as I drive down Main Street.

Cursing, I scroll down and dial Heston and luckily, he answers on the second ring.

"Sup."

"Where are you?"

His tone instantly changes, recognizing the urgency in my voice. "Tire shop."

"Tripp with you?"

"Yep. Something happen?"

"We're about to find out. Can you follow me or do I need to pick y'all up?"

"They've still got my truck in here. Swing by."

He hangs up and a few minutes later I pull up next to the tire shop. Jogging out of the building, Heston and Tripp both jump in and I take off running the yellow light out of town.

I pull up Justin's number after filling them in on the current situation.

"Hello?" his voice rings through the cab of my truck as we fly down the dirt road. Dust and gravel kick up and are probably doing a number on my truck's paint, but it's the least of my worries as I speed toward Savannah's house.

"Hey. Might be nothing, but just giving you a head's up," I say.

"What happened?"

"I can't get a hold of Savannah. Been since last night, and then she wasn't at work today."

"Want me to stop by her place?"

"We're headed there now to check it out. I could have waited to call," I say nervously. "But I have a weird feeling after what happened with the vandalism a while back."

"I get it man. Damn," he breathes out and then thinks for a moment. "Call me when you find out."

"Thanks, Justin."

I stab the button on the steering wheel to end the call and take the last turn before her house a little too tight. Tripp grabs the handle above the passenger side door and shoots me a look.

"Kill us before we even get there, why don't you?" he says as he shakes his head.

"Better than jumping out of a motherfucking helicopter," Heston mumbles from the backseat.

"There's her car," I say, pointing out the windshield. I feel bad tearing up the driveway by driving a little bit too fast, but I press down on the gas pedal anyway. As soon as we slow to a stop, I jump out.

"Savannah?" I call out. No one seems to be around, and no one comes out of the house. Tripp and Heston both open doors on opposite sides of her car, checking the inside. They both turn and shake their heads in my direction signaling that she's not in there, so I take off toward the house.

At first, nothing looks out of place. But I run toward the front door anyway. When my hand meets the doorknob, it's unlocked and turns easily.

"Savannah?" I call out as I step inside the house.

It's all one open space with no rooms or extra spaces to search through. It only takes me a minute to check the shower, the bed, and the kitchen to realize that she's not in here either. In a rush, I move around several chairs and plants. Logically, I know she can't be hiding behind those things but my brain is not functioning properly and I don't know what else to do.

"Check the backyard," Tripp suggests. "I'll go back and look out front again."

"Okay, give me your phone real quick," I say. "I'm putting

the security app on it and logging in. If we get separated, you can use it if you need to."

He tosses his phone and I catch it with one hand. He gives me the password and my fingers fly across the screen as I get it set up.

When Heston and I step into the backyard, I scan the space and head straight for the greenhouse.

I hear the door to the shed right next to the greenhouse creak open and Heston yelling Savannah's name.

"Where are you," I whisper desperately.

"Warren," Heston yells from outside and I jog out hoping to see that he's found her. But he's holding up an empty shell and my heart sinks. As long as I've known her, Savannah has never mentioned owning a gun.

I walk up toward him and take it out of his hand, inspecting it closely.

"Standard nine mil," Heston says. "Probably shot recently."

"How do you know? It's not hot," I ask him.

"Still smells like gunpowder."

I look around, searching for blood on the ground. I don't see any, but there are definitely some sporadic tire tracks behind the greenhouse now that I'm looking closer at the ground.

"This is my worst fucking nightmare, man," I groan while rubbing a hand over my face. Despite my effort to stay calm, I know that my voice is shaky right along with my hands. I let out another string of curses and anxiously shift my weight from one foot to the other.

"We'll find her," he reassures me. "Might want to call it in."

I nod, knowing that it needs to be done but hating the idea because it means I have no idea where she is right now or if she's hurt.

A sick and twisted part of me is relieved to know that Savannah wasn't ignoring me or scared off. But right now, I'd let her keep pushing me away and avoiding me for another decade in exchange just to know that she was safe.

"Want me to do it?" Heston asks.

"I'll do it. You call Gage and Blythe."

He pulls his phone out of his pocket and turns to walk back to the house.

I start walking around, looking for anything else that could help me find Savannah while I hold my phone to my ear and wait for Justin to answer.

"Anything?" he says after the first ring.

"She's gone."

32

SAVANNAH

With my knees tucked close to my chest, I hold my hand out in front of me and squint. There's a faint outline of my fingers and palm, but for the most part, I can barely see anything even if it's close to my face. The basement is pitch black without even a beam of moonlight creeping in through the single window.

It feels like days have passed although I know it's only been several hours. I'm not entirely sure what time it is, but I have a hunch that midnight has come and gone.

I let out a groan, shifting my hips to try and relieve the tension in my strained back. Sitting on the concrete floor with only a beam to lean back against has done a number on my joints already.

Deciding to stand and stretch again, I lift myself from where I was sitting. The chain clangs against the ground, reminding me of my confinement. The black scenery around me blurs as I sway back and forth on my feet. It's a familiar dizziness that I now know is from the poison.

It's a wonder I'm still alive after ingesting as much of it as I did. I don't know what type of poison it is, but Emma must have had the intention of disarming my abilities rather than sending me to a quick death.

The chain only stretches far enough for me to reach the unfinished bathroom, and I consider trying to kick the toilet, breaking the porcelain, and using it as a sharp weapon. Tears spring to my eyes as I try and calculate how much brute strength that would take.

If there were anything else down here, I might have more ideas about how I could defend myself. Without so much as a chair or maybe even something like a paintbrush, my options are nonexistent.

I take a few more steps into the dark space, twisting my upper body to hopefully pop my back and relieve some of the tension there. My stomach rumbles from a mixture of sickness and hunger, but I ignore it completely. I don't know how long I'll be down here and if I pay too much attention to the fact that I have no food to eat, I'll go insane.

"Mind over matter," I whisper.

My hands run over the fabric of my sundress, and it reminds me of yesterday. It's easy to fall into a state of delirium after the lack of food and sleep. I can almost feel Warren's hands roaming my body. Hear the words that he said to me.

I try not to think about what he's doing right now. There's no doubt in my mind that he knows I'm gone, seeing as how I never made it back to the ranch last night. As it stands, it looks like I won't be showing up in Westridge for work tomorrow either.

My heart flutters with hope realizing that along with Warren, friendships I've made recently all but guarantee that they'll realize quickly that I'm gone. They'll be looking for me.

That's a new feeling that I hadn't experienced in the past. Sure, I've never gone missing before. But if I had, I doubt anyone would have noticed, including my own family. Now I know that many people will be turning over every stone to find me.

Although the basement probably isn't as bad as the rest of the house, it's still hot down here, making my hair stick to my skin and sweat drop in beads down the side of my face. If it were cooler maybe my stomach wouldn't turn so violently.

At first, I wasn't sure if I was going to throw up, but I eventually made myself do it. I wanted any bit of the poison that was in that drink that Emma gave me to get out of my body as soon as possible.

Apart from the distant low sounds of the city and the beat of my own heart, it's deadly silent. I've screamed a few times, hoping that someone might hear me. But in this small, secluded suburb with no apparent residents, my cry for help has gone unanswered. I'm not giving up on hoping that someone hears me, but I've given up for now with it being the middle of the night.

I move toward the beam in the middle of the room and sit back down. My knees pull up to my chest and I lean my chin on them, hugging my legs close to my body.

"They're looking for me," I whisper out loud.

33
WARREN

"It'd be best if you stuck around here to help answer questions. Let the officers and the Search and Rescue team do their job, Warren. Things like this can get complicated and even dangerous in a hurry," Justin says.

"Sure thing," I lie. I'm not going to sit on my hands and wait for them to assemble their team. I get that they need to do things by the book, but I won't be wasting any time. I'm going to look for her myself the second Gage gets here.

"I know what you're thinking," he glares at me. "Just know that meddling can mess up the process and slow things down. I'm just trying to help you, man. This sucks but I'm going to do whatever I can to help."

"Thank you, I appreciate it. And what about her car? Any clues there?"

"No," he shakes his head, "but we've got forensics on it. And we've got a guy coming to look at the other tire tracks out back too."

"Did you get a hold of the owner of this house? She lives in Savannah's apartment in the city. Maybe she went there. Maybe—"

"Not yet," he cuts me off. "We've got this. We'll find her." His hand lands on my shoulder, but I just nod and look toward the driveway.

We've been here all day and the sun has long since set, but the entire front yard of Mesa's property is lit up with red and blue flashing lights. They were skeptical at first since she still hadn't been missing for even a full day when I called in to file a missing person report. But after I checked the security camera again and found the old footage from before I checked it the first time had been scrubbed, it was enough evidence of foul play for them to come investigate the property.

As soon as Justin shakes my hand and then walks away to speak with a few other officers, I drag a hand down my face. I can't make myself move from the spot on the front porch while waiting for Gage to get here, despite wanting to run off and scour every inch of this county while yelling her name.

"He's here," Heston says as he steps up behind me with Tripp on his left. They've been looking around for clues while I gave my statement to Justin.

My head snaps up to see Gage's truck coming up the drive. He parks in a hurry next to a few cop cars, hops out, and jogs toward us.

"Did you get everything?" I ask.

"Yep," he replies, slightly out of breath. He hands me a piece of paper that looks like it was torn out of a notebook. "Got the address and phone numbers for her parents and brother, her apartment address, and her car license plate. Oh, and my guy who looked into the scrubbed camera footage says that no one hacked the system. The archive was accessed from her account and the feed from yesterday was deleted right from her phone."

"And now her location is off," I sigh.

"Yep."

"What the hell?" Tripp says.

Gage's eyes harden and I wait for him to say what he's thinking. I don't want him to say it because I don't want it to be true. But he's seen this sort of thing before with the people that he used to deal with in his past life. He knows what's going on here.

"She didn't run away. Someone took her and they obviously have her phone. They texted you from it, deleted camera footage . . . Do you have any idea who it could be?"

"*Fuck,* I don't know," I say with a defeated sigh.

It wasn't even a year ago that my sister had been taken by some guys who were trying to get to Gage. It was one of the worst days of my life not knowing where she was or if she was safe. Now, I'm dealing with a mix of PTSD and déjà vu with Savannah gone.

At least with Blythe and Gage's situation, we knew exactly what to do and things escalated quickly. Right now, we're in the dark with no clear direction and it's only a matter of time before I lose my mind and start tearing shit up inch by inch until we find something.

This is my fault. I feel like a fucking idiot for not clocking this last night.

The concept of *"never let her out of your sight"* has never been my style even when I wanted to hog her to myself 24/7. Savannah is a grown woman who knows herself better than anyone, and I thought I was doing the right thing, not freaking out right away like I wanted to.

Now I wish that I had.

"Where's B?" I ask, trying to refocus on fixing this instead of dwelling on what I could have done.

"In my truck," Gage answers. "She wants to help but I'm not taking any chances until we know more about what the hell we're dealing with here. She's on the phone with your parents trying to keep them in the loop, I think."

God, I hadn't even thought about calling my parents with how jumbled my thoughts have been. I nod and look toward the truck over his shoulder, tucking my restless hands in my pockets.

"Cops give you anything?" Heston asks.

"No. I doubt they're going to know anything soon. Justin pretty much asked me to stay out of the way. If he does learn something though, I feel like he'll let me know."

Heston shakes his head and Tripp laughs knowing we will not be able to stay out of the way.

"Alright," Gage places one hand on his hip and one rubbing the outline of his jaw. "Let's get a plan together—"

"Oh, Warren," a female voice cuts him off. It sounds like she's crying and as she gets closer, I realize that it's Emma. "I came as soon as I heard."

I didn't expect to have my ex show up with tears in her eyes as she launches herself into a one-sided hug with me.

Heston and I make eye contact above Emma's head as she clings to my shirt and sniffs dramatically. He rolls his eyes and I try not to look too annoyed.

"We're going to get through this, and everything is going to be okay," she cries, trying to console me. Then she moves her hand to rest on my chest, hitting my last nerve.

I pull a hand out of my pocket, grab her wrist, and push her arm away. She takes a few steps back and looks up at me. Her eyes are slightly bloodshot and her pupils are dilated. I scowl at her and cross my arms to keep her from touching me again.

"You've got some nerve," Tripp mumbles. He walks away and Gage and Heston follow closely behind. One thing they can all agree on is not being able to stand a second around this woman.

"Can I be honest?" Emma whispers with a smirk. How she's gone from crying to a deranged smile in less than ten seconds is scary. I don't reply to her, but she continues anyway. "We could both use some rest after this crazy day. Why don't we go get some food and take a breather?"

"No," I shake my head. "Go eat if you want to. Hell, go take a nap for all I care. But I'm not going with you. Come to think of it, Emma, I'm never going to go get food with you or go home with you. I get the feeling that you don't understand that and I'm sorry, but I'm with Savannah. You've got to move on."

Anger flashes across her face and my head juts back when she fists her hands at her sides and forces air out of her nose like a fucking bull.

"Do you see her anywhere?" she grits out while waving her hands around. "Savannah is *gone*. She *left* you, but *I'm* right here. *I'm* the one you can depend on."

What the fuck?

"It wouldn't matter if she were in another country or standing right next to me. That doesn't change the way I feel about her," I say pointing to the center of my chest. "You are going to find someone someday who is right for you. I'm sorry if this hurts you, but you need to find a way to get rid of your tunnel vision and realize that person is not me."

She huffs louder than I thought possible and stomps her foot like a child, turning toward the sidewalk behind her and then turning back to me again. She scratches her arm and stumbles over a small rock that made its way onto the porch.

Her expression turns vacant like the words I just spoke to her have already evaporated from her memory.

I narrow my eyes and lean toward her. "Are you high right now?"

"What do you care?"

I watch as she turns and stumbles over to her car. As she slams the door shut and takes off down the driveway, I walk over to Gage's truck where he stands with Tripp and

Heston. Blythe is leaning her forearms on the passenger door where the window is rolled down looking devastated. I ruffle her hair to make her smile. It doesn't work, but it was worth a try. In her defense, I don't feel like smiling right now either.

"Any ideas?" Heston asks.

I nod. "I'm going to follow Emma. Be ready to meet me somewhere if shit hits the fan."

I kept my distance the best that I could. She was driving so fast, though, that I had no choice but to match her speed to keep up. I knew immediately by the direction that she was headed that she wasn't intending to drive to her house in town.

I realized my mistake in blowing my cover by driving too fast behind her when she slowed suddenly and took a sharp U-turn right before getting on the highway.

"*Shit*," I mumble.

Her driving is erratic as she turns back toward Westridge. Swerving, braking, speeding, nearly taking out a mailbox or two. That's when I remember Mesa's destroyed property and a lightbulb goes off in my head.

I continue to try and follow Emma but carefully scroll through my recent calls at the same time, finally finding Justin's contact and tapping on his number.

"Hey, I was just about to call you," he answers.

"Why? Did you find something?"

"No," he sighs. "Figured something out on those tracks though. They don't match Savannah's vehicle, any of the police cruisers, or anyone else's car that's been here to help in the search. We've got the treads in the database and should be able to match them if we get a suspect though."

I clear my throat and stare at the speeding vehicle in front of me.

"Okay. I have a bad feeling about Emma. She showed up totally blitzed while you were talking with some other officers at the house earlier and I followed her out toward the highway when she left. I think she noticed me following her and she turned us back toward Westridge. How fast can you make it into town to catch up with us and pull her over?"

There's a pause on the line and my fingers curl around the steering wheel, squeezing until I can't feel them anymore.

"I can't pull someone over or do anything else for that matter based on a bad feeling, Warren. You know that. Some protocols have to be followed."

"Savannah could be right under your nose and you'd have no idea!" I yell. I'm not actually angry at him, I know that. But I'm frustrated, scared, and at my wit's end. "Wait around if you want," I grit out. "I'll find her myself."

"I know it's hard, but you have to be patient with these things—"

He tried to convince me to dial it down a notch, but I'd already hung up on him and sent a text in the group chat. The Police Department might be willing to take their time to avoid a bad outcome, but my friends don't typically take the risks involved into account like most normal people. We've never turned down a fight if it meant helping each other.

3 4

WARREN

I thought Emma might run off the road a few times as I followed her home. The back end of her car slid back and forth on the dirt roads, she never used a blinker when she turned, and it's a wonder she didn't hurt anyone as we drove through her neighborhood once we finally made it to town.

When she stormed out of her car, she looked around before walking inside her house. It was clear that she'd noticed someone following her when she was headed toward the highway, but I kept a better distance after that hoping she'd think she lost me. I parked my truck at the end of the street several houses down from hers.

The lights flicker on in her kitchen and she doesn't waste any time before storming toward a console table and grabbing a glass vase to throw it against the wall. I wince when it crashes and falls to the ground in pieces.

Should I have seen this coming? I'd known since day one that she liked me more than I liked her. The real red flags though should have been the drugs and the jealousy. I don't know what made her obsession grow, but she hung on to it for dear life and hasn't been able to let it go.

I blow out a breath as a familiar vehicle pulls slowly behind mine and parks. One by one, Gage, Heston, and Tripp all step out. My boots hit the pavement and I close the door to my truck.

"The fuck is she doing?" Gage asks as we all walk toward her house. The streetlamps are on, but we stay as close to the shadows of the trees as we can.

We all watch as she paces back and forth in front of the windows pulling at her hair. I understand that she's upset with me, but this is more than that. Her movements are jumpy and she's destroying things in her own home. It's a psychotic break.

Tripp blows out a breath and adjusts his hat. "You think she's got Sav in there?"

"Hope not," Heston says. "Cause that's a fucking Glock."

He points toward the house and we all turn to look. Through the window illuminated by a chandelier in the living room, Emma pulls a handgun off the mantle and turns it over in her hand.

Gage pulls a gun out of the back of his waistband and checks the chamber.

None of us are surprised that Gage was packing, but I'd secretly hoped he wouldn't have to use it. The options of how to handle this start running through my head. With the guys as backup, I could walk up to the house myself and see if she'd let me in.

I have no idea if Savannah is there or not, but I'm not willing to risk waiting to find out when Emma clearly has a weapon.

With a sigh, I turn to Heston. "You got anything?"

He nods and Tripp starts laughing, pulling his hat off his

head and looking back at the truck down the street. "Man, I didn't bring anything."

"It's fine neither did I. So we'll split up," I say with a newfound urgency. I may feel a little helpless and not completely confident about what to do, but I have no idea whether or not Savannah is in more danger than anyone realizes, so the clock is ticking. I have to keep my cool and *do* something. "Heston, come with me to the front door. Gage and Tripp, y'all go around back. See if you can find a way inside to look around while we try and get Emma talking."

"Did you call the cops out here? Should we wait?"

"Yeah, they're trying to keep protocol. Not sure I have the patience to wait on their asses." I probably would have been willing to sit tight and wait for them to show up if I hadn't seen Emma through the window with that gun. "Let's go."

Tripp and Gage veer off to the side of the house, slipping through the gate in the backyard as quietly as they can. Last I knew, she didn't have a dog. So as long as they don't make enough noise to alert Emma that they're lurking around, they should be able to try the windows and doors for a way in.

I stalk up the cement walkway toward the front door with Heston slightly behind me. Before I reach up and press the doorbell, he reaches behind his back, adjusting his shirt over his gun, and then gives me a sharp nod.

It's silent for a moment once the ding of the doorbell echoes on the other side of the door. I cross my arms and take a deep breath, but then think better of it and put them back down casually at my side. If I'm going to get her to let us in and talk, I don't want to seem imposing.

When the front door swings inward, I bite down on my molars to keep me from stalking toward her, pinning her against the wall, and demanding some answers. One hand is behind her back, her hair is a ruffled mess, and she's chewing on the side of her lip relentlessly.

"Hi, Emma. I was hoping we could have a chat," I say in the most even voice I can manage at the moment.

Her eyes dart between me and Heston, but she doesn't open the door any wider or step back to let us in. "What's he doing here?"

"He was just with me when I decided to stop by and check on you," I lie. She still doesn't usher us inside, so I take a chance and gingerly step over the threshold.

Her lips form a thin line as I pass by her and walk into the house. She tries at first to close the door behind me, but Heston's hand shoots out and stops it from slamming in his face. Any person, man or woman, would cower at his expression. Emma twitches with annoyance, slumps her shoulders, and steps out of the way after realizing that he isn't going to take no for an answer.

As my gaze rakes over the dining room table just off the front entryway of the house, I spot several pill bottles and empty small plastic bags. She must catch on to what I'm looking at because she shuffles in front of me to cut off my line of sight. When she steps within a few feet of me, Heston's footsteps creep closer behind me.

I inhale through my nose and eye the hand behind her back. There aren't any sounds coming from the back of the house, so either Tripp and Gage are better at being quiet than I thought, or they can't find a way in.

"Emma. I need to ask you again if you've seen or heard from Savannah."

She narrows her eyes at me and in a flash, her once-hidden arm whips around in front of her. With the barrel of her gun in my face, I raise both of my hands in the air. Her chest rises and falls with an angry huff with the sound of

Heston turning the safety off of his gun behind me. He moves to the side of us with it trained on Emma.

"You'll never find her," she grits through her teeth, moving her aim between Heston and me frantically. "I *told* you. She's gone."

"Let's put the guns down and talk about it without anyone getting hurt," I coax her.

"No!" Emma screams. "Quit worrying about her and start worrying about *us*, Warren. I was good when I had you and I'm getting you back now. The problem is finally out of the way. You don't have to think about her anymore, don't you see? I'm right here and she's *not!*"

Her words are grating and rushed. I swallow hard, mulling over what she could mean by *the problem is finally out of the way*. My patience with her is wearing thin and I want to demand information, but my options are limited. Any further escalation is going to result in someone hurt or worse.

With her free hand, she scratches the side of her face and her eyes begin to well with heavy unshed tears. It hits me that she is unwell, plain and simple.

"What else are you on, Emma?" My eyes flick to the table behind her.

"I—I'm not—"

She stumbles over her words while Heston and I remain silent. A few times, I chance a glance in his direction. His eyes are hardened and ready to step in if need be, but I'm still not going to give up on talking her down before shit blows up.

"You're not sober," I state with enough assurance for her to know that I'm no longer taking a stab at her current situation. She's as loaded as the gun in her hand and losing her mind. "We can get you the help that you need. But I need you to lower your arm and step back first."

Before she has a chance to think it over, red and blue lights shine in through the windows. Emma's breaths pick up in a panic and she raises the gun even higher, now pointing at my forehead.

"Emma," Heston growls. "It's over. Put down the fucking gun or—"

"It's the only way now!" she interrupts him. "In another life, it'll all work out, right?" Her sad smile is what sends off the alarm bells in my head. It's sick and twisted, but I think she knows that if she kills me, Heston won't hesitate to shoot her. Six feet under, but together just the same.

In the next five seconds, a window shatters at the back of the house, and my head turns. Emma takes that as her opportunity to pull the trigger, Heston lunges toward me with gritted teeth, and we both crash into the wall.

My eyes blink slowly, and I see nothing but blurry streaks of black and white. As hard as I try, I can't keep them open.

A door crashes open somewhere, I think, but it's a muted sound that comes from miles away.

35

SAVANNAH

M y head is turned to the side with my cheek resting on the tops of my hands. I'm lying on my stomach and by now, I'm sure the side of the handcuffs have left an indentation somewhere on my wrists and the side of my face. But this is the only position I can be in where I can't feel the emptiness of my stomach as much.

I've tracked the sun as its beam of light coming through the window crept across the floor. The closer that it got to me, the longer the morning dragged on. I was thankful when the sun came up. That bleak darkness and utter silence of last night did nothing to help me stay calm. Instead, I felt more on edge.

I haven't drank any of the water in the bucket that Emma left for me out of fear that she'd poisoned it, and my throat is feeling drier with every passing hour. I'm thirsty, hungry, and exhausted from crying and getting no sleep.

More than once, I've wondered what would happen if Emma never came back. Or maybe worse—if she did come back but never set me free.

My visions have consisted of her wiggling her way back

into Warren's life now that I'm out of the way. I thought about how she'd used my brother, not only for making Warren jealous but evidently for drugs too.

I've had plenty of time to rehearse the speeches that I may never get to give.

You've hurt me for far too long with your condescending words and awful attitude toward me. I've done nothing to earn that from you and all you've done is join in on our parents' tendency to belittle me, I'd tell him.

In my head, I stand tall and confident facing my demons. No one coaches me through it, I just spell out exactly how I feel without holding back a single emotion.

I've learned about love. And when people love you, they do everything within their power to understand you instead of trying to mold you like clay and then voicing your embarrassment of them publicly when they don't act exactly as you demand. I don't deserve the way you've shut me out emotionally and yet still held me to an unreachable standard in your stupid circle of high society, I'd say to my parents.

Maybe I'll tell them one day. Maybe I won't get the chance. With the ability to speak freely to myself while I'm stuck down here, I thought of what I'd say to Warren too.

I don't have the heart to go over it again in my mind. It's too painful wishing I could say it to his face while wrapped in his arms instead.

My heavy eyes blink slowly as I stare mindlessly at the window across the room. But they snap wide open when something passes by outside, momentarily blocking the sunlight.

I study the window intensely and wait with heavy breaths. When the sunlight is blocked for a second again, a bolt of adrenaline surges through my body and I sit up in a flash. The chain attached to my wrists clangs against the concrete floor, and I yank it for some slack as I stand.

I only wobble on my feet for a second, working to find my balance.

My eyes roam the ceiling, wondering if it's Emma outside. I'd hear the front door and her footsteps entering the house if she was here. Did I miss hearing her car pull up? Surely, I would have recognized the sound of the engine. I don't remember hearing anything at all, but I also know that I'm so tired and famished that I almost feel drunk, so it's not entirely impossible that I wouldn't have heard a vehicle approaching the house.

My gaze flicks around frantically and I wait for another sign of life outside of this basement. When I finally hear something, it doesn't come from this house. I think it's coming from the one next door.

There's a rhythmic tapping sound. Faint enough for me to know that it's not extremely nearby, but still loud enough to be within earshot. A hammer?

When it stops, I lose control over my reactions and instincts take over. I drop the slack of the chain that I was holding and it crashes to the ground. My mouth opens, my eyes slam shut, and I let out the loudest possible scream that I can manage. It's hoarse at first, but I clear my throat, take three massive breaths, and try again.

I'm throwing the chain against the metal beam and growing light-headed from the blood-curdling screams, for what felt like several minutes, when I finally hear footsteps upstairs. Their echoes grow closer and at a quick pace.

With the very last bit of energy that I have left, I let out one final cry.

"Down here! Help!"

The footsteps quicken to a rapid pace and soon the stairs are shaking from the weight of a man in a neon orange shirt descending them.

"Holy shit," he yells.

I collapse to the floor, breathless and grasping at my throat with one hand and clutching my stomach with the other.

My vision is blurry, but I see the man turning and running back up the stairs. I considered for a second that this might be the end and that he's left me, just like the old version would have expected him to.

The new version of me pops into my line of sight. A hallucination that slaps me on the cheek and begs me to keep my eyes open and wait patiently. I'm worth saving. I'm worth sticking around for. And I won't be surrounding myself with anyone who doesn't believe that ever again. Not if I can help it.

36

SAVANNAH

To my relief, the sounds of footsteps descending the stairs fill the basement once again a short time later. The man returns to my side in a rush with a bottle of water and what I think is a bolt cutter. He sinks to his knees next to me and I part my lips as he opens the drink and brings it to my mouth. I wince when he snaps the metal binding my wrists, immediately pulling them to my chest and rubbing the red marks that they'd left.

"I'm going to carry you," he says. His voice is kind, but I can't help but react with a tear streaming down my face. "I'll get you upstairs, okay? We've already called the police."

He waits for my consent, and my nod is weak.

It's uncomfortable as he carries me through the house and he crosses the front yard toward his vehicle that's parked down the street. I'm relieved and lean my head forward in my lap when he finally sets me down in the front seat. The engine is running and my hands find their way to the vents in front of me, relishing the cold air.

"What's your name?" he asks from where he's standing on the curb, peering in through the open passenger door.

When I don't answer right away, he reaches into the bed of his truck and brings me another bottle of water. I nearly chug the entire thing, but he gently pulls it away from my lips.

"If you drink too much too fast, you'll be sick," he explains.

I hold my hand over my mouth, catching the stray drops of water dripping down the edges. He's right about the water because it hits my empty stomach and instantly begins to rumble and ache.

Sirens sound in the distance, and I turn my face to look at the man.

"Savannah Chase."

He smiles with a reassuring warmth. "You're going to be okay, Savannah."

In the next thirty minutes, several officers walked in and out of the house that I was trapped in with cameras and caution tape. A few of them took a statement from me, but I struggled to come up with a coherent description of the events. The nice man who found me offered a granola bar. I took a few small bites. Despite my hunger, it tasted dry and my appetite wasn't cooperating.

"We've contacted the law enforcement of Westridge, Miss Chase," a female officer says. "Emma Brooks was arrested last night on gun and drug charges."

My eyes widen and I listen intently.

"They'll add the charges of the events that took place here as well, don't worry. With the nature of the crime, she'll likely be denied bail. You're safe. You may need to provide more on your statement in the next few days if you don't mind. It'll help with the conviction and eventual sentencing. But you can go home after medical clears you. I'd be more than happy to take you. Or, is there someone you'd like me to call?"

"Jones!" Another officer shouts as he approaches the vehicle that I've been sitting in. The woman who was speaking to me turns her head in acknowledgment. "Gotta call from Westridge PD. They say there's a person on the line trying to get ahold of the victim."

"Her name is Savannah," the female officer corrects him. She takes the phone that was in his hand and passes it to me.

In a rush, I put the phone up to my ear.

"Hello?"

"She's on," a voice that sounds like Justin comes through the line. A smile breaks free on my face for the first time in too long. "Just a second, Savannah. It's good to hear you're okay."

"Sav?!"

My head jerks back at the shrieking volume that threatens to pop my eardrum.

"It's me," I say.

"It's you," she cries. It's Blythe's voice. I recognize it even through her shaky and tear-filled response. "Oh my fucking god, you scared me. Are you okay? I mean, of course, you're not okay. I'm so sorry. I miss you, *we* miss you. Can I come get you? Where are you?"

"I'm—near the city. Is Warren—"

"He checked out of the doctor's office just a little bit ago. He's got a little concussion but nothing serious."

My heart drops into the pit of my stomach.

"Concussion? What—"

"He's just fine, don't worry about him. A few nights of no sleep and then the tussle at Emma's house last night is all. He's knocked out on meds for the moment," her voice hitches while giving vague details about Warren and my eyes slam shut. "We'll focus on that later, you're what's important right now. We need to get you home."

"Okay," I whisper through the tears.

"They're going to take you to the hospital, okay? We need to make sure you're alright but I'll be right there with you."

"No, I feel fine, I just want to—"

"Savannah. I'll take you to see Warren the *second* the doctors give you the clear. I promise."

B lythe met me at the hospital in the city, which wasn't far from the house I'd been held in. I tried my best to protest, but it seemed like a necessary part of making sure law enforcement had every bit of information they needed about my well being after being found.

After eating, a few hours hooked up to an IV, and no visible bodily injuries to speak of, they couldn't come up with a strong enough reason for me to stay any longer than an hour. Thankfully Blythe knew the nurses and assured them that I'd be taken care of at home.

She'd been on the phone with several people before we left. It nearly gutted me to hear her relay the well wishes from Gage and the boys, her parents, and a few other people. I hate that they were scared or worried and I can't even imagine how Warren was feeling too.

I should have been feeling guilty that they were concerned about me. I hate what happened. But in a twisted way, I felt warm after hearing about their concern and relief. Even the fact that they went out of their way to check in . . . I felt loved.

It wasn't lost on me that neither my parents nor brother had called. I know my phone was still MIA and they probably didn't have Blythe's number. But they could have figured out a way to make contact if they wanted to. I didn't dwell on that for long because I knew I had the right people in my circle now.

I drifted in and out of restless sleep during the drive out of the city and back to Westridge. Several times, as we slowed to a stop for an exit or a turn, my eyes snapped open hoping we'd made it back already.

There's a crick in my neck, dry tears stain my cheeks, and my body is beyond the point of utter exhaustion. But I'm holding onto the tiny reserve of energy that was unlocked the moment I was finally safe in this car and headed home.

I once considered the city that we just left to be my home. Now the very thought of it stirs up a painful cluster of emotions that I'd like to never experience again.

Now, home is no longer just a place to me. It's my people. The same people that I had missed so dearly in that basement. Their laughs, smiles, hugs . . . even their jokes never once left my mind when I was coming to grips with the fact that if things with Emma went terribly wrong, I may never see them again.

More than anyone else, Warren had consumed my every thought. And I'm buzzing with anticipation knowing I'll see him again in—I check the clock on the dashboard—twenty minutes.

The few minutes it took for us to stop for food on the way had slowed us down a bit, unfortunately. But that first french fry might have been worth every second. Maybe I was starving, but I swear it was the hottest, saltiest, and freshest golden fry of my life. I'd licked my fingers like a feral creature.

I perk up at the sound of the blinker in the car and lift my head from where it was resting against the window. Blythe eases her foot on the brake and exits the highway, coming to a four-way stop. I sit up in my seat, feeling a sudden rush of excitement as she turns right on a dirt road.

She turns her head and smiles in my direction when we pass a green road sign that says that Westridge is 18 miles away. Her right-hand reaches across the center console, and I meet her in the middle with my left hand.

Our palms squeeze together for that agonizing stretch of road until Westridge finally comes into view. My heart flutters as we drive through town, past the places that I've grown to love. None so much as the ranch, though. And when we finally pull through those glorious gates, I almost open the door, get out, and kiss the damn ground.

My seat belt is already unbuckled when the bunkhouse is still a few hundred yards away. The tears start when I see them standing out front.

Heston with a hand in his pocket and his dog, Lucky, sitting obediently at his feet. Gage leaning against the front door. Tripp, all smiles, and holding a beer in his hand. Warren . . . jogging toward us.

"Stop the car," I whisper. "Stop the car!" My voice grows louder and more desperate.

Blythe pushes the brake pedal to the floorboard, thinking something is wrong with me at first, but she laughs when she realizes. I push open the passenger door and don't even bother closing it behind me.

Everything hurts, but I don't care. I run anyway.

The world around me turns into a blur and I fight to hold back tears so that I can see where I'm going. Thankfully we weren't far apart, and I made it without tripping and falling flat on my face.

Within seconds, our bodies collide. He plants his feet in the dirt, skidding to a stop as I launch myself into his arms and slam right into his chest. My legs wrap around him. His arms circle my hips and the back of my head, cradling me with his signature blend of tenderness and rough possession.

I'm smiling into his neck, but I'd rather look at him, so I

try and pull my face away. His hand around the back of my head holds strong, keeping me in place.

"Don't move. Not yet," he says.

I squeeze his neck hard enough that it could choke him and he laughs. It's a strained sound, but it's one I've been dying to hear. It can't erase what happened, but it soothes every part of me that's hurting.

I'm so happy to be in his arms that I almost miss it, but he starts swaying back and forth slightly like he's feeling dizzy. I remember what Blythe had said to me on the phone about him having a mild concussion and quickly unwrap my legs, forcing him to set me down on the ground in front of him.

His hands move up to cup either side of my face while he leans down to press his forehead against mine. It's as if every part of me that has been locked up for so long, sealed tight and stored away for my own protection, officially opened up in that moment. I released a heavy breath and let go of every inhibition with it.

Something about being faced with the possibility of never speaking to someone again, then getting the chance after all changes you. You stop caring about the repercussions or what they might say back.

I open my mouth to give life to the words on the tip of my tongue, but Tripp's voice fills the space around us instead.

"Super fucking cute, guys. But can we all go inside now? Y'all both look like you're about to fall flat on your asses."

"You brought a gun with you?!" Blythe gasps as she spins to face Gage. They're both standing next to the sink as the guys fill us in on what went down last night.

I'm sitting on the end of the couch in the bunkhouse living room while Warren lays his body across the cushions next to me. His head is in my lap and I mindlessly run my fingers through his hair. His eyes are closed, but I know he's awake and listening to the conversation.

"What do you think?" Gage looks at her like she should know better than to assume he wouldn't be packing.

I giggle and see a smile turn up the corners of Warren's mouth too.

I thought if I ever made it out, I'd be an inconsolable mess of tears. Instead, it's peace that I feel. And hearing about the events of last night isn't ripping through me like a knife or striking me with fear like I'd expected them to. It helps to know that Emma is in custody and that Warren has so far refused to let me go untouched for even a second of time. I'm safe here. I'm with my people.

I wasn't happy about the fact that Heston had to tackle Warren to the ground when Emma shot at him for telling her that she needed to get help and that the cops were going to take her in and get her into treatment. They didn't know she'd kidnapped me at that point or that the drug problem was just the tip of the iceberg. According to Warren though, he knew in his bones that she had something to do with me being gone and they chased her down hoping it'd help them find me.

I shudder at the thought of Warren being shot at and then hitting his head hard enough when he and Heston crashed to the ground that he needed medical attention. I push my hand through his hair, study his chest rising and falling, and memorize the weight of him in my lap to push away that vision.

Blythe rolls her eyes at Gage, lets out a long sigh, and goes back to peeling the potato in her hand over the colander in the sink.

"It was just in case. I didn't shoot anyone this time, honey," Gage says with a kiss on her cheek. "I did pull it out and almost popped her when she tried bolting from the cops though," he chuckles.

"*This* time?" I ask with a shocked look on my face.

Heston and Tripp are each sitting in a recliner on either side of the couch and make eye contact with their lips rolled into their mouths like they're trying not to laugh.

The room is silent for a minute but then Tripp and Gage burst out in laughter.

"It's not funny," Blythe says without looking up.

Warren covers his face with his hand, and I begin to realize I'm the only one who has no idea what they're talking about.

"Long story," Warren looks up at me and says with a sigh.

Tripp stands and heads to the fridge for a beer. Walking back to the living room, he stops next to me, and tiny splashes of liquid spray from his hand as he pops the top of the can. Holding it in the air, he turns in my direction. "All you need to know, Sav, is that around here? Not a single bitch has ever fucked around and not found out."

With a wink, he chugs half of the beer and sits back down. The rest of the room is laughing, and I can't help but smile. Sure, I've learned they're a little deranged at times. But I've grown to love them all just the same.

While expectations follow me everywhere else that I go, the bunkhouse is *come as you are*. It's turned into a safe haven for me, and there's nowhere else that I'd rather be.

My bedroom door clicks as I push it closed and turn the lock. We'd already taken a shower, changed into clean and comfortable clothes, and ate a big dinner with everyone. But I'm glad to finally be back in a quiet room alone with Savannah.

She pulls back the covers on my bed and slides her body underneath. Her eyes close and I watch with a smile as her entire body relaxes and she lets out a long sigh.

I crawl across the mattress and lie down next to her. "Comfy?"

"Almost."

I scoot closer to her, wrapping an arm around her waist and pulling her against my chest.

"There," she whispers. "Now I'm comfy."

My nose buries itself into her hair and my hand trails across the waistband of her shorts.

"Did you talk to your family yet?"

She sighs and snuggles closer to me. "Yeah. They finally got Blythe's number and called while you were in the shower earlier. They were glad to know that I was safe but warned that I should choose the people I surround myself with more carefully. Like this whole thing was somehow my fault."

"No offense, but your parents are awful."

"I know," she laughs softly. "It doesn't bother me as much as it used to. I had a lot of time to think about it while I was gone." I squeeze her tighter while I listen. "They have other priorities in their little bubble and don't want to deal with my messes all the time. Spencer has always been the same way too. I don't want to think about them anymore, you know? I'll talk to them about it one day, maybe. It'll be like airing my grievances to a brick wall, but I need to say my piece. They can apologize or treat me differently if they want but either way, I'm ready to move on and live my damn life. And I like how my life is right now. With you."

Hearing her with so much clarity on the subject makes my chest feel tight. I'm proud of how she's beginning to understand that she deserves to be loved.

She turns to her back when I lift my body, position my knees between her legs, and hover over her.

"I'm sorry about everything that happened," I say with my forehead resting on hers.

I know I'm not responsible for Emma's issues. But I was part of the reason this all happened, even if her unhinged obsession and substance abuse was out of my control. I should have seen the signs and I never should have let Savannah go over to her house alone. Guilt settles in my stomach, and I have to focus to keep breathing and not let the emotion take over.

Savannah lifts her chin, kissing me long and slow.

"It's not your fault. It's not mine either, and it feels good to let myself believe that." Her thumb runs the length of my jaw and I shake my head in wonder.

This is all I ever wanted. For her to love herself and let me love her too.

To have her here and safe in my bed.

To just be with her.

Instinctively, my hips press down on hers and I kiss her like it's the only thing in the world that matters to me right now.

"Fuck, baby. Sorry. I know you're tired and I want to make sure you're okay—"

"I don't want to talk about what happened. I want to think about the future instead," she whispers against my lips. Her hands trail down the front of my chest and down to my briefs. She pushes them down as far as she can, and while I sit up and get them the rest of the way off, she takes off her shorts and throws them to the side of the bed.

Settling back down on top of her, our mouths meet again. I run my hand along the side of her leg while she wraps it around me. She lifts her hips, begging for the friction we're both craving right now. I'm dying to scoot down and bury myself between her thighs to taste her, but I don't know if I can put off being inside her for another minute.

"Warren, please. I need—" her breath hitches and her sentence is cut off because I'm way ahead of her.

Right when I'm about to push into her, my movements still. "*Fuck*. Condom."

I'm practically panting above her and trying to think of the last place I saw the box of condoms when she fists the hair at the back of my neck to bring my attention back to her.

"I'm on the shot. And I want to feel you, Warren. *Now,*" she pleads.

After hearing that, there's no stopping it.

With one slow hard thrust, I'm inside her. Her nails rake the back of my shoulders, I hold my breath trying not to collapse from how wet and tight she is, and our bodies meld together like they were made to never be apart.

"God, Savvy. I'm not letting you go," I growl into her ear while pulling my hips back and sinking back into her once more.

"I'm right here. I'm not going anywhere."

Lost in the need in her eyes and the sensation of having nothing between us, my body completely takes over. Her hips tilt up for a deeper angle, and I slam into her again and again. A few times, I worry that I'm being too rough after everything that's happened. But I can't help it and she urges me on any time I think of slowing down.

"*Yes*," she moans. "Don't stop. Don't you *dare* stop."

"Come on my cock, Savvy. I can't last any longer, you feel too fucking perfect."

Without slowing the thrust of my hips, I brace one hand beside her head and move the other to her mouth. My thumb pushes in gently between her lips and her tongue swirls around it.

I'd like to keep it there longer, but that can wait for another time. Right now I'm focused on feeling her come undone. I pull my thumb from her mouth and lower my hand, making slow circles around her clit.

In the next minute, the whole world could be ending right outside this door and I wouldn't have a clue. Electric shocks zip up my spine as she clenches around me. Every nerve in my body explodes right along with hers, and she kisses me with such force that my lips go numb.

I'm breathless when she finally pulls away, but I study the sweet flush in her cheeks and the softness in her eyes.

She's safe. She's the most beautiful thing in the world. And she's mine. It's everything to me.

"It's no tractor seat, but the bed was fine, I guess," she teases.

"I'll bend you bare ass naked over a hay bale next time and you'll be wishing it was a bed," I quip back with a smirk.

She kisses my jaw in three different spots. I roll onto my side, bringing her with me to lay on my chest. I lift my forearm to cover my eyes, as the exhaustion I forgot about seeps back in.

"Missed you," she whispers through a massive yawn.

My hand rubs circles in the middle of her back.

I look down at her in my arms and clench my jaw to keep from getting choked up. "Missed you. So much."

SAVANNAH

"If you study another second, your eyes are going to fall out," Gage grumbles.

I'm sitting next to Blythe at the dinner table and we both have our laptops open. It's late, and we've been sitting at the table in our pajamas working for a few hours. I took the rest of the week off work since getting back to Westridge.

I didn't want to miss anything important at the firm, but a week to rest and spend time with Warren seemed like the best thing for me right now. I've tried to keep up as much as I can remotely.

"Shouldn't you be grilling or something?" Blythe quips back.

I cover my snicker with my hand and I see Tripp twitching with amusement to my left. Gage glares at her computer, then reaches across the table and slowly shuts it. He and Blythe make eye contact and I wait for a fight to break out. He hates it when she works too much because she's prone to stress. But she hates being told what to do, so conflict emerges often.

They can't help but smile at each other after a beat, though.

"Fiiine," she groans.

Gage puffs his chest, packs up her things for her, and heads for the door with her close behind. They hold hands on their way through the living room and I shake my head with a laugh. A perfect match, those two.

With a sleepy yawn, I shut my computer just as two strong hands land on my shoulders. My eyes close as he rubs the sore muscles on either side of my neck. When he stops, I tip my head and look up at him. "Hi."

"Hi," Warren says back in a whisper and a kiss on my forehead.

Remembering the fresh steaks in the fridge, I turn my gaze toward the door before Gage and Blythe have a chance to leave. "Y'all can eat dinner here if you want. Heston got groceries earlier."

"Yeah, I checked the fridge already. No thanks!" Blythe calls over her shoulder.

Heston is lying on the couch but pops his head up slightly. "What? I did good."

"Beer is not a side dish, dude," Tripp says without looking up from his phone.

Gage laughs and gives a wave. "See y'all later."

The front door closes behind them and Warren resumes rubbing my shoulders.

"I got something for you," he says in a low voice.

I look up at him again and arch an eyebrow. "What is it?"

"Just something for what I've been thinking about for a while. I'll get it."

While Warren strides down the hallway, I shove my notebook, pen, and laptop back into my bag.

"I'm headed out, don't wait up," Tripp says as moves toward the door to pull his boots on.

Heston shakes his head but gets up too. On his way to his

room for the night, he stops by the table. I look up at him wondering if he needs something.

"Doin' good?" he asks. One hand is in the pocket of his jeans and the other rests on the back of a chair at the table.

"Yeah," I smile. "I'm doing good. Thanks, Hes."

Without another word, he nods and disappears down the hallway.

We've never had an in-depth conversation before, but I think I have more in common with Heston than anyone else here. There's pain behind his eyes. He's steady and loyal, though. And I hope he fights off whatever demons I suspect he has one day.

I start to get up from my seat to grab some water to take to bed, but Warren slides in behind me and I sit back down. He's holding what looks like a small stack of paper and envelopes.

"If you don't want to do this, you don't have to," he explains. "It's just an idea."

I laugh softly at the apprehension on his face and reach for the papers in his hand. "What are you talking about?"

"You said the other day that you weren't ready to talk to your family yet."

I tilt my head and nod, remembering the conversation about my family after everything had happened with Emma. I have so much to say to them, but keeping my distance has been the best decision that I've ever made. I've grown, opened up, matured, and been happier than I've ever been without being around them.

"Well, I don't think it'd be good if you kept all those feelings bottled up any longer. You can write it down, and get it all out. Send it to them if you want or keep it for yourself. Either way, I thought maybe it could help put it all behind you. I hate the idea of you having anything swirling around in your head that makes you sad or forget how amazing you actually are. It kills me and I know it's damn near killing you too."

He lifts the papers toward me. They're off-white and slightly textured with a subtle shimmer when the light hits them just right, making me think they weren't cheap.

"Where on earth did you find beautiful paper like that?"

"I ordered it a few days ago. Just got here today."

For a split second, my brain shoots down the idea. It's easier to ignore my demons rather than face them, even if it's just on paper and not in person. But I can't heal if I pretend I'm not hurt. I can't move on if I hold the emotions hostage.

It's less frightening this way.

I step toward him slowly and place a hand on his chest. He bends down to kiss me, soft and sweet.

"You don't have to do it right now," he whispers. "Or ever, if you don't want to. I'm not pressuring you, I just want to help."

I lock eyes with him and count my lucky stars. I never imagined being with someone so thoughtful. Handsome. Relentlessly caring. He's everything I ever needed. "You're a once-in-a-lifetime man, Warren."

His dimples crease on either side of his smile and he kisses me again. Part of me wants to deepen the kiss and stay inside my comfort zone by heading off to bed with him for the night and ignoring the scary urge to write out these letters. But the brave part of me knows that I shouldn't push this to the back burner. I pull away with a sigh and place my hands on my hips. "I'm going to do it. Right now."

"You want me to stick around or give you some privacy?"

"I need to do this on my own," I say with confidence.

He slaps the papers on the table and wraps his hand around the nape of my neck, pulling me in for a hug. "Fire away, baby."

SAVANNAH

With the back seat of my car stuffed full of mainly shoes and handbags, I drive through the gates of Prairie Rose Ranch. Blythe is in the passenger seat with her tan bare feet propped up in the corner of the open window. It's not a refreshing breeze, being as hot and humid as it is. But it's a beautiful day nonetheless and I like the feeling of our hair whipping in the wind as we make our way up the drive.

"Is this crazy?" I ask her as I grip the steering wheel extra hard.

She pulls the green Popsicle out of her mouth and whips her head in my direction. "Oh, it's crazy alright. Good luck with laundry—these boys do five loads a day and there's still dirty clothes in the mud room. It's a hillbilly frat house, girl. Godspeed." She salutes and then bends forward to put her sandals back on.

"I don't care about that. But moving in with Warren . . . It's fast. I don't want to mess this all up by rushing everything."

She takes a sip out of her water bottle and then points it

to me. "You already pretty much live here. You're here every single night."

"True. You Farrows and your damn love spells. I give up fighting it and trying to take things slow."

Blythe clutches her stomach as she laughs. "I know I have no room to talk. If you're really that worried about it, you could move in with me," she suggests. "The bed in the guest room is comfy and I just put the cutest rug in there."

The car comes to a stop as we pull in front of the bunkhouse. I lean forward to look out the windshield and take a deep breath. I know it's not forever, but right now, it feels like home. Despite the comforting feeling, I can't help but worry about the future.

The proposition of living here was a mixture of wanting to spend more time with Warren and wanting to feel safer at the same time. We'll still take care of Mesa's place until she's back, of course. But even with Emma no longer being a threat, I didn't want to live alone.

"So I can listen to you and Gage going at it all night upstairs? I think not."

"Okay," she laughs. "So, you'd rather hear Tripp's girls screaming his name right across the hall. Got it."

My face scrunches up and I push the sunglasses to the top of my head. "Ugh. I'll take an extended stay at the bed and breakfast off Main Street for 200, Alex."

Blythe smiles but then lowers her voice to a more sincere tone. "Do you have second thoughts about my brother?"

"No," I say immediately. "It's just . . . I've never been so scared to ruin something good."

And that's saying something. I've been scared of ruining plenty of things before. But never as much as this.

"You should always go with your gut. But in my opinion, there's no timeline for love. The first time Gage and I were together, I knew in my bones I'd be sitting on a back porch with gray hair and an iced tea in my hand next to him in fifty years."

"The first time you saw him? Really?"

She shakes her head and rolls her eyes. "Oh, no. He was a blubbering mess the first time I saw him," she laughs. "I'm talking about the first time we knocked boots and he—"

"Okay," I cut her off and open the driver's side door. "It's not late enough in the day for me to hear about your sexcapades."

"Fine, but the man can bone. That's all I'm saying."

After a beat of silence, I form my lips into a tight line and take a cleansing breath.

"You know what? I'm going to stop being a nervous nelly and embrace it. I'm happier than I've ever been, and moving in with Warren isn't going to mess anything up. It's going to make it even better."

It feels good to step out of the cage of anxiety and say that out loud.

Blythe's jaw drops, but then her mouth lifts in a grin. "Who are you and what have you done with my friend?"

"Shut up," I laugh.

As we round the car and open the trunk, we each grab a moving box full of my things and bring it inside. It takes several trips for us to empty the car, but luckily I didn't have any large furniture to bring along.

"This feels right," I admit, staring at the stack of boxes in Warren's room. *Our* room.

Blythe squeals and claps her hands. I can't help but smile and laugh along with her.

"God, it needs a little redecorating though," I say. "First thing to go is the set of bachelor navy sheets."

"Shit," she mumbles with a hand over her eyes. "I forgot something in the car, be right back."

"I think we got everything—" I start, but she'd already run

out of the room. I shrug and turn to survey the room again, making a plan in my head for how we can spruce it up a bit.

I have no intention of erasing the simple charm or Warren's personality in the room altogether. A little brightness and color wouldn't hurt, though.

"Found it," Blythe says as she runs back into the room and stops in front of me. "Here. It's for you."

I reach out to take the small box from her hands. It's pink, of course. Shiny gold foil flecks cover the white tissue paper on the inside. I set the lid down on the dresser next to me and unfold the tissue paper to reveal what's underneath.

A tiny handwritten note sits atop a bracelet. Instead of opening the note first, I'm unable to resist the beautiful gold chain underneath. I lift it from the box and hold it out in front of me.

"What in the world?! B, this is so beautiful!"

A tiny charm hangs in the middle of the bracelet. I bring it close to my face, admiring the intricate details. It looks familiar and my brows pull together trying to piece together where I've seen it before.

"It's a prairie rose, just like my necklace. See?"

My gaze snaps up to see her holding the identical charm hanging from her neck.

"The necklace was a gift from my parents, and Gage named this ranch after it. It's special to me, and I thought . . ." she stops mid-sentence with a soft smile. "Well, I think it means something to both of us now and that you might like the bracelet."

"It's—" I swallow to clear my emotions. "It's gorgeous and I want to put it on right this second. Thank you. You're so thoughtful, it's the perfect gift."

I shake my head in wonder while fumbling with the chain to try and clasp it around my wrist.

"Hold on, silly! Read the note first."

"Here," I huff as I hand her the bracelet to hold for a moment. Taking the note out of the box, I unfold the delicate paper and read out loud.

"Will you be my bridesmaid?" I don't know how to be a bridesmaid. I've never been asked before. But visions of standing next to my friend on her wedding day flash through my mind and I have my answer. "Hell yes, I'll be your bridesmaid. Oh my *god*!"

I step forward to pull Blythe into a warm hug, and she squeezes me back hard enough that I almost can't breathe.

"It's going to be the wedding of the century," I choke out. "I can't wait and I'm so happy for you."

"I need you there with me," she whispers.

"I wouldn't miss it, B."

3 9

SAVANNAH

"He looks happy, doesn't he?" Blythe points out.

We're standing together in a crowd of people that are gathered outside of Farrow Equipment. Westridge doesn't get a new business in town very often. So when they do, they pull out all the stops, complete with local media coverage, a ribbon cutting, and a commemorative photo opp.

Leading up to today, Warren tried his best to brush it off like it wasn't a big deal. But I knew deep down that he was looking forward to this more than he let on. Between the dimples in his cheeks and the crinkles at the corners of his eyes, it's hard to miss his excitement.

"He does," I reply with a smile. I hold my phone out in front of me and snap a picture of him standing underneath the grand opening sign.

After shaking hands with the representatives from the chamber of commerce and city council, he turns to scan the crowd. Butterflies flutter beneath my chest when his eyes finally land on me. I hold his gaze for a beat, trying my best to let him know with just a look how proud I am of him.

It's been a few weeks since we moved in together, so we

see a lot of each other. But I still haven't tired of seeing that smile of his. Not one damn bit.

Everyone in attendance erupts in a roar of applause as Warren finally cuts the ceremonious red ribbon. I may not have a voice come tomorrow, but I can't help cheering along with everyone. His dream is coming true right before my eyes, and I swipe at my cheeks to erase the stray happy tears.

When the photographer positions people at the front for a photo, Warren cups his hands around his mouth and shouts over the bustling swarm of people in front of him. "Family! Get up here for the picture!"

Wade and Gayle are the first to reach him, each giving a heartwarming hug with proud smiles on their faces. They shuffle to the right side of him, taking their place for the photo. Blythe comes next, giving him some sort of cute secret handshake/hug combo. Gage is right behind her and they find a place next to Warren on his left.

The smile I'd been wearing drops from my face and is replaced with a watery and emotional expression when Heston and Tripp walk up to congratulate him. True to form, Tripp brings Warren in for a massive hug with a few slaps on the back and then steps in line next to Gage. Heston shakes Warren's hand, firm and steady, and grips his shoulder a few times before moving to stand next to Tripp.

They know they're his family and it's the sweetest thing I think I've ever seen. I clear my throat to steal back my emotions and lift my phone again to take a video this time of them all standing together. The photographer waves his hand, motioning for the few city people to scoot closer to fit into the frame. Everyone is all smiles except for Warren as he looks up and down the line of his family on either side of him.

"One second," he says to the photographer. He looks right at me then and holds his hand out. "Savvy! Come on, babe."

Without hesitation, Blythe's face lights up and she scoots over a little bit, making room between her and Warren. My body instinctively moves toward him, placing my hand in his and letting him pull me into his side.

We didn't get much of a warning before the flash on the camera went off. When the photographer looks at the tiny screen on the back of his camera and seems satisfied with the result, the crowd claps and I look up at Warren. But he was already fixated on me and I'm not sure he looked at the camera at all.

"Look at all of this," I whisper with a smile. "You did it."

He bends down closer to my face and tightens his hold around my waist. Our lips meet in a long kiss. I inhale through my nose halfway through, wishing we weren't in public at the moment.

When I place a hand on his chest and gently pull away, he pulls his bottom lip into his mouth with a roll of his tongue. His eyes bore into mine, sweet and intense all at once.

"I'm glad you're here," he says. "Now let's go inside and celebrate. Quickly, because I'd rather celebrate with you on top of me."

I slap him on the pec but laugh as he pulls me through the front doors of his business that's now officially up and running. A whoosh of cold air conditioning blows my hair over my shoulders as we step inside and walk through the main lobby and into the shop.

There are several white tables scattered around the spacious shop. Music plays above the laughter and conversation, coolers of beer and other drinks line the walls, and two big smokers send wafts of delicious food in the air from just outside the large garage doors.

"Do you want to mingle around for a little bit?" I ask. "Kiss some babies, shake some hands?"

"Plenty of time for that later. Eat with me first."

Warren leads us to the table where our crew is sitting. Tripp takes a bite of a slider while Heston leans his chair back on two legs, staring at his phone. Gage and Blythe are having a hushed conversation, laughing at each other between sentences.

Before we sit down, Warren's parents pass by, each holding a full plate of food.

Gayle lovingly squeezes my forearm and leans toward me. "Hope you're feeling better, dear. It's so good to see you. Love those shoes."

I look down at my heels with little cream-colored bows on the backs above the heel and smile.

Wade nods in my direction. "You ever need anything stop on by. No need to call."

"Thank you." It's all I can say without letting the tremble in my voice take over. They love their kids so fiercely and have shown an infinite amount of unconditional kindness toward me. They have no idea, but it's healed something in me, and I love them for that.

Speaking of love, I reach into my purse and pull out one of the letters that Warren gave me to write on weeks ago and slip it into the back pocket of his jeans. For good measure, I slap his ass and when he turns around wondering what the hell I'm doing, I smirk and casually take my seat.

He feels in his pocket, pulls out the envelope to inspect, but then slides it back into his jeans. It isn't until a few hours later when the party has mostly died down and we've cleaned up that he pulls me into his office.

"If you brought me in here to bend me over your desk to christen your office, I approve."

"I'd rather clear it off and lay you on your back so I can watch when I slide inside you, but if you want it from behind I'm happy to oblige."

I laugh as he locks the door and then stalks toward me.

The overhead light is off, but there's a lamp in the corner lighting up the room enough for me to look up and see the sharp angle of his jaw as my arms circle around his neck.

He pulls the letter from his back pocket and holds it in the air. "What's this?"

I shrug wearing the same smirk on my face from earlier. In a rush, he pulls away and tears it open.

"Well, don't rip it to pieces."

"Sorry," he chuckles.

It's amusing seeing his large fingers trying to open the thin delicate paper. When he finally retrieves the letter from inside, it only takes a moment for him to read it in its entirety seeing as how it's only three words.

It was the first letter that I wrote that night. Before the ones to everyone who'd caused me so much pain. This one wasn't a way for me to open up and vent into the void so I could let go of my past. It was a love letter to Warren and a way for me to take hold of my future.

Without a word, he folds the paper. His hands grip it tight and I hold my breath hoping he says something soon. I step closer to him, moving my hands to either side of his face.

"Warren—"

"I love you too."

My eyes start watering and a lump of emotion gets stuck in my throat. Suddenly, his arms are around my waist and he's lifting me off the ground. I feel like I'm floating as he spins us around one time. I don't fight the tear-filled giggles that bubble out of me, and it feels good to permanently remove the urge to hide how I feel.

When he stops I see the look on his face—so full of longing and promise. Like he thinks it's a privilege just to hold me.

"I love you," I say for the first time out loud. I know he just read the words but I want him to hear it too.

"Again."

"I love you," I say louder this time. He laughs and sets me down on the ground so that he can place one hand under my chin and the other threaded through my hair.

"I'd request that in writing, but I guess I already have that too," he smiles and leans down to hover his lips over mine. I rise to my tiptoes to deepen the kiss.

It's playful and sweet—smiling and kissing at the same time. I love it. I love *him*.

When I left the city, I'd hoped a change in my life would come that would ease the emotional pain and disappointment that I'd suffered through for so long. More times than I could count, I'd closed my eyes and wished for a new chance to become who I wanted to be. With people that lift me, not bring me down.

Somehow, someway, it all came true.

I step back and take Warren's hand. "Let's go home."

EPILOGUE

WARREN

SIX MONTHS LATER

Hours are long in the shop this time of year. They're never short, to be fair. But it's great for business and I can't complain too much. It makes walking through the doors of the bunkhouse at night feel that much sweeter.

I'd hoped Savannah and I might be moved out by now and have a place of our own. My savings account is looking good, and we could buy a place tomorrow if we wanted. But we agreed we'd like to build a house exactly how we want it on some land close to my family and the ranch. Nothing has come on the market that we love yet, so we're just waiting for the right spot to pop up.

For now, we're happy at the ranch anyway. It feels like home and in some ways, I think it always will, even when we eventually leave.

I arch an eyebrow seeing a sea of vehicles in front of the bunkhouse when I pull up. Tripp's Bronco and Heston's truck are parked in their usual spots next to Savannah's SUV. It's the blacked-out van with two sedans behind it that has

305

me cutting off the engine and jumping out of the driver's seat.

No one gets on this ranch without Gage knowing, so I'm not too panicked. Still, I stride quickly toward the door and swing it open. I wasn't prepared for the scene in front of me in the living room.

Formal clothes hanging on mobile racks, flowers, and wedding decorations. *Everywhere.*

Heston stands on a short pedestal, nostrils flared and scowling at the man bending in front of him who's holding a tape measure between Heston's legs. Colorful swatches of fabric litter the entire surface of the sectional, mood boards line the wall, and several men and women with tablets in their hands shuffle around the room.

The rustic bunkhouse has been transformed into a fucking bridal store.

"Mr. Farrow?" a middle-aged woman with a silver sharp-edged bob asks.

I nod while trying to hide a laugh as Heston huffs and holds his arms out on either side of him to be measured.

"Over here, please."

I follow the woman through a clutter of flowers and ribbon. We stop by the dining room table, and she turns toward me to size me up.

"Hmm. You have a cool undertone. This won't do," she mumbles while tapping on her tablet.

A pair of giggles come from the kitchen and I slowly turn my head to see Blythe and Savannah sitting on top of the counter, each holding a glass of wine. Their feet dangle play-fully, swinging back and forth and they're covering the fit of laughter with their hands over their mouths.

My eyes narrow, but I smirk. Of course, they didn't warn me about this and planned the ambush perfectly.

"We're going to need a different color for the best man's

corsage so that it doesn't clash with his complexion. The cornflower blue with a smidge of cream, maybe. Are you okay with that darling?" The woman who is standing in front of me asks.

Her question is directed toward Blythe who looks at me for a moment, then leans back on her hands and nods with a smile.

Me?

Gage has a brother that I've met once before. They aren't close, I don't think. I figured he'd probably come to the wedding though and aren't brothers usually the best man?

Women tend to overthink this kind of stuff, but I haven't really given it much thought. Gage is my best friend even if I'm sitting in the crowd when he ties the knot with my sister.

Right on cue, Gage and Tripp walk down the hallway and into the main area of chaos, each wearing a suit. Gage pulls at the collar of his shirt but Tripp struts like he runs a billion-dollar company.

"Oh dear," the silver-haired woman gasps. "Oh no no no. These are much too tight in the shoulders for you. And you," she looks to Tripp, "button up your shirt so I can put a few pins in."

I laugh and catch Savannah hopping off the counter to grab a beer from the fridge out of the corner of my eye. She pops the top and walks toward me, eyeing me from head to toe.

"You're going to be hot in a suit," she says in a sultry voice that's smooth as honey and makes my pants feel tighter than they are.

I take the beer that she offers but set it on the table instead of taking a drink. Grabbing her hand and whirling her into my arms, I lean down and leave an open-mouthed kiss on the side of her neck. Her hands squeeze my biceps, and she lets out a breathy laugh.

I recognize Savvy's ringtone as her phone buzzes across the kitchen island counter. With a hand on my chest, she gently pulls away and skips over to it. Her face lights up when she reads the caller ID.

"Hey!" she says as she answers the phone. I wonder who it could be calling her after work hours, but I don't have much time to think it over as two people show up on either side of me and lift my arms to run a tape measure from my hands to my shoulders.

"Oh, of course! I'll text you the code."

Savannah brings her phone away from her ear and types on her screen.

"Who's at the gate?" Gage asks, no doubt getting a notification on his phone that someone is here.

"It's Mesa. She's trying on Keanna's dress since they're the same size, remember?" Blythe answers.

Keanna is Blythe's best friend. She's a resident in Baltimore and I think I remember Savannah mentioning that she wasn't going to be able to make it down here until the week of the wedding.

Gage nods, recognizing Mesa's name. Blythe saunters off to the other side of the room where a few long silky dresses hang on a rack.

Not a minute later, a loud series of knocks echo through the bunkhouse. Savannah takes off toward the door, opening it with a smile.

"You don't have to knock, silly."

"Well, I didn't want to get shot at."

I cock an eyebrow and tilt my head. "Fair enough."

"Come on in," Savannah says as she grabs Mesa's hand. "I'm so glad you could come because B is spiraling about her friend's dress fitting."

Mesa follows behind her toward our room to try on their dresses. She's wearing frayed denim overalls cut off above the knee and an olive green cardigan hanging off of one shoulder. Her hair is tied up into two buns on either side of her head, a few red strands framing her face.

I turn to look behind me when I hear a low whistle.

Tripp's gaze follows Mesa as she walks down the hallway. His lips part and he pulls at the collar of his suit coat. Just as he pulls a stick of gum out of his pocket and unwraps it, I step in front of him to cut off his line of sight.

I love the guy, but I know his game. Hit it and quit it.

In the last few months since Mesa has moved back into her house just outside of Westridge, she and Savannah have become good friends. It means the world to Savannah and I don't want any rifts happening between them because one of my buddies had a one night stand with Mesa and then ghosted her.

"Don't even think about it."

"Don't know what you're talking about," Tripp says with a grin while popping the gum into his mouth.

A few minutes later, Mesa and Savannah walk back into the hallway, wearing matching dresses.

I pull my lower lip into my mouth as I study Savannah, and I hope to god she doesn't end up wearing that dress to the wedding because it will be shreds on the floor before the reception if I have to stare at her in it during the entire ceremony.

It's made of smooth rose-pink-colored silk with thin straps, hugging every single mouth-watering curve on her body.

I watch her twirl around in her dress and bare feet while taking a slow drink of my beer. Forcing more air into my lungs does nothing to even out my blood pressure from the sight of her.

309

"You and you," the lady in charge directs, "stand next to each other."

"Me?" Mesa asks, pointing to herself. But Tripp has already stepped toward her and held out his hand.

"Careful. Blythe might ask you to be in the wedding if we look too good next to each other," he teases her.

I swallow hard and pretty much give up whatever plan I had to keep him from hitting on her when she laughs and reaches her hand out.

"That wouldn't be so bad. I'm Mesa."

Tripp takes her hand and doesn't drop it even after a subtle shake. "I know who you are."

"Okay, turn this way," the lady says to them while waving her pen in her hand. "And walk forward a few steps."

Tripp lifts his elbow and Mesa loops her hand through, resting it on his bicep.

Not the fucking bicep. I know he's flexing right now, and I shoot him a look. Barely lifting his free hand, he flips me off and leads Mesa forward. Next to me, Savannah smooths a hand over my back and reaches for my drink to steal a sip.

"Absolutely stunning," the lady exclaims with a gasp. She lifts her tablet and taps on it several times. "All good here. The only thing left is the final fitting for the best man and then we'll go over final reception details next week."

"Thank you so much," Blythe says as she pulls her in for a quick hug and then turns toward Savannah. "The dresses are exactly what I envisioned. I could not be happier!"

"Are you sure?" Savannah bites her lip. "I love them too, but I'm not sure about how it fits around my hips."

"That's why we had you try it on so that we can tailor it to fit you!"

Savannah huffs out a laugh. "Tailor it to fit me, I like that. I was worried I'd have to change my diet or something."

"Never! I wouldn't change a single thing about you," Blythe says as she pulls Savannah in for a hug.

I thought brides were supposed to be angry and demanding. Maybe cry a lot, too. All Blythe wants to do is hug everyone.

"I would," I say as I take another drink.

Each girl's heads snap in my direction and Blythe glares. "Warren. Don't be silly. What could you possibly want to change?"

"Her last name."

THE END

AUTHOR'S NOTE &
ACKNOWLEDGEMENTS

I've done plenty of hard things before, but very few of them have been as emotional for me as writing Savannah's character in this story. If her struggles resonated with you, please know that your anxiety may be part of you, but it is not who you are.

While writing this book, I was lucky to have a village of author friends who listened to my many panicked voice messages, offered feedback, and encouraged me along the way.

I hope you know that I am here for you and your projects as well and would stop at nothing to support you in any way possible. It means the world to me having your opinions and helping one another has been the greatest joy of my author journey so far.

I hope I don't forget anyone, but thank you from the bottom of my heart Amanda, Karley, Chelsie, Margaret, Ansley, and Hannah.

To my editor Dani, thank you for your hard work, unending patience, and for putting up with my millions of revisions and borderline insane first drafts.

To Sonia, I love you to the freaking moon, and I'm so lucky to get to work with you on my covers that mean so much to me!

I put everything into this book, heart and soul. The nights were long, emotions ran high, and the tears were plentiful. A special shoutout to my husband is imperative because without him, I would have given up on this dream long ago. Thank you a million times over.

To my readers, thank you for your grace, kindness, and enthusiasm. This series is nothing without you and if you enjoy the bunkhouse boys as much as I do, it's a dream come true for me. I hope you're ready for Tripp and Mesa!

ABOUT THE AUTHOR

Lainey Lawson is a romance author living in a small southern town. She writes sweet and spicy rural setting love stories. If you're a long time reader, then you know to always expect a flair of suspense and unexpected twists and turns in her books - it's her favorite part!

Follow Lainey on her Amazon author page, Instagram and TikTok: @laineylawsonromance, and sign up for her newsletter for updates about the rest of The Bunkhouse series!

Also by Lainey Lawson - Smoking Gun (Gage & Blythe)

Coming soon
Up in Smoke (Tripp & Mesa)
Down in Flames (Heston & Hattie Jo)

CONTENT WARNINGS

Main character with anxiety
Toxic family members
Main character arrest
Kidnapping and gun violence
Side character substance abuse and poison usage
Explicit language and sexual content.

Printed in Great Britain
by Amazon